A Curiously

Hannah Hendy lives in a small town in South Wales with her wife, their daughter, and two spoilt cats. A professional chef by trade, she started writing to fill the time between shifts. She now writes cosy crime fulltime, a dream job! She is the author of the bestselling cosy crime series, The Dinner Lady Detectives, published by Canelo Crime and Canelo US. Hannah is represented by Francesca Riccardi at Kate Nash Literary Agency.

Instagram - @hannahhendywrites

Facebook - @hannahhendywrites

Twitter - @hendyhannah

Website – hannahhendywrites.com

Also by Hannah Hendy

The Dinner Lady Detectives

The Dinner Lady Detectives
An Unfortunate Christmas Murder
A Terrible Village Poisoning
A Frightfully Fatal Affair
A Gravely Troubling Discovery
An Extremely Unlikely Death
A Curiously Convenient Demise

A Curiously Convenient Demise

HANNAH HENDY

CANELO CRIME

First published in the United Kingdom in 2025 by

Canelo Crime, an imprint of
Canelo Digital Publishing Limited,
20 Vauxhall Bridge Road,
London SW1V 2SA
United Kingdom

A Penguin Random House Company
The authorised representative in the EEA is Dorling Kindersley Verlag GmbH.
Arnulfstr. 124, 80636 Munich, Germany

Copyright © Hannah Hendy 2025

The moral right of Hannah Hendy to be identified as the creator of this work has been asserted in accordance with the Copyright, Designs and Patents Act, 1988.
All rights reserved. No part of this publication may be reproduced or transmitted in any form or by any means, electronic or mechanical, including photocopy, recording, or any information storage and retrieval system, without permission in writing from the publisher.
No part of this book may be used or reproduced in any manner for the purpose of training artificial intelligence technologies or systems. In accordance with Article 4(3) of the DSM Directive 2019/790, Canelo expressly reserves this work from the text and data mining exception.

A CIP catalogue record for this book is available from the British Library.

Print ISBN 978 1 80436 476 5
Ebook ISBN 978 1 80436 477 2

This book is a work of fiction. Names, characters, businesses, organizations, places and events are either the product of the author's imagination or are used fictitiously. Any resemblance to actual persons, living or dead, events or locales is entirely coincidental.

Cover design by Ami Smithson

Cover images © Shutterstock

Printed and bound in Great Britain by Clays Ltd, Elcograf S.p.A.

Look for more great books at
www.canelo.co | www.dk.com

For the Mayor and Mayoress of Chepstow, long may they reign.

Prologue

Eleanor had always thought that if a town was a person, then a museum was the beating heart at the centre of it all. The sort of place that went by tirelessly working in the background, collecting memories. Unnoticed by anybody until some information was needed, or until it was suddenly broken and in need of saving. And that was what would happen soon, she thought sadly. Her funds as depleted as the rooms would be after she finished selling all the artefacts off. All chance of help washed away in the letter she had received that morning.

It was no good her asking for the money again. The only person she had left to ask had already said no. Eleanor had found herself turning wildly from any other vague offers of help, pushing people away. That didn't make her rude or cruel, like Cecilia had suggested, Eleanor thought to herself as she deftly arranged the auction numbers smartly in front of her. She had just run out of luck.

She had put her life's work into protecting the past while other people flounced around into the future as if it hadn't happened. As if what they were doing wouldn't also become history that Eleanor would one day weave around the museum.

She had always been this way – as a child, she had refused to play with toys to keep them nice. Some would say that was an unusual, perhaps even depressing way for a child to think, but the boxed toys graced some of the shelves in Dewstow Museum and Eleanor made Cecilia dust them weekly. So, who was laughing now?

Not her, she realised, with a grimace. Not after her grandfather had found out she was selling the Dewstow Heritage Vase, and told her exactly what he thought of her. But she believed in that old motto: sell one timeless historical piece to save the rest. Or, to put it another way: save the future by selling the past. Big corporations did it all the time. Why couldn't she?

At the rate they were going, however, she barely had enough to scrape together Cecilia's next wage packet. Cecilia was loyal to a tee, Eleanor knew, but loyalty could sour as soon as there was no money to buy bread with. Even on her mediocre wage as museum assistant. Cecilia was already showing signs of rebellion, which Eleanor intended to continue to squash. How dare she talk to her like that? Eleanor would need to continue to take a firm hand with the woman.

To save the day, Eleanor had agreed to host the Summerview Secondary School auction – for an upfront price, of course, and a large percentage of the profits for the museum. It had seemed a good idea at the time; hindsight was twenty-twenty after all, Eleanor sighed as she gave the room a scornful once-over. The school classrooms and hallways were clean and tidy enough and the canteen was certainly spotless, but everything behind closed doors was old and worn and dirty. The cramped, dark storage room behind the stage was no different. Out of sight, out of the mind of anyone who possessed a vacuum or a cloth. Eleanor had barely wanted to put her items down on the sad, scuffed table.

The walls were hung with old posters and the floor was littered with glitter and remnants of old drama costumes. It certainly looked as though Rose ran a tight ship, but a sterner glace showed off the smudges and fingerprints underneath it all. The dust swept behind the curtains and the mould and rot covered by a fresh coat of paint.

Unfortunately, the Summerview school auction was a necessary evil. Rose wasn't an idiot, by any means – Eleanor might even have respected her under different circumstances – but her awareness was annoying in this situation. Eleanor had needed to make foolproof plans to make her money back right under Summerview's headteacher's nose and that was not an easy thing to do. Eleanor somehow wished that she could tell everyone about it, so they could all see how cunning and clever she really was. Instead, she said nothing and let the residents of Dewstow all go on as they were, unaware that Eleanor was plotting in the background.

It was a shame Timothy Fitzgerald had died, Eleanor had thought more than once. Old Tim would have flogged the vase on under all of their noses three times over by now from one of the dusty shelves in his antique shop. Eleanor had needed to resort to the internet for the real sale, which would be covered up by the auction.

The storage room door creaked open behind her and Eleanor turned her head slightly, turning back to the vase in dismissal as soon as she had seen who it was with a tut of displeasure.

'Oh, it's you,' Eleanor told them, going back to her careful polishing. 'Shouldn't you be out in the studio with the rest of the rabble? Don't let me keep you.'

There was no reply. Eleanor found her annoyance growing, but refused to give her visitor the satisfaction of turning around to tell them.

Really, was it too much to ask that everyone be where they were supposed to be when asked? Dewstow really was a stupid place filled with stupid people. It annoyed her that she had become trapped there among them all, sorting things for the WI and throwing ridiculous events like this auction. No one in Dewstow could even appreciate what they were selling. Even her grandfather didn't know why he wanted the vase, not really. Only Eleanor appreciated its true value. He just wanted it because she had it, and in Eleanor's book that wasn't enough of a reason to do anything.

Eleanor didn't get the chance to say or think much of anything else. Instead, she found herself flying across the room, feeling weightless for a millisecond before she collided with the table the vase rested on. All the air smashed from her lungs for a second before she wheezed them back to life. She clambered back up to her feet.

'What are you doing?' she gasped, once she had caught her breath. She turned again, clutching for the vase on the table in front of her, but then snapped her head back at the sight of what rested in the intruder's arms. 'You could have broken it! Wait...' Eleanor turned to see if she had seen correctly. 'Is that... is that another vase?'

A sudden and shocking crack of pain arrived on the top of her head and radiated back through her body as she flailed in shock. Eleanor stumbled backward again, gripping the table to steady herself, nearly smashing the vase and feeling sick with the feeling that her skull wasn't sitting right over her brain any more. She held her hand up to defend herself, a moment too late, the world spinning around her eyes.

Something smashed onto the ground next to her as they panted and reached over her for the vase Eleanor had been lovingly polishing, still sitting safely on the table.

'Stop,' Eleanor tried to say, but all that came out was a thick gurgle, her mouth filled with the taste of iron, her spit suddenly too thick to be contained.

She lay there on her back like a downed turtle. Her head whirled and her eyes found the lines of the old, cracked ceiling, following them as she gasped for air. Her head becoming cloudy as she gulped. Something had been important. Her thoughts tried to click back to life, but she couldn't remember what. Her fingertips reached out, feeling the shards of porcelain cutting into her hands and her head and the slippery wet floor above her before everything else switched off.

Chapter One

'Stop pulling, Clem!' Margery said as they traversed the canteen carefully, avoiding the sharp corners of tables and the extensive sauce-sachet section that Margery had always been particularly proud of. 'We'll never get it there in one piece.'

'Nonsense,' Clementine scoffed, but she did stop tugging quite so hard. 'Even if we drop the plates and they smash, I'm sure we can just write "ceramic jigsaw" on the box. Someone will bid for it, Margery! You know what it's like! They're scavengers, the lot of them.'

Margery rolled her eyes, but that didn't stop the chuckle leaving her mouth. She lowered her handle of the bag to the floor and unlocked the canteen kitchen door. They hadn't wanted to come back to work on a Wednesday evening, but as she often said, sometimes needs must.

Since Rose Smith had taken over as headteacher there seemed to be a lot more work for the dinner ladies, whether they wanted it or not. Today's extracurricular activity was stacking all the auction prizes donated by the dinner lady team into Margery's office, which was also the canteen kitchen's dry store. Rose hadn't seemed particularly concerned about food safety regulations or where Margery was going to store her bags of flour. She had just told them both that she believed in them and then waltzed off to give someone else a job they didn't want.

Margery knew that they should say no whenever Rose suggested anything, but Rose had become a good friend, and it was hard to immediately dismiss an idea when she was using it to try and improve the school. Anything that raised money for extracurricular activities or textbooks or computers was all right in Margery's book, and Rose had been doing a decent job since she took over the role of headteacher, diving in headfirst. She was currently miles ahead of where her husband, James Barrow, had left off. By the end of his reign, he had been flailing around in the darkness of his office and pretending there were no murders happening under his watch.

The dinner ladies had managed to scrape together an interesting collection of items for the auction, although some were much more valuable than others. Sharon and Karen had both donated prized Dewstow Fun Runners T-shirts and matching socks. Ceri-Ann had supplied baby Nick's old travel system, as he had now grown out of most of it. It was in good condition still, and Margery could see that someone might bid for it, especially as all the donations were going to fund the school's sports and chess teams. It was all for a good cause. She wasn't entirely sure that anyone would bid for Gloria's collection of shed snake skins or Seren's wallpaper steamer, which she had assured them all 'only leaked into the plug socket and fused my house once!'. Still, you could never be sure what would happen. One year, the highest donation had been for a single shuttlecock painstakingly painted in school colours by one of the students with nail varnish, which Margery still wondered the reasoning for when they were sold as a set of six in the local sports shop for less than a pound. Regardless, you just never knew what might happen.

This year could be different, Margery thought to herself. Rose had hired an outsider to set it all up, someone who had professional experience with this sort of thing. Things might be a bit more interesting.

The precarious bag for life full of ugly plates was the last thing for the pile, and one of Margery and Clementine's own donations. In fact, they had donated quite a bit. Most of it came from their former friend Mr Fitzgerald's shop, which he had left to them in his will.

At first, they hadn't known what to do with the shop after his death. But they eventually decided to rent out the large shop floor for a small fee that just about covered the electric and water bill. It was now a buzzing community centre on the high street, used for all sorts of classes and groups. The council had managed to find some funding, which Margery and Clementine had used to make the place safe for human habitation. Mr Fitzgerald hadn't thought much of health and safety. The entire building had been a maze of loose floorboards and nails sticking out of walls. They hadn't known what to do with most of the strange items the shop had held for stock, so this was a perfect way to pass them on without feeling guilty.

'Where's Maria with the painting?' Clementine sighed, looking around for her sister, but not seeing her anywhere. 'Honestly, you give her one thing to do!'

'She was right behind us,' Margery said, looking back in confusion. 'I'll go and check she hasn't got lost. You sort out those plates.'

Margery left the dry store and made her way back through the kitchen. Maria had been a sore spot of contention since her surprise arrival a few months ago – a spongey bruise on their otherwise happy marriage. Clementine, of course, had been ecstatic to see her and hear all her stories from her travels over the years. Margery had not warmed up quite as quickly. Maria was moulded by her time on the run from the law, and didn't see the need to conform to society's norms and regulations. Margery had found that admirable at first, but it was becoming increasingly difficult to deal with.

Margery arrived in the canteen, just in time to catch Maria entering with the strange reproduction oil painting of the *Mona Lisa*. The Mona Lisa in this version didn't have the same wry smile as the original. In fact, Margery thought that this version had the much more terrifying grimace of someone with incredibly painful trapped wind. Margery was certain that Mr Fitzgerald had painted it himself.

'There you are,' Margery said, reaching out to help Maria with the heavy gold-framed painting. 'We were wondering where you'd got to.'

'Just admiring the school,' Maria said, although there was a note of disdain in her voice. 'It doesn't look like it's ever been updated. What did you say this auction money is going to again? It can't possibly be wallpaper. The entire place looks like an asbestos risk. I bet if they looked in the roof they'd find sixteen generations of bats.'

'I'm sure Rose has some good plans for it,' Margery said, trying to sound neutral. It wouldn't do to annoy Maria, who could be as fractious as Clementine. Not when she wanted to get on with it and then go home to happily have an easy dinner and watch some of the soaps they had recorded for later. They shuffled the painting into the dry store, where Clementine helped them to heave it up on top of the plates on the chest freezer.

'Well, thank goodness that nightmare is over till Friday,' Clementine said, wiping her hands together as if to rid them of the smell of the old painting. 'Hopefully we can find someone to take it all back out of here for us. I don't think I can bear the idea of carrying all of it over to the drama studio.'

'We've still got to get fish-and-chip Friday done, and I'm not sure how I'll reach the mushy peas,' Margery sighed sadly, looking at the cans of peas and big sacks of potatoes, which were half hidden underneath a pile of donated tennis rackets. 'I wish Rose hadn't let the rest of the departments leave their auction things here.'

'Only the terrible things,' Clementine said with a scoff. 'All the good stuff is elsewhere.'

Maria turned, suddenly interested. 'What do you mean?' she asked Clementine, her eyebrows raising quizzically.

'Rose has all the good stuff locked in her office cupboard,' Clementine told her. 'That's why we've ended up with... well... all this.'

She gestured around at the assortment of items, each less useful than the last. Maria nodded without saying anything, but Margery could tell that her interest was piqued.

They left the dry store and made their way back to Margery's car. It had been a struggle to fit all the donations inside. In fact, she had needed to pile both the backseats and front passenger seat of the Nissan Figaro with items and ask Clementine and Maria to meet her at the school.

Clementine opened the passenger side door and moved the front seat forward for Maria, who shook her head.

'No need,' she said cheerily, waving them off. 'I'll walk from here, it's a nice evening.'

'Is it?' Margery asked before she could help herself, watching Maria twirl the umbrella in her hand.

She looked up at the darkening sky. It looked a lot like rain to her, but she supposed she wasn't one to judge. Maria had been through a lot, perhaps she was still getting used to her freedom. Maybe she simply didn't mind a bit of rain. Living in a cold, damp van, she was probably used to it.

'We'll see you at home.' Clementine smiled, before climbing into the car.

Margery got in the driver's side, and they drove off, leaving Maria sauntering along beside the car for a moment before she disappeared from view entirely.

'Do you think Maria's doing all right, Margery?' Clementine asked, as they turned the corner onto the main road down the steep hill into Dewstow town centre. She wrung her hands together like she was trying to wash soap from them. 'She hadn't said anything, but I can tell she's not happy.'

'I really don't know, Clem,' Margery said. 'She seems to be doing okay to me?'

Margery wasn't sure if Maria had the capacity for real happiness any more. Not since her son had died, and he had been barely out of his teenage years at that. She didn't know Maria well at all, but she could imagine that would ruin anyone's life. Margery always selfishly hoped that she would die herself before Clementine, so she wouldn't have to live in a world without her wife. She imagined that pain would be tripled for a mother losing a child, even if they had been estranged. Maria hadn't said anything to her about how she felt, but Margery knew she must blame her for Thomas's death. Clementine had spent a full year reminding her it was an accident, and that if Thomas hadn't tried to kill Margery, then he wouldn't be dead. It ate away at her conscience, filling it with guilt that clouded all her thoughts.

Clementine and Maria had reconnected immediately, though they argued so much it was like they had grown up together. They were similar in the way that they both had to be right, all the time. It drove Margery mad, but even with all her trepidations, she had to admit to herself that it was nice for Clementine to have a family member to stay. She was conflicted about it, of course, but she still didn't feel as though she should get in the way of their fun. It had been nice to have an extra seat at the table to fill the Christmas just gone. Anyway, if a member of Margery's family had turned up at the house and asked for help, Margery knew Clementine would have invited them in with open arms. It was only fair that she did the same for her.

Some of the other residents of Dewstow hadn't been so welcoming. Apart from their neighbours open annoyance about Maria and her van sitting on Margery and Clementine's driveway for months on end, there were often other whispers that followed Maria. Clementine seemed oblivious to them, but Margery noticed, her ears always pricking at the sound of her or Clementine's names. They were well known in Dewstow, but Maria did not seem well tolerated.

'I just don't know if we're doing enough to help her.' Clementine shook her head, holding her own hands very tightly. 'We should be doing so much more.'

'We've got her a job and somewhere to live for now,' Margery reminded her.

'I know, but she doesn't want to be a cleaner, does she?' Clementine shrugged. 'I wish we could give her a job in the kitchen.'

'There's too many of us as it is,' Margery reminded her.

It had been hard enough to secure Maria's place on the Sanitation and Contamination Removal Experts team at the school. It had been lucky that Gosia was due to go on maternity leave, or it never would have happened at all. As it was, Maria was not terribly good at appearing at work, sometimes deciding that she'd rather spend the day out doing whatever it was she did. It was difficult for Margery to not feel embarrassed, seeing as they had got her the job in the first place. 'I don't think you should worry about that. Eventually she'll find her feet and I imagine she'll want to get back into a restaurant kitchen or similar. Do some real cooking. I'm sure being a dinner lady would bore her.'

Truth be told, she could tell it sometimes bored the rest of the team, too. Officially titled Education Centre Nourishment Consultants, the dinner lady team prepared food for 1200 students, teachers and support staff each day. It was not always an easy feat, although every day looked much the same. Any slight diversion in their careful routine might mean that they weren't ready for lunchtime. Everything revolved around lunchtime when they were at work. Margery tried to keep it interesting for her team, but there was really only so much she could change things up.

Clementine nodded, but she didn't look convinced by Margery. Margery had tried to get Maria to teach one of the classes at their community venue, but Maria had turned her down. Margery thought that if she had taught a few cooking lessons then Maria might have been able to turn public opinion around. As it was, even if Maria arrived for work at the cleaning job, she was often late. She seemed to spend most of her free time drinking at the Bell and Hope. Margery wanted to be helpful, but deep down she wondered what else they could really do.

Chapter Two

Maria didn't return that night, and neither Margery nor Clementine knew where she could have gone. Clementine had been beside herself all evening, though she had pretended she wasn't annoyed. Margery could see the worry that permeated the surface. And Margery was yet again embarrassed and annoyed the next day when Louise, the head of the Education Centre Sanitation and Contamination Removal Experts, had come to ask her where Maria was.

It had been obvious all day that Clementine was upset and was even worse now that lunchtime was over and they were preparing the food for the charity auction, which had arrived much too quickly for Margery's liking. The canteen kitchen did not feel like its usual busy hustle-bustle without Clementine's good humour. Margery found herself clock watching, wishing they were at home, while simultaneously realising how much work they had left to do.

Margery hadn't wanted to say 'I told you so' to Clementine, but she had suspected that there was more to Maria's sudden arrival and disappearances than she was letting on. She had initially given Maria the benefit of the doubt. Of course Maria had an aura of chaos about her. She was related to Clementine, who was the grand master of chaos as far as Margery was concerned. At least

Maria didn't put washing in the machine and then forget to take it out, Margery reasoned. She didn't mind sharing their facilities with her, especially since she spent most of the day shut away in her campervan. However, it really annoyed her that Maria would just up and leave without so much as a word to Clementine, who would then spend hours pretending she needed to go and return a spoon to Dawn Simmonds or peering through the gap in the curtains on the pretence that she had seen a delivery van when she was really just watching to see when her sister would return.

Admittedly, Dawn had a point about Maria's van being an eyesore. The Mazda Bongo was frighteningly rundown. Margery refused to believe it had ever been for a service or had an MOT in years. It had an old, rusted awning that Maria had put up as soon as she had arrived, and a washing line that extended from that. It constantly flapped like a flag under the weight of all Maria's socks and pants. Margery had suggested that perhaps she might want to use their washing line in the back garden or their clothes horse in the spare bedroom, but to no avail.

Clementine had repeatedly offered the spare room itself, but Maria had politely refused, telling them both that she had everything she needed in the van. This was what she was used to. Margery hadn't been convinced, had kept the door on the latch just in case, but Maria had managed out on the driveway for most of the winter now and in a month or so it would be spring again. Margery hadn't quite got used to it yet, though, and it was still a surprise to open the living-room curtains of a morning and see Clementine's doppelgänger smoking a cigarette outside in the front garden with their cat Pumpkin sat at her feet.

More than a few Dewstow residents had mistaken them for each other already, calling hello to Maria because they thought she was Clementine and then doing a double take when they realised that she was not. Maria and Clementine looked alike, which was confusing in itself, even though Clementine kept her hair its natural grey and Maria dyed hers the same as Clementine's had been before time had taken the colour out of the brunette waves. Margery wondered if the townspeople had simply decided Maria was too uncanny valley for them or if they had heard about Maria's long-ago escape from the police. Either way, her presence wasn't celebrated.

'I wish we didn't always have to prepare so many tiny things,' Gloria said as she rolled the next lot of arancini balls in breadcrumbs. 'We should just throw a few Victoria sponges together, that would be much easier.'

'We should do protein flapjacks,' Sharon suggested, from where she was trying to wrestle the huge mixer off its stand so she could roll out the scone mix. 'Then I might beat my parkrun personal best as well as making a delicious canapé.'

'How many of them are you planning to eat?' Karen scoffed.

Sharon burst into tears so immediately, Margery refused to believe she had had time to process the comment at all.

'Please, ladies,' Margery said. 'Karen? Help Sharon get the raisins into that mix. It won't do to have a raisin-less scone. Sergeant Davis is going to be in attendance.'

'Raisins just remind me of spiders without legs,' Seren said sadly. Ceri-Ann gave her an incredulous look, looking up from where she was cutting perfect chunky chips for the fish-and-chip canapé.

The menu had seemed much easier to prepare when she was writing it, Margery thought, as she wrung her hands together and looked at the prep list written on the white board behind Gloria's head. Clementine had been next to no help today, clearly still concerned about her sister. Margery had taken her off general prep because Clementine had cut the fish so small that they would have to serve fish fingernails instead of fish fingers. She had moved her onto sweets, but instead of icing the cake pops, Clementine was skulking around burning the custard for the miniature trifles and just generally being a nuisance. Margery wished she could send her home, but feared what Clementine would do if Maria wasn't there when she arrived. She'd probably go to the pub to find her and cause a scene. Thinking about it though, it might be worse if Maria was home, leading to another argument about Maria missing work.

Clementine and Maria did usually get on like a house on fire, but sometimes there was a little too much fire for Margey's taste. She didn't want them to argue without her there to referee; both were hot-headed people. It all made her feel incredibly old.

Her hands had always been tough after years of kitchen work, with thick calluses and dry palms, but even they were beginning to show more lines and spots of age. Worse still, whenever Margery complained about any of it, Clementine told her that she was being silly because she was as beautiful as the day they'd met, and anyway, 'the alternative is much worse, isn't it? I'd rather look like a squashed-up Christmas stocking satsuma than be dead'. Margery supposed she had a point.

'Why does every charity event at the school need us to make the food?' Clementine groaned. 'Honestly, the kids don't need any more sugar. They get enough from vapes and energy drinks and whatever else they can get their sticky hands on. That's why they're all so strange.'

'There won't be any students there,' Margery reminded her, ignoring Gloria nodding in agreement at Clementine's comments. 'It's adults only. That's why it's all canapés and wine.'

'We should just give it all up,' Clementine moaned miserably, sounding like a very upset ghost. She was stirring a third lot of custard, which Margery could smell had already burnt to the bottom of the pan. 'Leave the school and all move on – there won't be any need for cooking then…'

'What would we do, though?' Seren asked, her eyes wide at the very idea of it.

'Well, unfortunately you're all trapped here with your mortgage payments,' Clementine said. She shook her head at the sadness of that. 'But Margery and I can start charging for detective work, leave you all behind with the cakes and the jelly and whatever.'

'Will you actually work out what you want to charge people?' Gloria scoffed, starting the arduous job of rolling the next batch of risotto rice into balls. 'Your website still says you'll do it in exchange for the person who's hired you coming to mow your lawn.'

'We'll charge on a day basis,' Clementine said. She leaned back on the nearest prep table, forgetting the custard on the stove completely. Margery was sure it wasn't entirely intentional. 'And then it'll all go up on a sliding scale… you want a dramatic monologue after we've caught whoever? That's twenty pounds. You want us to just tell them what we think they've done, only ten…'

'What if they don't want a monologue, but they want you to sing the murderer a song after?' Ceri-Ann asked, in a way that made Margery suspicious that she might try and hire them for this reason alone.

'Neither of us can sing for tuppence, so we'd need lessons first,' Clementine said, furiously stirring the burning custard. 'That's probably at least a few hundred more and an extra week or two of planning…'

'This will all be over soon,' Margery said, stepping forward to turn off the gas burner before the pan caught fire. She was not entirely sure if that was true either. Picking up the clipboard again revealed another list of things they hadn't even started to make yet.

'Gosh, we'll be here till midnight at this rate,' Gloria gasped as she saw Margery's prep list over her shoulder.

'Yes, and even if we manage to get this all done, I'm not sure I've ordered enough tea bags,' Margery said, worrying her lip with her teeth.

She knew that one catering bag containing a thousand teabags would probably be enough, but you could never be sure. Before she had time to check over her ordering again, there was a sharp rap on the fire-escape door. The dinner ladies all turned to look at each other.

'Who could that be?' Seren asked, her eyes as wide as dinner plates. 'We're all here!'

Margery decided that there were enough of them to fight off any mystery intruder, so she could open the door. Maria stood outside on the fire escape, panting hard. Her eyes darted around the playground as though she was worried that she had been followed. Sometimes only the dye in Maria's hair gave away that she wasn't Clementine, and the long wool coat that she always wore.

'Maria,' Margery cried. 'Where have you been? Louise has been going mad, she said she had to clean the entire science department on her own...'

'Is Clem here?' Maria gasped, trying to catch her breath and grasping for her knee in a way that made Margery worry.

'What are you doing here?' Clementine stepped past Margery to confront her sister. 'Are you all right?'

'Oh yeah, of course, fine...' Maria hissed, her knuckles white as she grasped the railing.

'I mean, you don't look fine,' Gloria called in concern from behind them.

'I'm great,' Maria gasped, rushing into the kitchen and leaning heavily against the nearest table, taking deep breaths.

'Have you been running?' Karen asked her.

Sharon eyed her suspiciously. 'You're not trying to beat our personal best around the school playground on Strava, are you?'

'Nope, all good,' Maria said, wiping sweat from her brow. 'Your personal best is secure. I don't even carry my phone on me most of the time. It's in my locker for emergencies. I don't want Elon Musk or whoever looking at my emails, do I?'

'You don't carry your phone around?' Ceri-Ann asked incredulously. 'What do you do when you aren't doing anything?'

'Oh, you know,' Maria said, finally straightening up and looking slightly less unwell than she had. 'Read, do crosswords, sometimes I just stare off into space...' She turned to Clementine. 'Look, Clem... I've been here a while, haven't I, if anyone asks? All day really… just helping you out, making sprinkly cakes or whatever else it is you do.' She gestured with her fingers in the air as if sprinkling glitter out onto the floor.

'What do you mean?' Clementine asked, her brow furrowing. 'What have you done?'

'There might have been a very minor misunderstanding—' Maria began. She was interrupted by a knock on the kitchen door. The dinner lady team turned to see Summerview school's headteacher, Rose Smith. She entered the room on her heels, followed by a much older woman who was dressed the way Margery imagined 1800s gentry still would if they ever had the opportunity to rise up from their graves.

Margery recognised the apparition as Eleanor Black, the matriarch of the Black family, and just as cold and shrewish as her predecessor. Margery and Clementine had always tried to avoid her, unless it was inevitable. Once, Eleanor had spotted them walking past Dewstow's museum and had dragged them inside to show them her new display of ancient petticoats. Since then, they had skirted around the museum entirely on their walks. It wasn't hard to avoid it, as the building was at the very bottom of the town and out of the way enough to skirt past, but it was impossible to avoid its owner entirely. Eleanor had a finger in a great number of pies.

When Margery and Clementine had reopened the antique shop as a central communal hub for Dewstow, Eleanor had been there on opening day with her clipboard and environmental health questions nearly getting the place shut down before it could really begin. Mrs Mugglethwaite, Dewstow's local gossipmonger, usually gushed about how much she liked Mrs Black, and her best friend, Evelyn, said very much the same, but Margery had certainly seen another side to Eleanor that day. Margery feared that Eleanor had simply taken umbrage to Clementine's breezy demeanour and their excitement and decided to make things more difficult for them. The only reason the shop was still open to the public was because Dawn Simmonds had talked Eleanor down at their behest in a very rare moment of cooperation. They had been forced to host all of Dawn's WI meetings after that, which had been nearly as upsetting as Eleanor's complaints. However detestable Margery and Clementine found her, the rest of Dewstow seemed to be very much in her pocket. They had never heard a bad word about her from anyone else, leaving Margery wondering if they had overreacted. They hadn't, she knew. She remembered the cool look in Eleanor's eye as she had given their shop a once-over.

'Hello, Mrs Butcher-Baker.' Rose sighed, looking between them all. 'Do you think we could have a word with Ms Glover?'

Maria seemed to shrink at the mention of her name. Clementine stepped in front of her, blocking her from Rose's view.

'Whatever you need to say, you can say to all of us,' Clementine said. She glared at her and then gestured around at the rest of the team.

'Why don't we all go for a break and have a cup of tea?' Gloria suggested, leading Sharon and Karen away from the ovens. 'Let's go to the staff room.'

'Are we allowed in the staff room?' Seren said, looking bewildered. 'I don't even know where it is.'

'We'll just have to search for it together,' Gloria said, smiling through clenched teeth.

The team left the room, and Rose and Eleanor stepped out of their way, although Ceri-Ann looked as though she wanted to stay and hear what was going on, her exit reduced to a very slow shuffle. Once the babble had finally left the kitchen, Rose turned to Maria again, who was still half hidden behind Clementine.

'I'm so sorry, Margery… Clementine,' Rose babbled, her voice rising in a way Margery had never heard. She seemed thoroughly rattled, her usually pristine silver bob looking frayed under the fluorescent glow of the kitchen lighting. 'But it's been brought to my attention that Ms Glover… well… Eleanor, did you want to say what you had to say?'

Eleanor sucked in air through her teeth in annoyance. 'I don't see why I should. This is your school, is it not?'

'Yes…' Rose said. 'But I'm not the one with the complaint.'

'How do you stand up without a spine?' Eleanor scoffed, shaking her head. 'I found her' – she pointed a sharp manicured finger towards Maria – 'rummaging through the items for the auction.'

Even Clementine turned to look at Maria in surprise.

'What?' Margery asked. 'What items? We've got them all in our dry store.'

'No, you don't,' Eleanor said, with a dismissive wave of her hand. 'Your headmistress has kindly allowed us to store valuable items in her office, which is where your colleague was found earlier, with her hands all over the Dewstow Heritage Vase.'

'She's my sister,' Clementine told her, 'and she wouldn't do anything like—'

'I just wanted to have a look at it!' Maria cried from behind Clementine. Clementine whirled around with her eyes wide. 'There's no crime in that, is there?'

'Do you know how much that vase is worth?' Eleanor said, ignoring Maria's outburst. 'It's practically priceless. The auction isn't for another day, and the vase already had several anonymous bids in the thousands! So, you can keep your grubby mitts off it.'

Maria was very quiet for a moment. Margery thought she saw a flicker of guilt and regret cross her face before it left again as quickly as it had arrived. Instead, Maria scoffed, with a shrug that told them all that they were all overreacting.

'So, what if I did touch it?' she said, folding her arms across her chest and looking over at Eleanor and Rose in defiance. 'What are you going to do about it?'

'You admit you were in the office?' Rose asked, her face a picture of surprise, her eyebrow raising.

'I can't believe you,' Clementine said, shaking her head and stepping back from Maria. 'Why would you want that vase? There are probably a million nicer ones at the supermarket. Honestly, Maria, you don't want anything from the auction. It's all trinkets and weird coats of arms – things a vampire would want to get in a Christmas stocking...'

Both Eleanor and Rose spluttered at that.

'I suspect this isn't the first time you've broken into anywhere, is it?' Eleanor accused Maria. 'You got that door open easily enough and it was firmly locked.'

Maria shrugged, but her face fell. Margery thought she reminded her more of one of the teenage students than a woman in her sixties. The way Maria sulkily refused to even look up at Eleanor told her she had indeed broken into many places. Maria breaking into Rose's office after Margery and Clementine had told her that was where Rose was keeping the important auction items was suspicious indeed. Margery thought back to a few days ago. Maria had suddenly had the money to take them for lunch and they had all gone out to a cafe nearby. When they had returned home, Margery had gone to the old teabags tin that acted like a moneybox and lived on top of the fridge, so that she could ready the cash to pay the milkman, but she had discovered that the tin was gone. She hadn't said anything to Clementine at the time, hadn't thought too much of it at all really. Margery had assumed that perhaps Clementine had used the cash for something. But now it seemed much more sinister.

'Mrs Black doesn't want to involve the police,' Rose told Maria, her voice implying how very lucky she was that they weren't taking this further. 'So, this will end here. But please would you stay out of the office.'

'I'll be keeping a very close eye on you…' Eleanor said, ignoring Rose's calm tone. 'Especially given your record.'

'What's that supposed to mean?' Clementine spluttered at the same time as Margery gasped. 'Maria was absolved of everything that happened. She's been innocent for years.'

'Innocent people don't break into locked rooms.' Eleanor smirked. With that she turned and left.

Rose watched her go, putting her hands to her temples and massaging them.

'She'll be on the warpath now,' Rose sighed. 'Sorry about that, ladies, but she insisted.'

'It's quite all right,' Margery said, at the same time as Clementine turned to Maria.

'What were you really doing in the office?' she demanded.

Maria rolled her eyes in defiance. 'Nothing!' she said. The way she flicked her hair behind her ears told Margery everything she needed to know.

'You can't just say that and not explain,' Clementine said. 'It makes you look even more suspicious!'

'Stay out of the office please, Maria,' Rose said. 'Eleanor will have us all imprisoned if anyone else goes near her precious vase, and regardless, I'm sorry but you've been given a great number of chances now. Let's not make this the beginning of anything more.'

Maria nodded, but didn't look Rose in the eye.

'What's so nice about that vase anyway?' Clementine asked.

'That's what I wanted to know!' Maria exclaimed, waving her arms and nearly knocking the custard from the stove. 'Everyone keeps banging on about these "high-value items"' – she made air quotes as she said the words – 'and all I saw was a load of dusty old rubbish. I bet you had better stuff in your old shop.'

'Well, Eleanor is right about the price and the mystery bidders,' Rose said, running a hand through her hair. 'The sooner this is all over, the better. If I'd have known being headteacher would mean more than a good parking space, I might have reconsidered it.'

'You're a liar. You love the power and the parking space,' Clementine scoffed. 'You're absolutely mad with it. Remember last week when you made Seren iron and starch all your socks?'

'She used to do that for me anyway.' Rose smirked, looking much more herself than she had when she had first arrived in the kitchen. She turned to Maria again. 'Please, let's start a clean slate.'

Maria held her hands up in defeat, but Margery wondered if she would stay true to her word.

Chapter Three

The school drama studio was a babble of people. It could have been the beginning of one of the smaller student plays, Margery thought, if only she closed her eyes and focused on the noise. It was only the gathered crowd's eveningwear that promised something more entertaining.

The studio had somehow been transformed from a basic and boring room, which usually hosted nothing more than a few governors' meetings and the smaller Year Eleven shows, to a glamourous convention centre. Margery had no idea how Rose had done it, or where she had borrowed the nice tables and chairs from. They certainly weren't the old, scuffed ones the students usually sat on. She suspected that Mrs Blossom – Rose's archnemesis and secret best friend – had had a hand in it somewhere. Mrs Blossom was standing next to Rose on stage in front of the closed curtain and they were both surveying the scene in cocktail dresses. Mrs Blossom's dog, Ada Bones, was wearing a matching black dress with glittering headband, but Rose's dog, Jason, had been spared the indignity of matching her outfit. He was wearing a sparkling new collar, though, the diamanté catching the light from the mirrored ball that hung on the studio ceiling.

'Crikey,' Gloria said, looking around at the spectacle in front of them as they served coffee from the hot drinks station. 'Rose has really outdone herself with this one, hasn't she?'

'She really has,' Margery replied. 'It's even better than the Christmas concert was.'

'Yes.' Gloria nodded. 'And that had Jason playing all the animals in the stable, didn't it? This is even better. I feel so underdressed!'

Margery smiled to herself. Gloria was Margery's hard-to-please second-in-command. If she thought something was impressive, then it must really be so. Usually, an event of this calibre was kept well away from Dewstow and Summerview school, and could only be dreamed about being held at Ittonvale school. The last few auctions had certainly not met this standard. Ittonvale's headteacher, Mrs Hallow, was mingling with all the other guests, having let her deputy head take the lead in greeting parents from Ittonvale school. She seemed to be having a much better time than she usually did at these things, Margery wondered if she realised that the champagne was non-alcoholic.

Margery looked around for the rest of her team, who were dotted around the room. Karen and Sharon were serving drinks while Ceri-Ann and Seren handed out nibbles on silver serving trays. Clementine was on rubbish duty, which meant she had spent most of her time chatting to guests and doing no work at all and had currently disappeared into the group.

There were a lot of parents Margery didn't recognise in attendance – probably from Ittonvale school – with a few students accompanying them.

An icy hand grasped for her wrist, startling Margery out of her thoughts. She twisted to see who it belonged to.

'Maria—' she began. Maria interrupted her. Her eyes were wide and frightened, her gaze darting past Margery's face and over the room at the gathered crowd.

'Where's Clem?' Maria asked. Margery shook her head. 'Oh, please, Margery, I really need to speak to her. This is important, where is she?'

'She's here somewhere,' Margery said, taking Maria's panicked face seriously. She scanned the room for any sign of her wife. 'She was chatting to one of the governors the last time I saw her.'

Maria gave her one last long look and then sighed, turning away. She let go of Margery's arm and disappeared into the crowd.

'What was that about?' Gloria hissed.

Margery didn't know. A wave of unease washed over her. She should have realised that her leisurely walk home the other afternoon was an excuse for Maria to case out the expensive auction items in Rose's office. She shook her head, wishing the thoughts away. Clementine trusted Maria, and so Margery should too. Even if it was becoming harder and harder to the more that she got to know her.

'Ladies and gentlemen,' the DJ called over the PA machine, and his microphone squealed with feedback. Margery looked up, and recognised him as one of the particularly annoying Year Eleven students. 'Please put your hands together for our school dictator— I mean... Summerview Secondary School's headmistress, Mrs Smith!'

Music blared from the speakers for a minute, before Rose stepped forward onto the stage holding a handful of cards, ready to begin the auction.

'Thank you, Max,' she said, glaring towards where he sat in the cupboard that contained the audio-visual equipment. 'Welcome, all, to the fourteenth annual Summerview school charity auction!'

Margery clapped along with all the others, looking around again for Maria and not finding her. She had well and truly slipped into the crowd and disappeared.

Up on stage, Rose described some of the great wonders hidden behind the curtain, and waxed lyrical about how everyone had been incredibly generous with their donations. Margery was amazed at how much had been donated in the first place. It gave her some hope that the school would continue to thrive under Rose's control. Mr Barrow had always done his best when he had been headmaster, but without much success, and Rose's predecessor, Ms Cooper, had only made things worse still, but with Rose at the helm things had taken a drastic upward turn. Margery even had enough money to buy the more expensive disposable crockery for lunchtimes, the sort that could be recycled. Such details may have seemed small and petty to outsiders, but it meant that they were finally hitting the school's environmental targets for the year, and in Margery's mind that was nothing to be scoffed at.

Margery decided to ignore Maria's needlessly dramatic entrance and enjoy the show. Maria could find Clementine herself if she wanted her that badly, she decided. It had been annoying enough that Maria had upset their neighbours constantly over the past month; now that she had brought them trouble at their workplace, Margery was just about ready to wash her hands of the woman entirely. The only thing stopping her from talking to Clementine about asking Maria to leave was that it would destroy

Clementine if Maria was kicked out of the auction. The sisters had taken so long to get their relationship to where it was now. If Maria left angry then it might be damaged forever and take Clementine's future happiness with it.

'Without further nonsense from me,' Rose said into the microphone, 'let's get on with the auction. Please allow me to introduce to you our auctioneer for the evening, Mrs Black!'

There was a round of applause that seemed to go on forever, slowly trailing off as the crowd realised that Mrs Black hadn't yet appeared. Rose stood on the stage, looking around at the crowd in confusion.

'Mrs Black?' she called into the microphone in a sing-song tone. The feedback from her voice hummed around the walls as the crowd began to murmur among themselves. Rose stood away from the microphone, covering it with her hand as she hissed something to Mrs Blossom. She shrugged, still holding her glass of champagne. Rose shooed her, and Mrs Blossom rolled her eyes, but left the stage, presumably to look for Mrs Black. Margery wondered how you could be late to something you'd spent so long organising. Eleanor Black had donated many of the precious items that were available for bidding.

'Well, while we wait for Mrs Black,' Rose said, beaming widely, although her grin seemed rather forced to Margery, 'why don't I show you what you're playing for?'

One of the Year Seven students began the arduous process of drawing the curtain back. It squeaked along the rails as she pulled on the rope.

Margery was always a bit wary of stages after what had happened to the school's music teacher, Mrs Large, a few years earlier, but the drama studio had a prebuilt stage that was integrated into the hall. Rose had assured them all that it was robust enough to host as many school shows as she could physically manage.

Margery leaned forward to better see the wonders hidden behind the curtain, as did the rest of the crowd. She saw Rose's husband, James Barrow, and several other teachers jostling for a good look from their corner at the back. Even Ceri-Ann put down the cheese-and-pineapple-on-a-stick she was meant to be handing out.

Rose gestured with a flourishing wave, the wide sleeves of her dress flapping like a flag, her eyes closed in rapture. They slammed open again at the gasp from the crowd. Rose whipped her head around to stare behind her at the empty plinths, her mouth dropping open. She screeched as though she had just found a spider hiding in a bunch of supermarket grapes and dropped Jason, who ran around her in circles, yapping.

'Where?' Rose said. She staggered over to the empty tables, running her hands over them manically, as though the auction items would suddenly become visible if she searched hard enough for them. 'Where is everything?'

There was a horrible grating scream from elsewhere. It took Margery a moment to place where it was coming from. It sounded again and the gathered crowd turned their heads towards it.

'What was that?' Gloria asked. Margery had already begun to make her way towards the double doors that led into the main school building at the side of the stage. She was drawn towards the sound, rushing towards the scream, which cut through the murmuring of the crowd. Before she could place the source of the noise, Mrs Blossom appeared suddenly in the room in front of Margery, almost falling through the double doors into the studio and staggering to hold on to the bottom of the stage, Ada Bones yapping at her feet.

'She's dead!' she wailed. 'Dead!'

Rose rushed off the stage to comfort her. The crowd parted easily, backing away from them as though whatever Mrs Blossom was afraid of was contagious. The room began to murmur to themselves. Margery met Rose's eye and found that she looked just as confused as Margery felt. Mrs Blossom continued to weep.

Margery didn't waste any more time. She made her way past the stage and opened the door into the hall, deciding that whatever Mrs Blossom was reacting to needed to be sorted out. Her heart began to pound despite herself, the hairs on her arms rising at the memory of Mrs Blossom's scream and the panic in her wide eyes. She picked her way gingerly down the hallway and looked inside the nearest open doorway.

Inside the small, dusty storage room, a figure lay face up on the dreary carpet, no life left in her eyes. The floor was covered in shards of colour and for a moment Margery's eye imagined it to be a scattering of mosaic, until she realised that the fragments were pieces of ceramic. From the Dewstow Heritage Vase that Maria had tried to steal. Margery gasped at the biggest chunk of ceramic, reading the letters inscribed into the pieces.

A shiver ran down her spine at the sight of Eleanor Black's body. Her arms were twisted under her in a horrible unnatural way, and her eyes wide and unseeing as she stared forever at the last view she would ever have, the long strip lights of the storeroom.

Chapter Four

Margery sat at one of the old plastic tables in the canteen and tried to wait patiently. Mrs Blossom had been hysterical by the time the police had arrived, and not even Rose had been able to calm her down. The crowd had been split into two halves by the police and Clementine had gone with the other side of the room to be interviewed. Margery very much wished that they had stayed together. It was already past one in the morning and the darkness through the canteen windows was making her feel sick with anticipation. She hadn't been able to speak to Clementine since Mrs Blossom had found poor Eleanor Black's body. Margery hoped Maria had found her and been able to ask her whatever mad thing she had wanted. It was a good thing, in a way. It meant that Clementine had been spared the fate of seeing the dead woman's open staring eyes.

Mrs Blossom had been in no state to answer questions, and the building was in lockdown after Eleanor had been found. Every person on the scene needed to be interviewed about what they had seen... if they had seen anything.

Margery didn't think most people would have seen much at all. If it hadn't been for Mrs Blossom's abrupt entry to the studio, then Margery wouldn't have suspected a thing was wrong. Eleanor might have lain dead and undiscovered for much, much longer.

Margery grimaced at the memory of the woman's faraway gaze and twisted expression. She had always heard that death was supposed to be peaceful, once it had happened. None of the people that had died on her watch had seemed particularly peaceful. Margery had always thought that being dead as a concept seemed fine enough. Hopefully, when it came, she wouldn't know much about the actual act of being dead. She couldn't remember anything from before being alive so she assumed she wouldn't mind. The dying itself was another matter entirely and she wasn't looking forward to it at all.

Locked away with her thoughts, she didn't expect the shadow to fall over the table. Margery looked up to find Officer Mark Wilkinson staring down at her judgementally and seeming terribly out of place under the bright lights of the canteen kitchen. Ceri-Ann's boyfriend, Officer Symon, stood behind him, eclipsed by the man's large arms. They had already taken down Margery's version of events. In fact, she had been one of the first to be interviewed. Symon looked stressed, Margery thought.

'Hello, Officer,' Margery said, at a loss for any other words and wondering what he could possibly want now. 'Are you… do you want to interview me again?'

'Mrs Butcher-Baker,' Officer Wilkinson replied gruffly, like he was about to announce that he was, unfortunately, in attendance to drive her to a surprise colonoscopy. 'No, I'm just come to give you a bit of news.'

'What news? What's going on?' Margery asked, her stomach sinking at the sight of Officer Wilkinson's stern expression.

He seemed annoyed by her outburst. Possibly he thought she was getting in the way of his job running smoothly. He was not known for his kindly demeanour. Margery and Clementine had certainly had a few run-ins with him since he had taken his post, but they had come to an uneasy truce over the last year. They didn't trust him and hadn't since his mismanagement of Mr Fitzgerald's death. Mr Fitzgerald's murderer had been found in the end, but the police had been little to no help. All except Officer Symon, who had been forbidden to investigate by Officer Wilkinson, and so had hired Margery and Clementine to find the murderer for him. It would have been much easier with the police's resources. It had been hard to trust any of Dewstow police force since, except Symon, of course. Officer Wilkinson had got away with keeping his badge, but Margery was not convinced that would be the last time they came up against him. The worst thing about it was that she knew that Officer Wilkinson would hide his wrongdoings much better next time.

She wished Clementine were with her, and suddenly found herself worrying about why she was not. She assumed that Maria must have found her and that they would be together somewhere, but it was not like Clementine to not have come and found her.

Officer Wilkinson sighed dramatically, but Margery thought he seemed secretly quite pleased. The shadow of a smile lurked at the corners of his mouth. 'I won't beat around the bush here. Once we find her, we'll be taking Ms Glover into custody.'

'Mrs War— you can't mean Maria?' Margery gasped at the same time as Symon grimaced behind him. 'You can't possibly be serious?'

'Yes.' Officer Wilkinson nodded. 'Unfortunately, Ms Glover's whereabouts at the time of Mrs Black's death are unaccounted for and we'd like to ask her a few more questions.' He paused as though considering what to tell her. 'Ms Glover's fingerprints are all over the room and also the broken vase that was found with Mrs Black. We're DNA testing now. I suspect we'll find more evidence once that's done.'

'I can't believe it,' Margery said, shaking her head. 'You can't possibly think that Maria murdered her, just because she was nearby when it happened. You should just arrest us all if that's the case.' Officer Wilkinson looked for a moment as though he would rather enjoy arresting her, but Margery continued. 'DNA certainly doesn't prove a thing. Mine was probably all over the scene too, I was the next person to find her…'

'I'm not talking about touching-Mrs-Black's-body-to-perform-first-aid sort of DNA,' Officer Wilkinson snapped. 'This is a very serious murder investigation.'

'Which Maria isn't part of,' Margery insisted. She stood from her seat, looking between them. 'She touched that vase yesterday, that's why her fingerprints are on it.'

'We also had a report of an altercation at the school yesterday because she had been looking at the vase,' Officer Wilkinson continued. 'Several of the cleaning team watched her argue with Mrs Black before it was broken up by the headteacher. They said Ms Glover rushed off after. Ran away to the canteen and asked her sister to say she'd been with her all day.'

'That was about something else,' Margery said, turned to Symon desperately. 'You can't possibly believe she'd kill anyone just for a little argument? And the DNA, well, that's probably wrong, isn't it? You'll just have to retest everything…'

Symon gave her such a pitying look that it made Margery's stomach writhe with worry.

'That remains to be proven either way,' Officer Wilkinson said, his expression neutral. 'Unfortunately, if the forensic evidence comes back as I suspect it will, then Ms Glover leaving through the fire escape down the hallway from the storeroom Mrs Black was found in is very suspicious. Wouldn't you say so?'

Margery found herself lost for words, opening and closing her mouth stupidly.

'How do you know she did that?' she managed to get out.

'All the fire escapes at the school have CCTV,' Officer Wilkinson said, the smug smile appearing finally as Margery knew it eventually would.

The doors behind them burst open, slamming against the wall. Clementine entered the canteen, looking terribly flustered and so unlike herself that Margery found fear running down her spine at the sight of her. Clementine was not someone usually so consumed with such anger.

'You can't possibly believe Maria did this!' Clementine snapped at the police officer, who stared at her in surprise. 'Hasn't Maria been through enough? She's been in enough police station cells for a lifetime, can't you leave her alone?'

'Her record for evading police custody is quite substantial and we already have a team searching for her,' Officer Wilkinson told Clementine firmly. 'I have it on good jurisdiction that she's only recently returned to the country after being on the run for a number of years.'

'Yes, but—'

'So unfortunately, we have no choice,' Officer Wilkinson told her.

'Call it off,' Clementine said, her hands uncurling from the fists they had been in and reaching for Officer Wilkinson in desperation. 'Call off the search, please.'

Officer Wilkinson shook his head. 'You know I can't.'

Can't or won't? Margery thought grimly.

'When you see your sister,' – Officer Wilkinson turned to Clementine, the nasty smile back on his face – 'you tell her to turn herself in. Don't try and hide her. We'll find her and then you'll go down too. Tell her, "If you're going to kill someone, you've got to be cleverer than that."'

—

They stepped out of the school into the cold night air. The wind whistled through Margery's hair and around her ankles, making her wish she had worn better shoes. Clementine began to walk, but Margery folded her arms tightly around herself and thought for a moment.

Going home immediately wouldn't answer any questions. Margery didn't think either of them would be able to sleep, and she needed something to do. The school was going to be closed on Monday, Rose had already sent the memo out to the school email. It had lit up Margery's phone, but it hadn't surprised her. Rose was no fool. Not like former head James Barrow, who had always insisted on the school remaining open even when there was almost certainly a murderer running around it, endangering students and teachers alike in his eagerness to sweep it under the rug and carry on as normal.

'Another murder,' Clementine said, stopping to poke her shoe into the nearest puddle. 'And it's barely been a year since Mr Fitzgerald died. Maria… she wouldn't have killed Eleanor. How could she? I know the police think they know everything about her past, but she didn't have a choice, did she?'

'I know,' Margery said, her head suddenly feeling heavy with it all. 'Where will Maria be? Would she have gone home?'

'No, I don't think so,' Clementine said, shaking her head adamantly. 'She's not as stupid as he thinks she is. Oh, Margery, I don't trust that Officer Wilkinson, do you? Not after all that cover-up with Mr Fitzgerald's death and now this.'

'No, I don't either,' Margery reassured her.

Clementine walked back over to her with a sigh of unhappiness.

'You don't understand,' Clementine said so quietly it was practically a whisper. She reached over and wound her fingers with Margery's own, the cold fingertips digging into the skin of her palm. 'Since Maria arrived, I've been waiting for it to all go wrong… and now it has. I was right to worry, and this just proves it.'

'No, it doesn't,' Margery told her firmly, squeezing her hand tightly. 'Nothing's happened yet. It'll all be a mistake.'

But she was beginning to wonder if perhaps that wasn't true. Maria had taken an interest in the vase, and she had argued with Eleanor Black the day before she was murdered. It was that sort of thing that made her very suspicious indeed, and that was without Maria's DNA being all over the scene of the crime. Margery closed her eyes and the vision of Eleanor on the floor came straight to the forefront of her mind.

'I always wanted a family,' Clementine said softly. 'Of course, I had Mum and Vincent, but I always wanted a sister to grow up with. I thought once she was here then I'd be happier, but I'm not. If anything, it's just made everything worse. I spend all my time worrying if she's all right, and now... well... now...'

Clementine trailed off and Margery decided that they couldn't just stand there and do nothing, and they couldn't go home and do nothing either. There must be more to this than they knew.

'Come on,' she said finally, beginning to walk and pulling Clementine along with her.

'Where are you going?' Clementine asked, but she let herself be led.

'We've got to find out what's going on,' Margery explained. 'Let's go and get some answers. We'll never find out what happened staying here.'

'But Maria...' Clementine began.

'We need to help her before the police get their claws into her,' Margery told her firmly. 'She's not going to be stupid enough to go somewhere we know. Now, come on.'

They got into the car and drove a short distance away, stopping in the street and hoping that the car lights and engine hadn't woken any of the neighbours.

Clementine knocked on the door and waited. Margery stepped back to survey the dark house. She hoped it wasn't too late.

Ceri-Ann had been at the studio during the events of the evening, but that didn't mean that she would still be awake – not with baby Nick being the handful he was. Ceri-Ann had returned from maternity leave a few months earlier, but she was still only in three days a week. Margery wished she could pay her the same money as before so she could work less and spend more time with her young family, but Ceri-Ann didn't seem to mind that much. She was always excitedly telling them how much Nick loved his sessions at nursery and showing them photographs of his adventures. And anyway, Ceri-Ann's and Symon's parents split the rest of the childcare between them to give her a break sometimes.

When Margery and Clem knocked at her door, Ceri-Ann answered, the baby monitor in her hand, the creak of the door hinges piercing in the calm night. She didn't seem surprised to see them still in their eveningwear – the opposite, Margery thought.

'Hiya, mate,' Ceri-Ann said, her face falling at the sight of Clementine's. Her warm smile didn't quite meet her eyes. 'I'm so sorry about Maria – it's crap, isn't it?'

Margery watched Clementine's shoulders slump at the apology. Ceri-Ann's fingers played with the baby monitor nervously, but her gaze stayed on Clementine's face, hoping for reassurance.

'Symon feels so bad about the search,' Ceri-Ann continued. 'He wanted to come and talk to you before, but obviously he couldn't… I haven't been able to sleep just thinking about it all. Mrs Black was grim, wasn't she? But she didn't deserve to die like that, no one does.'

'It's all right,' Clementine said, her voice a sail with all the wind taken out of it. 'It's not Symon's fault, it's just… I can't see Maria killing that woman. Why would she?'

'Come in,' Ceri-Ann said, stepping back from the doorway and gesturing them inside. 'I'll put the kettle on. You don't mind herbal tea, do you?'

'We're not keeping you up?' Margery asked, her mother's voice in her head telling her to watch her manners.

'Nah, can't sleep after all that,' Ceri-Ann said. 'I'm not the best sleeper anyway, to be honest. I think even without the murder, the look on Rose's face when she saw all the stuff was missing would have kept me up. Christ, I don't think I'll ever see anything that funny ever again.'

Inside, they sank down into the crushed velvet sofa while Ceri-Ann went into the kitchen. She left the baby monitor on the living-room coffee table with them, and Margery watched as Nicholas slept peacefully in his cot. Sometimes she wished she could go back to being that tiny. It seemed like a nicer life than the one they were living at the moment.

Ceri-Ann's living room had a comforting air. It was youthful it its decoration. And it all had a purpose – not like Margery and Clementine's busy living room that had way too many old, worn chairs, and a ridiculous amount of trinkets stuffed into the glass display cabinet.

The wall behind the sofa was a bright cheerful yellow and the rest of the place was all sage greens and golds. It should have clashed horribly, but it felt soothing somehow, like a splash of colour on a dreary oil painting. The unit beside the television contained all of Nicholas's books and the toy chest sat on the floor next to it, so full the toys on top looked perilously close to toppling to the floor. The dining table sat over in the other room. Beside it, Nicholas's highchair was set up for the morning, the splash mat underneath ready for his usual breakfast antics.

Margery had always had a soft spot for Ceri-Ann, but she had especially enjoyed watching Ceri-Ann grow into being Nicholas's mother. It had brought out even more of Ceri-Ann's already joyful nature and turned it into something stronger and slightly more sensible.

Ceri-Ann brought them in a mug of tea each, Margery watched the steam rising from her cup as Ceri-Ann left to get her own mug. She sat down on the floor in front of the coffee table and looked at them expectantly.

'Can you tell us what the police think happened?' Clementine began, not wasting any time. 'Other than Maria killing someone, which didn't happen. Have you heard anything from Symon yet?'

'Don't worry, mate,' Ceri-Ann said, 'I believe you. I think Symon does too from what he told me on the phone on his break, but he has to investigate. It's his job. But I reckon she'll be let off before they get her in. No evidence.'

'Except the fingerprints,' Margery reminded her. 'And the fact she's on the run after being witnessed near the murder scene.'

'Oh yeah.' Ceri-Ann winced. 'Yeah, that doesn't really scream "innocent", does it? Thing is, though, wasn't Maria trying to have a look at all that stuff for the auction? Didn't she break into the office to have a look? Not going to lie to you, but I was definitely trying to keep listening to your conversation when Gloria dragged us all off to the staff room, which we still haven't found by the way! We ended up all sharing a can of Coke from the leisure centre vending machine because we didn't have time to get our purses and we only had a pound that Seren found on the floor.'

'She did,' Margery said, remembering the altercation they had had with Maria and Eleanor. 'Do you think she might have touched some of the items?'

'She could have done, couldn't she?' Clementine said. 'She could easily have touched the vase that killed Eleanor even if she wasn't the killer.'

'Yeah, exactly, mate.' Ceri-Ann nodded along. 'Do you know why she cared about the vase so much, though?'

'What do you mean?' Margery asked.

'She asked me loads of questions about it last week.' Ceri-Ann shrugged. 'Obviously I don't know anything about stuff like that. I'd have just used the vase to put sunflowers in – it's a nice shade of blue for them, isn't it? But that would have probably spat in the face of about two hundred years of tradition or whatever, if you read the auction pamphlet.'

Margery wondered where their pamphlet was, it must still be at home somewhere. Maybe it would hold some clue about the vase, other than it being a historical artefact. People had kept saying it was one, but no one seemed any the wiser why. Eleanor would have known exactly what was so special about the vase, she thought grimly. That's why she was so worried about Maria sniffing about in the auction items, probably.

'Eleanor said that there were several secret bids for the vase, didn't she?' Margery said, thinking about loud. 'A few people must have been after it.'

'I can't see why Maria would want it,' Clementine said, the mug in her hand as full as it had been when Ceri-Ann handed it to her. 'None of this makes sense. It doesn't add up.'

'We'll have to see what she says,' Margery told her, trying to sound soothing. It didn't work and Clementine's face crumpled again. Margery suddenly had the worrying thought that Maria might well have wanted to take the vase. The school didn't pay terribly well, and Maria missed so many of her shifts she couldn't have much in her payslips anyway. And the money tin had gone missing... perhaps Maria was in financial difficulty.

An expensive heirloom vase would certainly have fixed that issue. Margery couldn't bring that up to Clementine, not yet. She would wait until Clementine had calmed down first.

'Symon rang me on his break,' Ceri-Ann said, looking between them both. 'He said that they haven't found her yet. But they're searching everywhere and waiting outside your house and shop.'

'She must have an alibi if she didn't kill Eleanor,' Clementine said abruptly, shaking her head. 'Why did she run?'

'Maybe she doesn't want them to know why she was really there,' Ceri-Ann suggested. 'Why would she have been in the hallway anyway?'

Margery shook her head at the same time as Clementine put her head in her hands.

'What I don't understand is why Maria would smash the vase if she was going to steal it,' Margery said. 'Surely that proves she wasn't trying to?'

'Yeah, exactly,' Ceri-Ann nodded. 'But where are the other auction things? Did she have a part in hiding them?'

'That's a good point,' Margery said, thinking about it. If Maria had tried to steal from the auction, why would she have stopped at the vase?

Clementine scoffed. 'Your point is a knife!' she snapped. She got to her feet and began to put her coat back on. 'None of this is helping, Ceri-Ann. I'm sorry we've wasted your time like this. Margery, let's go home.'

'We can't give up yet, Clem,' Margery said, looking up in surprise. She reached out for Clementine's hand. Clementine allowed her to grasp her by the wrist, albeit reluctantly. 'There's got to be something to do to help her. Where are the missing auction items? There's got to be something more to it all.'

'I reckon they're still at the school,' Ceri-Ann said. 'No one would have been able to smuggle them out. Not now they'll be searching all the cameras. I reckon they're hidden somewhere in the building.'

'But where?' Margery asked. 'Surely there's not that many hiding spots?'

'I dunno,' Ceri-Ann said with a sigh, suddenly looking very tired. 'That's what you two are good at really. I'm crap at this stuff. I'm always amazed by the ending of every episode of *Midsomer Murders*.'

'Yes exactly, we'll work it out,' Margery told Clementine, giving her wrist a squeeze. 'And if we don't, then Symon will help—'

Ceri-Ann made a noise in her throat. Margery turned to look at her.

'Sorry,' Ceri-Ann said, looking sheepish. 'Symon would definitely try and help, you know he would… Well…' Her eyes flicked to the baby monitor for a moment, as if she was considering something. 'The only thing is… he's got to do his job. He's so close to becoming a detective and he was on thin ice after the last time he helped you with Mr Fitzgerald's murder…'

'What are you saying?' Clementine asked her, looking down at Ceri-Ann with wide eyes.

Margery knew exactly what Ceri-Ann was saying and she understood. It was an unfortunate truth that they would have to deal with.

'Symon can't help us,' Margery said. Ceri-Ann looked relieved that she didn't have to repeat herself. 'We'll have to do this alone, Clem.'

'Are you joking?' Clementine asked Ceri-Ann, shaking her head in disbelief. 'My sister's wanted for a murder investigation and the only person who could help us, won't help us! Why?'

'Look, Clem,' Margery said, trying to placate her with a touch to her arm. 'Symon has a family to worry about. He can't lose his job for us.'

Clementine pulled her arm away with a sneer.

'I've heard enough,' Clementine said. She turned and left the room.

Margery watched her go in shock for a moment, before getting up herself to leave. Clementine slammed the door behind her, the glass rattling with the force of it. On the baby monitor screen, Nicholas stirred. Margery and Ceri-Ann gave each other the same sympathetic look.

Chapter Five

'I don't think we have much of a choice here,' Clementine said, her voice rising in fury as they made their way down through the town centre on Sunday morning. 'It's only a matter of time before the police find Maria. We need to be prepared for them to charge her and get ahead of them. That means an investigation of our own.' She turned to look pleadingly at Margery. 'You can't bow out, Margery. Please, I need your help.'

The police were still watching the shop. Margery and Clementine had been informed of that this morning. It had made things quite awkward for the classes that were being held inside the shop, but that couldn't be helped.

Margery had been dealing with a distraught Clementine since they had left Ceri-Ann's house early on Saturday morning and things hadn't improved. Clementine's temperament was always quite fractious, but this was even worse. Margery felt like she'd been spending the weekend trying to bowl down the pins of Clementine's anger using only marbles.

'All right,' Margery agreed for the ninth or tenth time that day already. It was much easier to simply go along with Clementine when she was like this, and really Margery wasn't convinced that Maria would kill Eleanor either. Why would she? Margery didn't trust Officer

Wilkinson either, not as far as she could have thrown him, which was about half a centimetre at best.

She knew that Clementine was just saying things now – she didn't have any idea how to help Maria either. The rest of the school CCTV was being scoured with a fine-tooth comb, Rose and the police both looking for the missing auction items. Surely something was bound to turn up on that before Margery and Clementine found anything out. They didn't have anyone to ask anything either – everyone they could have asked for information had been in the studio with them while Eleanor was murdered. But there must have been someone who had it out for Eleanor enough to kill her – and Clementine was adamant that wasn't Maria. Margery agreed with her in principle. It was just that there didn't seem to be any other suspects.

The town centre bustled with the Sunday market. The main road was always closed off the last Sunday of the month so the market stalls could be put out. It always made Margery really miss Mr Fitzgerald, who had always left his shop and sold his bizarre trinkets from a stall instead. There had never been a queue and Mr Fitgerald had always been eager to chat.

Margery saw Rose walking towards them up the hill with Jason behind her before Clementine stopped them. James Barrow, Rose's husband, was sauntering along next to them. Since James had stepped down from the headteacher position at Summerview, he had a much more relaxed air about him.

'Ladies,' Rose called, waving the paper shopping bag in her hand as she greeted them. 'Clementine, I'm… I'm just so sorry about Maria… I hope it all gets sorted.'

'Yes, it will, I'm sure,' Clementine said. 'Thank you.'

It was a rare genuine moment between them. Usually their conversations bristled along with Clementine trying to wind Rose up, and Rose taking the bait every single time. Margery wasn't sure what to say, looking between them and feeling awkward at intruding.

'So how does it feel to have your very own school murder investigation?' Clementine asked Rose, who groaned at the question. Margery watched as James hid his smirk behind his hand.

'Please shut up, Mrs Butcher-Baker,' Rose said, and Margery felt normality returning, although she could see the hint of a smile around Rose's lips. 'Honestly, the thing is...' She lowered her voice to a decibel only usually listened to by Rose's dog, Jason. 'I know you're not supposed to speak ill of the dead, but I didn't like Eleanor much. She wasn't particularly nice to people who didn't do everything the way she demanded. I'm actually not that surprised she's been murdered, but you didn't hear that from me!' She stood back at full height and looked around sadly. 'We've been at the school all weekend, it's going to be open from Tuesday, I think. But we decided to deal with the crime scene properly for once...' She gave James a look, and he held his hands up in defeat. 'The police have been in DNA testing and all sorts. It's nearly over now, although I don't think we'll be able to use that room any more. We might have to make it some sort of memorial to her.'

Margery couldn't think of anything worse than having an old, dusty cupboard be where visitors came to pay their respects to you.

'Has the CCTV shown any more of why Maria was there on Friday night?' Margery asked. 'She came to me in the studio just before Eleanor was found, but we didn't think much of it in the commotion.'

'I wish she'd told you why she wanted to see me,' Clementine said, her face falling. 'It's killing me not knowing. Maybe she needed help with something.'

Rose and James looked on as Margery patted Clementine's hand soothingly.

Before the moment got too awkward, there was a call from across the road. 'Yoohoo! Clem, Margery!'

Mrs Mugglethwaite made her way across to them, stumbling under the weight of her shopping and her hefty raincoat, which was so large the sleeves completely covered her hands. She looked like a Teflon-coated monster with bags for hands.

'Good Lord, let's escape before she gets here,' Rose hissed to James. Then, a little louder, she said, 'See you on Tuesday, ladies.'

They slipped away just as Mrs Mugglethwaite arrived at Margery's feet.

'I saw you and I just had to come straight over,' Mrs Mugglethwaite gasped. 'I heard all about it all with your sister, Clem, dreadful business! Now tell me, why did she kill Eleanor? Was it for the vase? Why did she smash it? Couldn't she have killed her with something else if she was just trying to steal the vase? Where is she now? Is she hiding in your shed?'

'She didn't kill her,' Clementine snapped. 'Honestly, Martha, have you got no tact at all?'

'I just thought, since I saw her at the museum last week… well, she was very elusive,' Mrs Mugglethwaite said, her mouth dropping in surprise at Clementine's outburst. 'She was snooping about one of the exhibits and asking me things about the school auction. I had to tell her, "I don't know anything about the auction... Now, the price of a book of stamps? That I can help you with."'

'What did she ask you about?' Margery asked, feeling her jaw drop.

Clementine stood next to her, staring at Mrs Mugglethwaite in interest.

'Gosh, all sorts of things,' Mrs Mugglethwaite exclaimed. 'What was the most valuable – of course I told her I didn't know. I don't know much about that sort of thing at all, but I pointed her in the direction of Eleanor, because obviously Eleanor was a great well of information, wasn't she? Knew everyone and everything, not like me, I like to keep myself to myself...'

'Maria didn't kill her,' Clementine told her firmly.

Mrs Mugglethwaite nodded in a way that told Margery she didn't believe a word of it.

'Well, a lot of people have it out for Maria, don't they?' Mrs Mugglethwaite said. 'Look at Dawn and her petition to remove her caravan from your driveway. I said to Dawn, "Dawn, it's Margery and Clementine's driveway. They can do whatever they want on it. If they wanted to put a pile of sand there and have beach parties on it then it would be well within their rights."'

That was true, Margery thought; a lot of people did have it out for Maria. Perhaps she had just been in the wrong place at the wrong time, though that didn't explain why Maria had been asking questions about how expensive things were of relative strangers. To her knowledge, Maria had only met Mrs Mugglethwaite once very briefly before when she had introduced them at a chance meeting in Tesco a few days after Maria's arrival. She eyed Clementine's face. She was nodding earnestly – desperate for proof that Maria had been set up.

'I wonder what Wilkinson will think once he realises, he's wrong,' Clementine mused.

'Don't talk to me about Wilkinson,' Martha said, her eyes suddenly glistening. 'Losing Woolworths from the high street all those years ago, that was dreadful… but Wilko? I still haven't found a new place I can buy both pick and mix and a dozen envelopes.'

'You work in a post office…?' Margery found herself saying, unsure why they were still entertaining the conversation.

Mrs Mugglethwaite didn't have any useful information, so they made their escape.

—

Later that evening, Margery finished the washing-up while Clementine plotted numerous timelines of the day of the auction, all of them useless. Without Maria home to tell them, there was no way to know where she had been when Eleanor was being murdered. Margery wished that Maria had stayed away from the school building entirely, or sat back and enjoyed the auction like they had all been planning to do. Now there was a missing piece where Maria had disappeared. There was a knock on the door.

'I bet that's Maria,' Clementine said, jumping up from the dining table to go to the front door. 'She'll be here to turn herself in. The police will realise she's innocent and let her go!'

Margery stepped back from the sink and was just taking off her rubber washing-up gloves when Symon entered the room. Clementine followed him, her face a dark cloud of disappointment.

'What's going on?' Margery asked Symon.

'I know Ceri said I couldn't help you...' he began.

Margery gestured for him to sit. Symon was still wearing his uniform, and he looked flustered and pale... even paler than usual. He sat at the dining table and Clementine sat opposite him, her eyes desperately searching his face.

'What's happened now?' she demanded. 'Where's my sister?'

'I'm here to warn you,' he said. 'Wilkinson's trying to chuck me off the case – too much history with you. But he's got plans for when he finds her. He wants to charge her then and there, and keep her until trial. He's already applied for the extended custody order.'

'You are joking,' Clementine gasped. 'She won't be allowed bail?'

'No.' Symon shook his head. 'Not with her history. He's really excited about it.'

Maria had run before, Margery thought worriedly. But she hadn't had much of choice last time, she had been framed.

'Look, even if she's not here, Maria's belongings are going to be searched tonight. Some of the auction items are still missing. I tried to stop them, but he won't have it,' Symon explained. 'They're on the way here right now. They'll search the house and the shop too.'

'You're really not part of it?' Margery asked desperately. 'Ceri-Ann said...'

'I know what she said, and she's right,' Symon said. 'The only way I can help you is if I stay under the radar. Wilkinson can't suspect I'm helping you again. He doesn't trust me after all that business with Mr Fitzgerald's death a few months ago. Well, he was the one who helped cover-up a murder, wasn't he? It's a joke, this station.' Symon shook his head. 'Listen, I'm doing what I can, please trust me on that.' He looked around again, as though Officer Wilkinson might burst in at any second. 'I just thought I'd let you know, just in case you had anything suspicious or if Maria is here. I can't help you if she is. They'll definitely search the house once they've finished searching the van. I'm sorry I can't do anything else.'

'We don't have anything suspicious and Maria certainly isn't here,' Margery said. Symon nodded.

'I didn't think you would, but you never know,' Symon said. 'I like you both. I don't want you to get into trouble too. The thing is…' He lowered his voice to a fraught whisper. 'The vase that was smashed at the crime scene, the one that was used to murder Mrs Black, it wasn't the real vase…'

'What?' Margery and Clementine exclaimed together.

'The one that was smashed wasn't old enough to be the real one,' Symon said, shaking his head. 'Wilkinson has a theory that Ms Glover stole the real vase and swapped it with a fake one. He thinks she was caught in the act by Mrs Black. And then Ms Glover killed her in a panic.'

'Maria wouldn't have killed anyone,' Clementine said for the hundredth time since Friday night, but her voice sounded weak and confused.

'Then where is the other vase?' Margery asked. 'Were they both smashed?'

'Not that we can tell,' Symon said. He looked tired and older than his years in the dim light from the kitchen bulb hanging above the table. 'We're looking for the real vase still. I tried to tell Wilkinson, how would Ms Glover have got the vase out on the CCTV without being seen? It's a huge vase. But he's convinced she stashed it somewhere.'

'Maria wouldn't have had time to hide it,' Margery said. 'Would she?'

'We thought that the most likely place it would be is at the school still. We've ripped the place apart searching for it,' Symon explained. 'Here's the thing, though – I think you're right. Officer Wilkinson seems to think she hid it in time somewhere, but I think that if she did do it...' He held his hands up before Clementine could profess Maria's innocence again for her. 'If it was her, then she must have either had an accomplice or been followed and they took the vase once she ran out of the fire escape, but none of that explains the fake vase.'

'So, someone else could have killed Eleanor?' Clementine said. 'I knew it.'

'My running theory currently is that Eleanor knew whoever killed her,' Symon explained, taking off his hat and running his hands through his light hair. 'There weren't many signs of a struggle, and... God, I really shouldn't show you this...'

He took a piece of paper out of his pocket and unfolded it. 'This is what was on the bottom of the fake vase. They've been piecing it back together in evidence,' he said in explanation. 'We reckon there's more going on with whoever this is. We're looking for them now.'

Margery strained her neck to look at the photograph. It was of a piece of ceramic that had been pieced back together and held the engraved initials R. J. E, the letters twisted together in cursive. It had obviously been painstakingly pieced back together from the thousand pieces of the vase that had been strewn across the floor of the storeroom they had found Eleanor inside. The same initials that Margery had seen on the storeroom floor the night Eleanor died.

There was a succession of thumps on the living-room door, and they all froze. Symon pushed the piece of paper into Clementine's hands.

'Mrs Butcher-Bakers!' Officer Wilkinson thumped on the door again, his booming voice bellowing through the house and into the quiet kitchen. 'It's the police.'

'Oh no,' Symon said, his eyes darting around the room as though looking for a place to hide.

'Go out through the back garden,' Margery whispered, quickly rushing to where the back door keys hung on the hook by the door. 'You can get through the estate down the alley behind our house.'

Symon nodded gratefully and Margery rushed out into the garden to unlock the back gate for him, her fingers slipping on the keys as she fumbled with them. She somehow managed to let Symon out into the alley and shut the gate again. She slipped the keys into her pocket and then went to the trowel that Maria had left lying next to the bed of rosemary she had recently planted. Margery had given up asking her to put the tools back in the shed months before and Maria wouldn't have a chance now. She looked sadly over the soil. It was still freshly turned. Maria had begun to label what things were but hadn't finished that yet either, leaving just a singular wooden stake sticking from the ground, still blank. Margery looked up from the soil as Officer Wilkinson took a step into the garden.

'Hello, Margery,' he said, looking at the strawberry plants, which were beginning to wilt. 'I'm sorry we're not here on a nicer occasion – but as I've just explained to your wife, this is essential police business.' He inspected the old fence between their garden and the neighbour's, running a finger over the worn paint, which flaked off under his touch. 'We're going to search your shop, the house and Maria's van. If you're hiding her then I think you ought to speak up now. It'll be better for you if you do.'

'Well, we don't have anything to hide,' Margery said, trying not to feel guilty about the lie when the key to the garden gate was in her pocket. 'Search away.'

'I don't believe that for a minute,' Officer Wilkinson said nastily. 'I think you're hiding something here and I can't wait to find it. Then we'll see how clever you think you are in front of a judge.'

Margery ignored him and rejoined Clementine in the kitchen. Clementine was so angry her face was almost purple, her arms folded across her chest so tightly that Margery would sure her nails would leave indents in her skin. The paper Symon had given them was hidden in Clementine's pocket. Margery hoped beyond hope that the police wouldn't decide to search their persons. There was no telling what they might do.

They sat at the table in silence as the police began to ransack the house. They might be here a long while, Margery thought. She and Clem were not the neatest of people, and they had a lot of odd things that would need searching through. Margery sighed and got up to make a pot of tea.

She had just finished pouring the water from the kettle into the teapot when there was a commotion outside the house. Her head turned instinctively at the hullabaloo.

Clementine was already out of her seat, running from the kitchen without so much as a look back. Margery abandoned the teapot, following Clementine through the living room and out the front door. Margery gasped as she saw what was laid out on the sheet in froCnt front of Maria's van.

'That's the silver candlesticks from the auction,' she said, shaking her head in disbelief. 'And the bag of gold sovereigns. Gosh, Clem, she must have stolen the lot!'

Clementine looked as though she might have a heart attack. Her face had gone a horrible, yellow-tinged white and she clutched her chest as she leaned against the wall to steady herself.

'And the crockery we donated,' Margery added, her eyes widening. 'What on earth?'

'Looks like your sister-in-law did help herself to a few bits after all,' Officer Wilkinson scoffed from behind them. Another of his officers left the van, dropping another bag onto the ground. 'Makes sense, with her history.'

'She could have just asked us for that,' Margery said, shaking her head. 'It doesn't make any sense to steal it. You can't possibly believe that she would just have all of this? And her history wasn't stealing, she did what she needed to do to survive.'

'You're lucky I'm not arresting you, too,' Officer Wilkinson said, raising an eyebrow at Margery's outburst. 'Who's to say you didn't know this was here?'

'You can't be accusing us of that,' Margery snapped. 'How did it even get here? Maybe it was planted here to make Maria look guilty.'

'She doesn't need any help to look guilty.' Officer Wilkinson chuckled. He lowered his voice so his team couldn't hear, bending down to speak into Margery's ear. 'Don't worry, there's plenty of time for us to find something on you as well. Just you wait… and even if I don't, well, I'm sure I've got enough to scrape something insidious together. Your meddling days are nearly over.'

Margery turned to Clementine, who was standing still between them, her hands clenched into tight fists. She had expected Clementine to have a harsh reply for the police officer, but instead she simply stared down at the ground in front of the van in disbelief. Margery felt a shiver of fear run down her spine at the sight. Officer Wilkinson continued to direct his team, sneering the entire time.

Chapter Six

The weekend slipped by in a stressful haze, and then Tuesday stormed past too, almost taking Margery's sanity with it. It was hard enough arranging the food order normally, but she had needed to reschedule everything for Tuesday instead of Monday. Some of her suppliers didn't usually deliver on Tuesdays and it had taken a great deal of convincing and some awkward phone calls.

It was very much like the worst sort of unplanned bank holiday that could happen, and neither the students nor teachers cared that Margery was struggling to change the plans. It only mattered that there was food. The dinner ladies blended into the wallpaper easily at the school, unless something went wrong in the canteen, and then a giant billion-watt spotlight seemed to shine down on them. There was nothing that could make a person angrier than the kitchen running out of baked beans and cheese for the jacket potatoes. Mrs George, the head of English, had slammed her dinner tray down so hard that it had almost cracked in two, and Mr Worle from IT had put his change into the charity box in such a fit of anger that the coins had gathered together in the slot. It had taken Seren twenty minutes to unstick them with a butter knife. By the end of the day, Margery had felt more like a controlling prison warden than a kitchen manager, and she knew that the dinner lady team were more than happy to slope off quickly at the end of the shift.

It would all be better tomorrow, now they'd caught up. Margery breathed a huge sigh of relief once they could retreat to her dry store office, which was now blissfully empty of auction items.

Well, it would have been much more blissful if the auction items hadn't all ended up on Margery and Clementine's driveway and then in a police van... and even more ideal if they knew where Maria was. But beggars couldn't always be choosers. She knew that the sight of the police officers bemusedly pulling hundreds of Argos catalogues out of their shed would stay with her for a long time.

'So, what have we got to go off?' Clementine asked, pointing to the whiteboard in Margery's dry store office space in the canteen kitchen. 'Firstly – Maria was interested in the auction items. Yes, that's true, but we don't know why. And then she argued with Eleanor before she died because Eleanor caught her touching all the things in Rose's office, which is probably where her DNA came from at the crime scene... and obviously we know now that she must have stolen some of them...'

'Or all of them,' Margery sighed, thinking of the piles of stolen belongings that the police had managed to bring out of the small vehicle. She was annoyed with herself that they hadn't thought to check the van before. Not that they really should be tampering with evidence, but it would have been much less of a surprise at the very least.

'And the police found the initials R. J. E. on the fake vase,' Clementine said, stepping back to look at the board, tapping the pen against her lip. 'But we don't know who that is and neither do they.'

'No.' Margery grimaced. 'If the vase that was shattered at the crime scene wasn't the real one then someone must have been trying to swap it, mustn't they? What was Maria doing in the office the day before? Eleanor thought that Maria was snooping about the vase, and Maria didn't exactly deny that, did she?'

'Well... maybe,' Clementine said, slumping back down onto her makeshift seat on a twenty-five-kilo bag of flour. 'Then it would definitely have her fingerprints on it, wouldn't it? But if her plan was to swap the real vase for a fake, then she could have done that then. That would have been the most sensible thing to do. Why wait till the auction? And the other thing is, she didn't have a vase on her when you saw her at the auction, did she?'

'No, she just had her coat on,' Margery said, tapping her chin with her pen. 'She didn't even have a bag.'

'Well, forget all that. We're supposed to be finding out how Maria didn't kill Eleanor, not trying to make my sister look more suspicious!' Clementine sighed. 'Maybe she did hide the vase. Gosh, I wish she could just tell us where she was before the auction. They found all the other auction items quickly enough.'

Margery hadn't said a word about Maria's potential guilt yet to Clementine, but there were several missing holes in the timeline. They needed to explore all the options before they came to the conclusion that Maria was guilty, but it was not easy.

'What do we do now, then?' Clementine asked. Her face was the picture of defeat.

Margery and Clementine had hoped that they might find Maria before the police did, but none of their usual searches had brought any results. They had visited the Bell and Hope pub several times, but each visit the owner had assured them Maria hadn't been in. The dinner lady team WhatsApp group was busy with messages of possible hiding spots, but no one had managed to form anything concrete yet. It was as though Maria had disappeared from the face of the earth. Clementine wasn't dealing with it very well.

They were interrupted by Rose. She opened the door to the office and poked her head around the door, her face lighting up with happiness when she saw them.

'Ooh good, you're still here,' she said. 'Could I have a word?'

'Of course,' Margery said, gesturing for her to enter.

They had called her after the police had raided their home on Sunday. Margery had demanded to know who had set up the auction and why they hadn't noticed that anything was missing. Rose had assured her that Eleanor had set the auction up herself, and she hadn't mentioned that anything was missing. That was extremely odd in itself to Margery.

Rose leaned against the chest freezer, somehow still looking every part the imposing headteacher she was, even slumped against it. 'What a terrible day. The police have ripped the place apart. I'll never get the science rooms posters back in the right order, the students will have to make a new display on the cell cycle...'

'They didn't find the vase?' Clementine interrupted her, her face hopeful for a moment before falling again at Rose's shake of her head.

'No,' Rose said. 'And I don't think they will. Whoever killed Eleanor will be long gone with it. Silly thing to kill someone over, but here we are! The people of Dewstow and Ittonvale have killed for far less, as you know.'

Rose gave Clementine and Margery a pitying once-over, as though unsure what to say next.

'You don't think Maria killed Eleanor?' Margery asked, her face twisting in confusion. She had been sure Rose would blame Maria. Clementine looked just as confused, but also as ecstatic as if Rose had announced that they would all be receiving a million-pound Christmas bonus.

'No, I don't,' Rose told her firmly. 'She was a complete mess, of course, and obviously bad style must run in the family, no offence, Clementine,' – Clementine shrugged, glancing down at her flour-covered apron and hot-pink kitchen clogs – 'but she wasn't a murderer. Anyone could see that. Maria was just a poor lost soul. There must be another cause for what happened. Of course, I was a bit annoyed when the auction items were missing…'

That was an understatement, Margery thought. At the auction, Rose had looked as though she might be about to explode.

'But they're all back, now, aren't they? Yes, maybe a bit of petty theft, but the vase? No. Eleanor's death? Certainly not, I just can't fathom it.'

'It's a shame we can't prove that she's innocent,' Margery sighed. 'The police certainly don't seem to agree. They ransacked our house, turned the entire place upside down looking for her and the vase.'

'They're still searching CCTV,' Rose said. 'Of course we don't have it in the studio and there were no obvious comings and goings from outside the building that Gary could see when we watched the footage.' Gary Matthews was Seren's husband, and the school's lone security guard. He spent most of his time reading books he'd borrowed from the school library and being outsmarted by Year Nine students playing *Knock Knock Ginger* with his office door. 'Whoever murdered Eleanor entered as a guest like the rest of the crowd and then must have left the same way as everyone else. I thought I'd check the timelines to see if anyone else left, but there was nothing.'

'No one left carrying a big parcel or bag?' Margery asked, feeling desperate for a glimmer of hope all of a sudden.

'Lots of people,' Rose said. 'You forget that people were still dropping off auction items. This is honestly a nightmare.'

'Don't you have any other CCTV?' Clementine asked. 'There must be something of Maria somewhere.'

'There isn't any of that storage room,' Rose explained. 'I did think about having a camera put there for backstage footage on the school play recordings, a little DVD extra, you know? Like the good old days before all the horrors of streaming things on the internet.' She paused, deep in thought, her brow furrowing. 'The problem is, there were so many people here that day, and we weren't monitoring the backstage areas. I assumed Eleanor wanted to be alone. Crikey, you should have heard her going on about the sacred space she needed to unpack and polish the auction items…'

'Maria's fingerprints were found on the broken vase somehow,' Margery said. 'It doesn't look good if we don't have any CCTV.'

'Don't you have a camera in your office?' Clementine asked Rose.

Rose paused for a moment, her eyebrows raising in a way that told Margery she wasn't sure what she should say. Margery thought she might be about to reveal some important information.

'I don't usually,' Rose said breezily. 'But that day, I was preparing my new... I mean...' She coughed in a way Margery found incredibly suspicious. 'Well... what I mean to say is I did that day. I'll check the footage.'

Margery asked, 'If Maria took all those auction things, then how did she get them off site? She certainly couldn't have walked them out of the building.'

Rose turned pale in a way that made Margery's stomach turn over horribly.

'She really took them, didn't she?' Margery asked.

Rose nodded. 'The police found the footage on the security cameras this morning,' she said. 'She brought a van around to the playground by the drama studio and then loaded it, right under our noses as we were preparing for the auction.'

'What!' Margery cried. Clementine gasped, but didn't say anything, her face falling.

'Why would she do that?' Clementine said finally.

'I don't know,' Rose said. She brought her hand to the bridge of her nose and squeezed. 'If it helps, she wasn't alone.'

'Not alone?' Margery said, feeling her jaw drop of its own accord. 'Who was she with?'

'She must have been coerced into it,' Clementine said with a firm nod. 'There's no way Maria would have done something like this without being pressured into it. That must be why she was looking for you, Margery, at the auction...'

Margery wasn't sure any of that was entirely true, but it didn't seem wise to say.

'They don't know who was with her,' Rose told them. 'I'll see if I can get a copy of the footage so you can see.'

Margery mumbled something about that being helpful at the same time as Clementine groaned.

'Gosh, what are we going to do?' Clementine threw her hands up in exasperation. 'We might as well throw Maria down the drain now, that's how useless we are!'

'It's not all lost yet,' Rose said, tapping her finger to her chin in thought. 'Have you been to the museum?'

'What, ever? Or like now for this murder?' Clementine asked. 'We try and avoid it if we can. Too many dusty coats of arms. I think we went once at school. A boy in my class called Percy fell down the stairs.'

Rose gave her a very long look that suggested she wasn't convinced that Clementine had graduated from school at all.

'That's true,' Margery said, thinking it over. 'Actually, Martha Mugglethwaite told us she saw Maria there… and that Maria was asking a lot of questions.'

'I only say because Eleanor owned the museum,' Rose said. 'I'm not sure what will happen to it now. Perhaps one of the Fishers will take it over, though I don't think there are many left.'

'Who are the Fishers?' Clementine asked, coming out of her sulk.

'One of the older families in Ittonvale,' Rose explained. 'Nearly as old as the Black family of Dewstow. Well, I suppose that family is smaller too now that Eleanor and Vivian have both passed, and I don't think there's many of the original Fisher family left that are younger than about ninety.'

Vivian had ended up weaved tightly into a difficult murder Margery and Clementine had solved the year before. It hadn't ended well for most of the people involved, including Vivian who had forfeit her place as the

Black family matriarch. Margery often wondered what had become of the family since, and who was now living in Vivian's huge summer house in Devon and the Black family mansion at the top of Ittonvale Hill. It was only a short drive up the road, but it might as well have been on another planet. It was worlds apart from Margery and Clementine's tiny end terrace, which had just enough room for them and two cats to live comfortably.

Rose went to the door and peered out into the hallway, checking they were really alone.

'I think there's a lot more going on here than we thought,' Rose whispered, 'but I don't know how to find out. Perhaps I can get you up to Ittonvale school for the day. You'll find something out if you work there for a day or so, I'm sure of it. There are still a few Black family descendants at Ittonvale, though I'm always amazed that they would be sent to a public school, the Fisher and the Black family are linked you see. The older Fishers all went to boarding school – perhaps the money for the fees isn't there any more for the younger family members. I'm surprised they sent them to Ittonvale though, when anyone with eyes can see that Summerview Secondary School is the obvious educational choice!'

Margery nodded agreeably trying not to look at the flaking plaster on the walls of the dry store.

'The museum it is, then,' Margery said.

'For now,' Rose promised.

Rose had an expression, Margery thought, that held a secret. She wondered what on earth Rose had been filming in her office. Whatever it was, maybe it could hold the key to solving the mystery of what had really happened to Eleanor Black and whether Maria was genuinely involved. Margery knew from previous experiences with Rose that there would be no point in pressing her for answers, however. They would have to wait for her to come back to them.

Chapter Seven

They had been worried that the museum might be closed and had disagreed what to do if it was. Clementine wanted to smash a back window, but Margery reminded her that they didn't know what they were looking for and they wouldn't be able to return if they were caught. Luckily, they didn't need to break in – the lights were still on as they arrived.

They rushed down the hill to the riverbank, following the footpath until they reached Dewstow Museum. It was a huge boxy building that had once been used as a hospital in the First World War for recovering soldiers returning home to Dewstow. It was much older than that, though. Margery didn't know much about its history, but she knew that it had once been a large family home. She'd never thought to explore any more about it. In fact, they had only been there once, and that had been as part of former kitchen manager Caroline's kitchen choir. They had sung outside the museum as part of the Christmas celebrations. Unfortunately, it had been quite far off the beaten track for the rest of the town and Caroline had only arranged it because it was very close to her house. Seren lived there now, and Margery could see the street that led to Seren's from the front of the museum.

'Hello,' a timid woman behind the till said as they entered. 'Are you residents? The museum is free for residents!'

Margery turned to look at her in surprise, somehow not expecting to see anyone now Eleanor was no longer here to run the museum. The woman was slightly taller than both Margery and Clementine, which was not saying much really. She looked a fair bit younger too. She was probably in her late forties or a very young fifties. Her hair was still red and youthful with only a few strands of lighter grey, and her cheeks were freckled in a way Margery had always been envious of on school friends.

'We are residents,' Margery told her. The woman beamed at them both before opening the huge book on the desk in front of her to sign them in. 'Are you still open? We thought you might be closed.'

'I was supposed to close a few minutes ago,' she said, 'but then I saw you both coming over! I said to myself, "Cecelia, you've got guests!"'

'Oh, you don't need to stay open just for us,' Margery exclaimed, feeling her eyes widening. 'I'm sure you want to get home...'

'Don't worry about that, I don't get many visitors!' Cecelia beamed, her hands clasping together in excitement. 'Would you like to sit in our Anderson shelter exhibit? I can put on a special CD of World War Two noises for you.' She smiled broadly. It lit her face. 'Sometimes I sit in there and have my sandwiches at lunch just listening to the CD and imagining it all!'

'Oh dear, no thank you,' Margery said in alarm. 'We just thought we'd have a look around at the local history. Do you have an exhibit for that?'

'Of course! How exciting, I'm always hoping someone will ask.' Cecelia jumped up and beckoned for them to follow. 'Come with me. I'll show you.'

Margery had hoped that they would be able to get in and out of the museum quickly with some answers about Maria's interest in the vase, but that became impossible as Cecelia began to give them a very intense guided tour. They followed her up the stairs and across the hall into the main local exhibit, which featured a large number of blown-up photographs of Dewstow and Ittonvale. Margery and Clementine had lived in Dewstow together for over forty years, but Margery wasn't a local originally, having grown up more than a few miles away. Clementine had told her own version of Dewstow's history over the years, but Margery had learned to take many of Clementine's stories with a large tablespoon of salt.

According to Clementine, the towns of Dewstow and Ittonvale had originally been one larger town revolving around the wall that surrounded Dewstow. Not much of the original town was left now, but there were still remnants dotted all over the area.

As the story went, Ittonvale had prospered, being on the industrial side of the river while Dewstow struggled as run-off from the factories killed the fish that Dewstow used to farm. Eventually they had been divided, separated by the tiny bridge that led over the river in between them. The bridge was still there, though it was only used as a footpath for walkers and cyclists now. The dual carriageway had been built nearby, and it towered over the river as it led up to Ittonvale.

Ittonvale might have been richer, but Margery always thought Dewstow was a tiny bit nicer. Dewstow had a real sense of community, with its still bustling high street and local events. The residents of Ittonvale had always seemed a bit more guarded to Margery, and she and Clementine certainly had never felt welcome there on their short visits.

'And of course this very building is where Mr Itton of Itton Fisheries lived so long ago. And here is his donated comb, which he used to comb his moustache with almost daily.' Cecelia gestured grandly to the ivory comb, displayed proudly in the display case.

'Almost daily?' Clementine asked. Margery realised that she had forgotten why they had come already. 'Why not every day?'

'Twice a week it was washed, conditioned and styled at the Thickett family barber shop on Dewstow high street! The shop is now a newsagent, but I like to walk past there sometimes and imagine how amazing it must have been… the sound of all the straight razors working in unison like something out of *Sweeny Todd*…'

Margery suddenly found herself wondering if Cecilia's favourite colour was magnolia. She seemed like the type of person to dye her hair the same exact shade it already was. If she had been an item of clothing, she would be a beige cardigan that had escaped from a wardrobe. In fact, Cecilia was wearing a cardigan in a light pastel pink today. It washed out her already pale skin. The freckles on her face hovered over nose like they had been drawn on with a biro, and the blue veins running over her cheeks and forehead were visible through skin so light it was almost translucent.

'Do you have anything on the antique vase that Mrs Black donated to the school auction?' Margery cut in. Cecilia immediately looked as though Margery had force-fed her a lemon.

'Yes,' she said, with a stammer. 'But it's not here any more. After what happened, you know…'

'We know what happened to Mrs Black,' Margery said kindly. 'We were hoping you might have any information about the vase. It might help.'

'How would it help?' Cecelia asked suspiciously. The pleasant woman who had been so pleased to show them around had disappeared. 'Oh!' The realisation passed over her face. She turned to Clementine. 'You're the murderer's sister!'

'She's not a murderer…' Clementine began but Cecelia was already shaking her head.

'I'm sure the newspaper will say otherwise,' she said, looking close to tears. 'I really can't help you with the vase. I already told the police that it's obviously been smashed to bits, hasn't it? An awful thing.'

'The police have been?' Margery asked, realising as soon as she said it that of course it must have been true. 'What did they say?'

'That they had identified a suspect, and that I wasn't to worry about the museum,' Cecelia said, twirling her hands in anxious agony. 'So, I just carried on as normal. It's what Eleanor would have wanted… she'd come back to life and kill me if she knew I'd shut the doors, even for a day!'

'Did they tell you who the suspect was?' Margery asked. 'Only, I didn't think that was public knowledge quite yet.'

Cecelia smiled a small, grim smile. 'I was there at the school that night,' she explained. 'I overheard them talking about her.'

Margery knew that Martha, with her husband so high up on the council, would have found out about Maria and of course most of the school staff would know by now. But still, Cecilia knowing struck her as odd.

'Did you see my sister here at the museum?' Clementine asked her. Cecilia nodded, her eyes wide pools of fear.

'I did,' Cecilia said. 'She was here a few weeks ago. I gave her the tour! Oh, Eleanor. How could she ever forgive me? I answered lots of questions. I'm probably why she's dead!'

Margery stepped back, slightly concerned that Cecilia looked as though she was mere seconds away from dropping to the floor and rolling herself up in the worn rug that ran the length of the exhibit. She nearly told Cecilia that it wouldn't matter if Eleanor didn't forgive her, seeing as she was quite dead, but managed to hold the words back. Clementine didn't manage to stay so quiet.

'What did you tell Maria?' she asked bluntly. 'We need to know.'

'I just told her the history of the vase, you know,' Cecilia said, with a wet sniff made of newly formed tears that didn't quite fall. Margery made a mental note of that. For all of Cecilia's outward anguish, there seemed to be something else going on beneath the surface. She decided to try a different tactic.

'What was Eleanor like as a boss?' Margery asked her. 'Did you like working for her?'

Cecilia's eyebrows rose and her brow furrowed for a moment before her smile returned. 'Oh yes! She was lovely. She took me on years ago and between us we've really managed to uncover lots of Dewstow and Ittonvale history.' Cecilia moved over to one of the displays and opened a drawer. 'She was an expert at restoring and reproducing historical documents. She taught me so much. Take a look at these.'

She pulled on a pair of white gloves and removed the parchment from the drawer, holding it up so Margery and Clementine could see. 'It's the original deed for the building. Fascinating!'

The parchment looked so fragile that Margery worried about standing too close. Her breath might cause it to tear in two. The ink looked almost fresh, the handwriting legible, which surprised her as whenever she had seen something written in old-timey cursive before, it had been impossible to read. Margery wondered if that was what the restoration meant. She couldn't say she knew much about any of that. Cecilia let them gaze at it for a moment longer and then carefully put it back in the drawer. She moved on to the next and opened it, revealing what looked like the same paper. 'Here's Eleanor's reproduction of it – uncanny!'

She put that back as well and then disappeared into another drawer again, this time bringing out a huge tome of a book, opening it to reveal another handwritten page.

'This is Dewstow's original Domesday entry,' Cecilia breathed.

Margery could feel the excitement pouring from Cecilia in waves. It was magnetic in intensity and almost contagious. She found herself smiling at the page that told her that the town was worth twelve pounds in its entirety.

'Aren't you worried you'll have to move on now?' Clementine asked, her brow furrowed as they watched Cecilia put the paper away again. Cecilia shook her head as she removed her gloves. 'Leave the museum?'

'No,' Cecilia said, matter-of-fact as she shut the drawer tightly. 'Eleanor always told me she'd willed it to me. I don't see why that would have changed. Of course, it's all been a bit strange. The police have been in and I haven't heard from the rest of the family yet...' Cecilia's eyes flickered around the room and Margery realised that Cecilia wasn't sure. She decided to take a chance on a more interesting question now that the woman was distracted with worries of the future.

'Do you know anyone by the initials of R. J. E.?' Margery asked.

Cecilia looked startled for a moment. 'Why?'

Margery didn't know what to say to that for a second, it seemed an odd way to answer a question.

Finally, Clementine answered for her. 'Well, do you?' she asked, all niceties gone.

'No,' Cecilia said, giving her a strained smile that didn't mirror the expression in her eyes. 'No, I do not.'

It was a lie, Margery realised at the change in Cecilia's demeanour, but there was no way to force her to tell the truth.

They left the museum and began to cross the street to follow the riverbank around to the main road again. Margery felt as deflated as Clementine looked and they didn't speak as they crossed the road and began to trudge home. Margery wondered for a minute if they should get the bus. The sky was dark and gloomy already, threatening rain.

'What's the verdict, then?' Clementine asked. She joined Margery in looking up at the dark clouds. 'It's a bit odd in there, isn't it? Mind you, it's never been particularly normal, has it? No one who spends their time around so much dust could have a fully functional brain. All I'd do was sneeze if I worked there.'

'She's certainly lying about something,' Margery said. 'I just can't tell what yet.'

'I agree,' Clementine said with a nod. 'The thing is, she would have known Eleanor the best probably, wouldn't she? All those years cooped up together.'

Margery nodded. 'Yes, and I'm sure she knows exactly who R. J. E. is, judging from her reaction.'

'Back to the drawing board, then.' Clementine sighed.

Chapter Eight

The lunch hour dragged by in an unusual slog. It was normally Margery's favourite part of the job, where all the fruits of their labours were enjoyed, and the hard work was worth it. But even the children seemed gloomier than they usually did, sullenly filing into the canteen with their trays. A bleak air had fallen over the canteen, not helped by Clementine's skulking or Mrs George's constant glaring at them from her place as queue monitor. The atmosphere hadn't been this strange since Seren had tried to book the thirtieth of February off work. Margery had needed to show her several calendars to explain why that wouldn't be possible.

Margery hadn't been able to catch Rose before the workday began, but was hoping they might cross paths at lunchtime. Any news about Rose's office camera would be very good news indeed.

Rose didn't always have time to come to the canteen at lunch since she'd become headteacher – she usually booked her food through the online system and had it delivered. Margery had to hand it to the last headteacher, Ms Cooper. She had been a menace, but she had managed to streamline certain aspects of the school during her very short tenure after Mr Barrow was forced to step down. Seren was on lunch deliveries today and so Margery asked her to pass Rose a note that explained that they needed a meeting.

Then she awaited Seren's return, doling out portions of potato wedges and spicy beef chilli while they waited. Seren arrived finally, all in a huff and a puff that Margery usually associated with broken vacuum cleaners and boiling tea kettles – and with no news of Rose.

'Do you know what I've been thinking?' Ceri-Ann said. 'The police got a warrant to search that pottery place in Ittonvale, but they didn't find anything. But obviously, the owner would have known they were coming, wouldn't they? They would have hidden anything incriminating.'

'What are you suggesting?' Margery asked curiously.

'I reckon you should go up there and have a look about.' Ceri-Ann shrugged. 'Can't hurt, can it? They do lessons there. You could book one and then, like, cause a distraction or something and have a look and see if there's any more stuff by whoever made that vase.'

'What if the owner recognises us?' Clementine said, piling the last of the cottage pie onto a plate and passing it over to a student. 'We're world-famous in these parts, you know. There'd be no good us just rolling up there. There would be pandemonium from the fans, we'd need to hire security…'

'The rest of the team could go and report back?' Margery suggested, before Clementine could exaggerate any further. 'Do they do group classes?'

'They do but that would be no good,' Gloria called from over by the till. 'We're not detectives, are we? We wouldn't know what to look for.'

'We're not detectives either – well, not professional ones,' Margery said weakly. 'How can we be when we work here full-time?'

'Stop solving murders, then,' Ceri-Ann said with a laugh.

Clementine began to rattle off the finer details of their website but was luckily interrupted.

'Hello, Mrs Butcher-Bakers,' a booming voice called from behind them, making them all jump. 'I received your note.'

'Rose!' Clementine cried, as Margery clutched her chest in shock. Sharon burst into tears and Karen dabbed at her face with a tea towel. 'What are you doing sneaking around back there? Creeping about the place like a mole! What if we'd all had heart attacks? None of us are getting any younger!'

'How's Jason getting on at daycare, Mrs Smith?' Ceri-Ann asked curiously. 'Is he settling all right?'

Rose sighed deeply, shaking her head. 'No, I did try what you said, but I just couldn't leave him there all day. He's meant to be here with me.'

'I felt that way when Nick first started nursery,' Ceri-Ann said, nodding in understanding. 'He'd cry his eyes out when I took him in and then later they'd send me a message on his online diary that said "Very happy Nicholas now". I'd click on it, and it would just be photos of him that the NSPCC could use for an advert.'

'I feel the same way,' Rose said. 'I'm sorry that we don't have the facilities for a nursery here, Ceri-Ann—'

'Oh, that's all right.' Ceri-Ann threw her hands up. 'He loves going now, just for the food.'

Rose smiled at her. Then she turned to Margery. 'Do you have time to come with me? You too, Clem.'

Margery and Clementine followed Rose into the dry store office and closed the door, leaving Ceri-Ann and Gloria to coordinate the end of the lunch hour.

'Is it about the camera in your office?' Clementine asked eagerly.

'Oh! Well… no,' Rose spluttered, her eyes opening wide. 'I did start looking at the camera footage last night, but I ran out of time.' Rose lowered her voice. 'But I've got something else you might be interested in.'

'Oh?' Margery asked. 'What is it?'

'The footage of Maria's van. And the names of the mystery bidders,' Rose explained. 'From the auction.'

'Ooh, good! Wait… what mystery bidders?'

'There were mystery bidders for the vase – it was one of Eleanor's conditions about doing the auction for me,' Rose explained. 'Anyone was allowed to email or text in and place a bid. Would that help you in finding who killed Eleanor? Surely if someone would bid secretly for that hideous vase then they might try and steal it. Maybe bidding was their back-up plan if stealing it went wrong. Of course there were a few bids for many things. The *Mona Lisa* replica had a few…'

'For once, you've had a great idea.' Clementine gasped.

Rose ignored Clementine, and continued. 'I was just tucking Jason up in my office for the day before I made my rounds, and I had the idea to check Eleanor's notebook. One of the bidders I can't identify,' she said, worrying her lip with her teeth. 'I don't have any idea who they are, and they didn't leave an address, but the other name I recognise. Eleanor passed on a copy of all of the auction information before the day of it. It was written down with all of that.'

She handed Margery a sheet of paper with a few names written alongside the bid amounts. Only one had any contact details.

'Louis Fisher?' Clementine asked from over her shoulder. 'Who's that?'

Margery wondered for a moment why Rose was so eager to help. After all, she didn't know Maria well. Rose could well have assumed that she had killed Eleanor. That was without the fact that it had happened on school grounds, and theoretically put Rose's new position in danger. Rose looked as though she wanted to tell her something for a moment, but instead she nodded back. Rose tapped her finger to her lips and thought about it.

'I'm not sure,' Rose said. 'But like I said before, the Fishers are an old family. They used to be in big business with Ittonvale, heavily involved in everything there.' She blinked. 'Oh that reminds me, Margery. I've managed to wangle you a professional development day at Ittonvale school, in their kitchen.'

'What?' Margery said. She felt the alarm of that creep up her neck and into her throat, her voice coming out in a small squeak.

'Yes, you just go up there next week and pretend you're learning their way of doing things, blah blah.' Rose waved a hand dismissively. 'But really you're finding out what you can about the Fisher family… and maybe see what Rhonda is doing while you're there. Just in case she's planning to steal another play from me. Do you remember Rhonda Blossom?'

'Your arch-nemesis and head of drama?' Clementine scoffed. 'Of course we do. It's all you've gone on and on about for the last million years. How is this going to help Maria?'

'Well,' Rose said with a sigh, 'the Fishers used to be big donators to the school. I imagine no one would tell me a thing if I asked, especially if it could lead to something bad for them. Perhaps I'll go and visit Rhonda on my own anyway, though. It'll be nice for Ada Bones and Jason to have a playdate. They haven't seen each other since last week.'

Rose's face lit up as she spoke about her dog. Margery decided to change the subject on the hope that Rose would forget all about it and she wouldn't have to go at all.

'Who are the other mystery bidders?' Margery asked, reading the rest of the page.

'I'm not sure,' Rose admitted. 'I don't think Eleanor would have seen it as important, seeing as Louis Fisher was the highest bidder. I'm sure she was planning to start the bidding at that number to see if she could get even more money.'

The price Louis Fisher had been willing to pay for the vase was astronomical, Margery thought. She could have bought the entire crockery department of a John Lewis store with it. What hold did the vase have over people? Why was it so special? She had seen it when it had been carefully transported into the school by Eleanor in the glass display case and it hadn't looked particularly special to her. Margery supposed that maybe she just didn't have the right sort of taste for such a thing. Her idea of a nice vase wasn't the ugly lump of clay that Eleanor had been so besotted by.

She looked back at the list and read through the names. None of them rang a bell. There was Louis Fisher, with a scrawled phone number and address under it and a Robert James Evans and a B. E. Ethels with no other contact information. That last one looked less like a real name the longer Margery stared at it.

'I've also got the footage of Maria's van.' Rose pulled out one of the school tablets from the oversized handbag she usually carted Jason around in when his little legs grew tired on their walks. She unlocked it so that Margery and Clementine could see the footage. The video was both clear as day and terribly damning. Onscreen, a van pulled up alongside the window to Rose's office. After a second, Maria emerged with an armful of goods, rushing them around to the back of the van and throwing them in through the doors.

'That's not her van,' Margery said.

It couldn't be. The van on the footage had all four working tyres. Maria's van was sitting on their driveway still, where it had been since she arrived. Margery's car was usually parked behind it, and even if it wasn't, the van was barely road legal. Maria had been saving her meagre wages from the part-time cleaning job for new tyres and to sort the rust that was blooming like black mould over the bottom and sides of the van. The vehicle was more science project than inhabitable space currently. There was no way that it could have been driven up to the school and then escaped again in one piece.

'No idea,' Rose said. 'The numberplate led the police to a van-hire place called Star Tours. The company had no record of loaning the van to Maria, had no record of loaning that van at all, actually.'

'An inside job?' Margery asked.

'Possibly,' Rose said, with a shrug. 'Well, I'd better get off. I hope some of this might help. I know it's a bit of a slog.' She turned to Margery, her usual businesslike demeanour returning. 'Mrs Butcher-Baker, try not to let me down at Ittonvale. I know you won't, but I've had to pull a lot of strings to get you in. They're very secretive about their catering, won't even tell me the brownie recipe.'

Rose turned to leave again.

'Rose?' Clementine called.

Rose swung back around.

'Thank you,' Clementine said, 'I really appreciate it.'

'Of course,' Rose said, sliding out through the dry store door and leaving them alone for a moment to think. Margery stared back down at the piece of paper Rose had given them.

'R. J. E.,' Margery said, realisation hitting her like a train. 'R. J. E.! Look, Clem, Robert… James… Evans,' Margery said, showing Clementine the writing Eleanor had scribbled down. 'R. J. E. Like the initials on the vase!'

'Oh!' Clementine exclaimed, throwing her hands around Margery. 'That's got to be the person who made the fake vase!'

'Gosh, it really could be the person who made it,' Margery said, still looking at the page, stunned. 'But who are they? Maybe we should try and ask Cecilia if she knows them again.'

Clementine shook her head. 'Well, we might be able to find out ourselves now we know his full name. Let's have a look in the phone book later.'

They left the safety and triumph of the dry store and made their way back out to the canteen. The hullaballoo was beginning to wind down for the lunch hour, though Margery suspected it might rise again during the afternoon break.

'What did Rose say?' Gloria asked as Margery arrived back at the serving counter.

'Not a lot,' Margery told her, the lie feeling heavy on her tongue.

'Really?' Gloria said, her eyebrows raising. 'She usually has so much to go on and on about.'

'Miss,' a voice called from behind the kitchen serving counter. 'Did we hear that you need disguises?'

'No,' Margery said. Ceri-Ann chuckled.

'Yeah, they do!' Ceri-Ann told the student who had asked. 'Why? What do you want?'

The student grinned. Margery had seen her before but didn't know her name.

'Mrs Smith told us to tell you to come to the art department at three, miss,' she said, 'She said she overheard you talking and we have to help you.'

'Help us do what?' Margery asked, but the girl had already skipped off with her lunch tray while Karen was ringing her items through the till.

Chapter Nine

They had searched for the mysterious R. J. E. in the phone book and Ceri-Ann had even scoured the Dewstow Facebook community page for him, to no avail. Whoever he was, he might not be as easy to find as Margery and Clementine had originally hoped. With no other options left, they made their way to the art department just before three in the afternoon, as they had been instructed. They didn't venture down to this end of the school very often – it was much too far from the beaten track for the dinner lady team, who would only occasionally venture down to deliver Ms Brush her preordered egg mayonnaise sandwiches. The art department was two large classrooms that faced each other, separated in the middle by the hallway that led to the fire escape. It was in the old building of the school and had large windows, letting in the last of the afternoon light. It beamed through the rooms and out of the glass partitions in the top of the classroom doors. Margery and Clementine stood awkwardly in the corridor, wondering where they were supposed to go now.

'She just said "art department",' Margery told Clementine. 'Nothing about where we should meet or who we were meeting... or even which classroom.'

'That sounds about right, doesn't it?' Clementine scoffed. 'You know these students. It's all mysterious drama nonsense this, wide-leg jeans that. I'm surprised she didn't just draw us a cryptic treasure map. Let's just get in and out so we can go and pay a visit to Mr Fisher, seeing as we have his address. The answers are all there, I'm sure of it. I bet he'll be able to tell us all about R. J. E..'

The door to the classroom on the left flew open and Rose sashayed out into the hallway in a dramatic flourish of scarfs, the long skirt she wore billowing along with her. The student from the canteen followed behind her, followed closely by Jason, who waddled along behind them as the tail of a bizarre parade.

'Took you long enough, Mrs Butcher-Bakers!' Rose said with a huff. 'Honestly, can't a woman send a vague message and expect it to be followed immediately?'

'We're two minutes late, if that,' Clementine said. 'Which you'd know if you ever looked at a clock. I've seen you winding that one in the school hall forward so you don't have to do assemblies for as long.'

'What would you have me do? Assemblies are dreadfully boring,' Rose scoffed. 'I can't always fob them off on James or make them into an interactive play. Best to keep them short and sweet. Anyway, this morning's wasn't boring, was it? Having to reassure all the students that they weren't about to be murdered as well. That was interesting enough not to need a song.'

'The recorder club played "Murder on the Dancefloor",' Margery reminded her.

Rose nodded in remembrance. 'It just seemed fitting, Mrs Butcher-Baker.'

Rose turned to disappear back into the classroom, nearly careening into the student as she twirled, shooing them back inside and then gesturing for Margery and

Clementine to follow them. She scooped up Jason and returned him to the table in the centre of the classroom, where it looked as though he was being fitted for an outfit.

'Look, guys, the dinner ladies are here!' the student cried as they entered, and Clementine shut the door behind them. Margery wished she had kept it open so they could run away if they needed to. The strange meeting caused goosebumps to rise up and down her arms.

Inside the classroom sat a group Margery recognised as Year Eleven students. They didn't seem annoyed to be there, which meant they weren't being forced. Margery wondered if they were part of a club. They were all seemingly engrossed in the masks they were painting on the table in front of them. Rose went to the back of the class and sat down heavily in the teacher's chair by the whiteboard. The students turned to look at Margery and Clementine with interest.

'Hello,' Margery said, feeling her voice emerge as a squeak.

'I'm Grace and this is Harry, Jack, Jessica and Noah.' Grace gestured around at the other students. Margery tried to commit their names to memory, but realised that she hadn't a hope of remembering which name went with which face. Grace spoke much too quickly for her to retain what she said. 'We're Summerview's costume department.'

'Did you make Jason's *101 Dalmatians* costume?' Margery asked. 'That was fantastic! We were all talking about it for weeks afterwards!'

'Yeah!' Grace beamed. 'We weren't sure if he had enough spots, but it looked good under the stage lights, didn't it?'

'Are you making him a costume now?' Margery asked, looking over at Jason, who was sitting very nicely as one of the girls attached a headband to his tiny head. It looked oddly like fluffy ears, and Margery instantly wondered if Rose would have the gall to perform *The Wizard of Oz* for the third year in a row, this time casting Jason as the Cowardly Lion as well as Toto the dog. 'What... I don't mean to sound rude... but what is it exactly?'

'Oh, miss, can't you tell?' The student turned Jason towards her.

Rose gave a dramatic cough, interrupting the moment.

'What has this got to do with us?' Clementine asked Grace, then glared at Rose in suspicion. 'This seems like a way for Rose to get us involved in another school play. Can I just remind you, Rose, that a woman died the last time you made us join a play, and we still can't even sing!'

Rose spluttered indignantly. Grace shook her head.

'Not for a play,' Grace began.

'Is it because we've got "rizz" and you think we'd make great costume models?' Clementine said, making large air quotes with her hands. The students cringed.

'Yes, that's right,' Clementine continued triumphantly. 'You can't hide anything from me with your young youthful youthfulness... I know all your slang!'

'I overheard Ceri-Ann talking in the canteen about visiting the pottery workshop, and how you were worried you might get recognised by the owner and I thought they could help you make disguises for your case,' Rose finally explained, waving a hand towards the students, who nodded. 'So, I sorted it. May I also suggest that you tell your little dinner ladies to discuss your illegal plans at a lower volume in the future? It's dreadful having to listen to how you're going to rob banks or whatever it is you do all the time. You'll give the students ideas, and I can't have an uprising at the moment. We've got GCSE exams to worry about…'

'Why would you help us?' Clementine said, looking at the students in suspicion. 'How can we be sure we can trust you?'

'For free chips!' Noah piped up.

Grace glared at him, and he grinned.

'I'm only allowed to do chips on Fridays,' Margery told them sadly. 'Don't blame me. Blame the government's healthy-eating initiative.'

'Free crisps?' Noah asked. The students nodded in agreement.

'This is way more important than free crisps, Noah!' Grace said, rolling her eyes at the boy, who looked back at her as though her words had electrocuted him. 'Miss, we need you to find the person who's stealing our costume supplies.'

'Your supplies?' Margery asked, looking to Rose, who nodded sadly.

'Unfortunately, there is a thief,' Rose explained. 'We haven't been able to find them yet, but rest assured we will. I'm having a CCTV camera fitted right outside this very room.'

'Do you have any idea who it could be?' Clementine asked Grace, who shook her head.

'No, miss, but they must be a student or something,' she said. 'Why else would they want our stuff?'

'What are they taking?' Margery asked.

'I'll send you a list of what's missing,' Rose told her. 'It's mostly costume bits and bobs and general art supplies. Nothing expensive, but the little things add up. At this rate we'll have to charge extra for the play tickets.'

'You already charge too much,' Clementine said. 'Especially since you added a booking fee to the school website – what on earth are you using that extra money for?'

'How do you think we put on such grand performances?' Rose scoffed. 'You have no idea the expense of running the backstage areas, the catering alone…'

'We do the catering,' Margery reminded her. 'I know exactly what it costs. I wanted to use cheaper bread last year, but you wouldn't let me.'

'Yes, well… you can't have a cheap sandwich, Margery, not for my stars.' Rose spluttered briefly before returning to her rant. 'Year after year, replacing the bulbs in the lighting rig, the elegant costumes, the very best acting I can find from the very limited pool of talent I have access to. It all costs a fortune.'

'Can you not just put on a simple show?' Clementine suggested. Rose's face turned an even darker shade of red. 'Ooh, maybe a nice hand puppet show? You could just make the puppets with socks and use buttons for eyes.'

Rose glared at Clementine in a way that made Margery flinch. Clementine was so used to Rose's wrath that she was oblivious to it, continuing to name different methods they could use to make puppets and what songs the puppets could sing.

'You know we're doing a new play this year,' Grace said. 'We all can't wait to show you—'

Rose jumped up from her seat at that, interrupting Grace with a huff. 'There's no need to bore the ladies with all of that! Come on, now, let's get started. Do you agree to the terms, Mrs Butcher-Bakers?'

'Yes,' Margery said. Clementine nodded.

'And do you, Grace?' Rose asked the student, who still looked a bit put out at the interruption.

'Yeah, all right,' she said, among the murmur of agreement from the rest of the students. 'Let's get started, then.'

'What are you going to do?' Margery asked in alarm.

'Well, for one you'll need a new face,' Grace said, stroking her chin as she considered them both.

Clementine threw her hands in the air. 'I like my face as it is! What are you planning to do to us?'

'Just give you both a false nose,' Grace said. Jessica and the others chuckled.

'It's worth a try, Clem,' Margery said, reaching out to touch Clementine's shoulder. 'Think about Maria.'

Something passed over Clementine's face for a second, an emotion Margery couldn't quite put her finger on.

'All right,' Clementine said with a sigh. 'But this had better be good. I don't want my fake ears falling off the minute we leave the school.'

'Don't worry,' Grace told her earnestly, 'it will be.'

Chapter Ten

An hour later and Margery and Clementine were finally able to leave the art department and make their way to Louis Fisher's address, having had their facial features measured and scrutinised strangely so the students could make the disguises while they weren't there. Ms Brush had arrived to supervise at half past three, surprised to see Rose, Margery and Clementine there, but Rose had told her that the dinner lady team had been roped into the school summer concert. Margery wasn't sure that Ms Brush would believe them, the summer concert was still a few months away and they had the usual spring festival to get through first. It wasn't an entirely unbelievable lie, considering that Rose had quite often coerced them into learning a song or five for a show. Although only once had she had trusted them with the curtain pull and lights. And on that occasion, Seren had managed to get the curtain stuck halfway across the stage while Ceri-Ann had accidentally set the stage lights to strobe right in the middle of an important soliloquy.

Ms Brush mentioned something about it only being right that they were involved in this particular play, which Margery wasn't sure the meaning of, but they hadn't hung around for long enough to ask her anything more about it.

They already knew where Louis Fisher lived from his address, and they had already visited the building many times before. Not that they visited the retirement community building often now, not since Clementine's mother had died anyway. But it was also strange to return for another reason. The elder Mrs Butcher had lived there for the last five or six years of her life, in a tiny flat that had been mostly trinkets and, for some ungodly reason, a numerous amount of casserole dishes she bought from charity shops. Margery had been sad when she died, of course, but she hadn't missed having to clamber over the piles of Le Creuset casserole dishes every time they visited. Mrs Butcher had unfortunately lost her battle with dementia many years ago now, but the family had struggled with what to do before she had passed. If it was right to sell the home they had all grown up in to pay for her care.

These things weren't easy, Margery thought. In fact, they could be so painful that she couldn't bear to remember anything about her own mother's end-of-life pathway. She had squished it all back down into the dark place where all her other fears and bad memories lived.

Clementine would often worry about going the down the same road as her mother, the fear of losing who you had been always lurking. Margery supposed it did for everybody.

They rang the intercom and waited for a moment. Margery felt the anticipation rise in her chest, as it always did whenever they went somewhere with the intention of asking someone unexpected questions. You could never be sure how the person would react, how they would feel being asked personal details by two strangers. Sometimes people were pleased to see them and happy to talk, but more often Margery and Clementine were ejected from the building in a rage at the questioning.

'Do you have the password?' The voice came over the line, almost hidden in the static from the intercom. Clementine lurched forward to hold down the speak button.

'It used to be "eggs Florentine",' Clementine said, her brow furrowing as she tried to remember. 'But we're looking for Louis Fisher.'

'Unfortunately, I can't let you in without the correct password,' the voice said in a crackle. 'That password's very old now.'

Back to square one, then, Margery thought, wondering what on earth they would do now. Clementine was on the warpath as it was, and Rose had taken great steps to get them here in the first place. It simply couldn't be another dead end. There had to be another way to find out who Robert was.

'Excuse me, ladies,' another voice called. 'Are you looking for me?'

They both turned and came face to face with a man, peering out at them from a ground-floor window. His face was full of deep furrows and lines – the smiles of the decades carved into the skin around his eyes. He was so thin he was almost skeletal, the windowsill digging deep white grooves into his bony palms, the skin stretched tightly over them. The skin at the corners of his mouth was both taut and crinkled in an alarming measure. The look of someone who had once been a long-term heavy smoker.

'Well… are you Louis Fisher?' Clementine called back.

'I am!' he said, with a cheerful wave. 'Would you like to come in? I don't get many visitors any more. Password is "Cheddar cheese"! Once you're in, I'm in flat 4b.'

They tried the intercom again, and sure enough the password was correct. The receptionist didn't seem entirely sure about the password debacle at the door, and their quick turnaround. Margery worried for a moment that he would refuse to let them in anyway, but then he buzzed them through.

As they entered, Margery looked over to Clementine, who was taking in the surroundings, her head probably swimming with memories as they traipsed down the familiar halls until they reached the door to Louis's flat. Margery raised a hand to knock, but Louis was already opening the door. He beamed at them and then hobbled back to let them inside.

Louis Fisher's room had yellowing walls where cigarette smoke had collected, and the stale smell lingered in the air. Louis wasn't a former smoker, then, Margery thought to herself. The ashtray on the coffee table contained more than a few used cigarette butts.

It was oddly comforting to Margery and it reminded her of her childhood, in the way that paraffin gas and hot water bottles always did.

'Come in, come in! Make yourselves at home,' Louis said, gesturing to the living area. 'Guests at last! I'll pop the kettle on.'

Margery and Clementine helped the man make drinks in the tiny kitchen area of the flat – if you could call it a flat. It was more like a large hotel room made to look like a flat, and it was serviced day and night by on-call staff.

Margery had always considered the home to be a nice in-between from living alone for Mrs Butcher. They had been lucky she had enough money to afford it. The end-of-life care had cost the family the money from the sale of

Mrs Butcher's bungalow and then some – but it had been worth it for the peace of mind it brought.

It had been sad, then, and that sadness still flickered to the forefront of Margery's mind every now and again. Had they done the right thing? Would it have been better for her to die at home? There were no right or wrong answers, only horrible lingering unknowns and questions that she asked herself late at night. However, she knew deep down that by the time Mrs Butcher had stepped foot in her little flat in this very building, her mind was no longer her own anyway. The stern widow who would have died before leaving her home no longer really existed.

But it was one thing to know that, and another to have to make those decisions. Clementine's brother had been away in Australia, as he still was, with a family of his own and a big corporate job he couldn't just drop. It had mostly fallen on Clementine's shoulders, with Vincent swanning over every six months for a week or two and then leaving them all to it again. Margery wondered if some of Clementine's determination to make it all work out with Maria was down to the distance between herself and her brother, in emotion as well as location.

'What can I do for you?' Louis asked, once they'd all finally sat down. The pot of tea on the coffee table in front of them billowed with steam when Margery poured it out for them all.

'We're here to ask some questions about the Dewstow Heritage Vase,' Clementine explained as Margery placed the cup in front of her.

'Oh, right.' Louis smiled. 'Well, what would you like to know? It's dreadfully old, you see...'

'Whatever you can tell us,' Margery offered. Louis beamed at her.

'The vase has been in my family for years,' Louis began. 'Well before any of us were even thought of and a generation or three before that. The vase is almost as old as Ittonvale is, of course, it was called Dewstow back then, but then you know they were split. I was born in Ittonvale, of course. Way before hospitals. My mother birthed me at Itton Manor. Do you know it?'

'You can see it from the riverbank,' Margery said, thinking of the big house on the hill on the other side of the water. She wondered how much longer that would be there for, subsidence on the cliffs would have to take it in the end.

Louis nodded. 'The vase came into my family's possession with Elizabeth Itton, who became Elizabeth Fisher, of course,' he said, his eyes glazing over as he tried to remember it all. 'Ending a long line of Ittons after Frederick Itton failed to produce an heir and Elizabeth married…'

'But how did the vase end up with Eleanor Black, then?' Clementine asked, her patience wearing thin after the day they had had already. Margery didn't blame her. She hadn't expected a history lesson either. Or seen the need for one.

Louis raised a wrinkled hand. 'I'm getting to that,' he said. 'The Black family won it in a New Year's Eve parlour game about, ooh, nearly two hundred years ago now, but they shared custody of it. Every New Year's Eve for over a century our two families would get together and play games to see who would win custody of it for the following year. That ended during the Second World War, too many men away, but after that they took turns. When

I came of age, I got it one year and then Billy Black used to take it for a year after that. We'd done that for years, of course.'

'What happened?' Margery asked, genuinely interested now.

'Well, until a decade or so ago, we would still meet every New Year's Eve. Either at Vivian and Billy Black's manor or at my home at Itton Manor… for the tradition of it all.' He smiled at the memories, looking fondly at the photographs lining the shelf above their heads. 'Then I did something stupid.' His face darkened as he thought about it. Before Margery could ask what he meant, he continued. 'I passed it down on my side to Eleanor to do the handovers. I'm getting on, sometimes I'm not up for the party. She was supposed to go in my stead.'

'But she didn't?' Margery breathed. Louis nodded.

'Exactly. She broke her end of the agreement almost immediately, saying it was hers now and she could do what she liked with it,' his lips pursed at the bitter memory. 'That's why she's dead. It's cursed, you see? We all promised to swap it until the last of us was gone, but she didn't stick to that.'

His words were cold and Margery found herself shivering at them.

'Did you kill her?' Margery asked, though she could tell he had not as soon as she asked.

Louis raised his eyebrows in surprise. 'No, of course I didn't, how would I?' He snorted. 'I'm a frail old man! I haven't left this building to go further than the garden for two years.'

'Frail old men have killed before,' Clementine said.

'No, but that woman did it, didn't she?' Louis said, with a nasty spit. 'The newcomer.'

Neither Margery nor Clementine said anything, but Margery could feel the resentment pouring from Clementine in waves.

'I'm not going to kill anyone for an old vase,' Louis snapped, taking a sip of the tea that was still much too hot. His lips smacked as he slurped from the cup and winced.

'Then why did you bid for it?' Margery asked, as Clementine continued to seethe.

'What do you mean?' Louis asked, his already wrinkled face crinkling in confusion. 'I didn't... no one got to bid on anything, did they? Were the auction items not stolen?'

'You placed a bid before the auction began,' Margery said, trying to remind him calmly. 'A mystery bid.'

'I certainly did no such thing,' Louis scoffed. 'I don't want the vase. I told Eleanor as much. When she didn't want to do the swap ten years ago, I told her she could keep it then, if she wanted it that badly. "Do whatever you want with it," I said.' He looked around the room sadly. 'Anyway, what use is any of that to me here? Maybe back in the day when I was still at home, but not now.' He looked around the room as though taking in his surroundings for the first time. 'Not here.'

'You definitely didn't place the bid?' Clementine asked, finally shocked out of her stupor.

'No,' Louis said. He shook his head, suddenly looking like a child who was frightened of something hiding in the darkness of the shadows under his bed. He turned in the chair with great difficulty and pulled a wodge of papers from his coffee table. 'Eleanor was being threatened by that woman, that's how I know she did it.'

He thrust the papers towards them. Margery opened the first one and read the horrible diatribe scrawled onto the paper. Whoever had written these words had really hated Eleanor. They must have done. And though she was the main suspect in all this, this certainly wasn't Maria's handwriting. Maria would leave Clementine a barely legible Post-it note every other day telling her she'd used all the milk or she was going out to the Bell and Hope. Margery knew that handwriting inside and out.

There was a ring from the intercom attached to the doorbell. Margery and Clementine jumped. Louis glared over at it with a huff.

'That'll be bloody Jeffery again,' Louis said. He took the papers back from Margery and quickly slid them away inside the coffee-table drawer. He dragged himself up from his chair with great difficulty using his walking stick. 'Sometimes it's better to be left alone, isn't it? Can't get anything done with him popping over all day every day, trying to help. You know, he finished my jigsaw for me – who does that? "Jeffery," I said, "I was saving that... what am I supposed to do on Saturday night now?"'

'Who's Jeffery?' Margery asked him, as he made his way to the door.

'He is... was Eleanor's brother-in-law,' Louis explained, with a wave of his hand 'Jeffery Black.'

'Wait... so how did you know Eleanor?' Clementine asked in confusion. 'You're related?'

'She was my granddaughter,' Louis said, with a wry smile. 'She married Cecil Black. He's gone now, of course. He was much older than her when they married. I told him that she should have settled down with someone more her age, but why would she listen to me?'

'Cecil Black? Vivan Black's son?' Margery asked. 'So is Jeffery Vivian's son, too?'

They had come across Vivian a few years ago but hadn't known her personally. The Black family was well known across Ittonvale, less so in Dewstow and only really by locals. They had kept to themselves in the last few decades, any of the former glory long gone. Margery doubted anyone from out of the area would have cared about the so-called prestigious families who owned most of the town's buildings and land. But Margery thought that maybe there was something more to it all. It didn't seem like a coincidence.

'Her youngest. And the baby of the family,' Louis told her with a shake of his head. It was obvious that he didn't think much of whoever was waiting on the other side of the door. 'Still acts like a big baby, if you ask me.'

Louis reached the door and opened it, revealing the man standing on the other side. Jeffery was in his late fifties or even early sixties, Margery supposed by the lines next to his eyes and his greying beard. Margery wondered what he thought about the troubles that had befallen his mother Vivian and her husband Billy but knew better than to ever ask. Behind him peered a teenage boy. His face was so pale his skin was almost translucent, his mouse-brown curly hair flopping over his forehead.

'Oh, you've got guests, have you?' Jeffery asked, looking around at them all and then picking up the full-to-bursting plastic carrier bags by his feet. 'You should have said, Lou. I'd have popped back later.'

Louis ushered him in anyway, ignoring their awkward silence while Jeffery began to unpack the gammon and potatoes from the bag.

'You've got to stop bringing me bits,' Louis said, shaking his head as he watched Jeffery work. 'I can get my own shopping, Jeff. I get them to do it online for me.'

'Let me help you, you old fool,' Jeffery said with a chuckle. 'Sorry to barge in.' He looked around at them both jovially. 'I'm Jeffery – but everyone calls me Jeff.'

'Okay,' Clementine said, reaching out to take his outstretched hand. 'I'm Clementine and everyone calls me Clementine. This is Margery, everyone calls her... er... they call her Margery.'

The boy stood behind Jeffery, eyeing them curiously. He didn't step forward to greet them. Instead, he stood back, rolling his hands together.

'Oh, I think I've heard of you,' Jeffery said. 'The dinner ladies who solve crime! There's probably a book in there somewhere, you know. Have you thought about selling your story to the *Daily Mail*? I'm sure there'd be some money in that.'

'We couldn't,' Clementine said. 'They might want to take photos of us and then we'd have to dust the living room.'

Jeffery laughed uproariously. 'Well, if you change your mind, I've got a contact who could help you. The family appreciates what you did for mother, by the way. I always meant to reach out and thank you.'

'No need,' Margery told him. 'We were just glad we could help.'

'This is Andrew,' Jeffery said. He clapped Andrew on the back, and the boy flinched. 'And I think that you met my older son, William,' Jeffery said casually, as he opened the fridge. 'Do you remember?'

'Yes,' Margery said, remembering the polite young man who had invited them into his grandmother's home and spoken to them at length very kindly about her. She could see the resemblance in both Jeffery and Andrew, the dark eyebrows and prominent chin that had befallen all of the Black family features since Vivian had introduced it with her genes.

It was funny to think about family resemblance sometimes. Margery could look at one of her nieces and nephews and see their parents, but also her parents and their parents and on and on and on. There was a great comfort in that. You could look into someone's face and see the memory of someone else. She was sure someone had once felt the same about her. Margery had a great-niece now, who looked exactly like a mix of Margery as a baby and her mother. A living historical artefact.

'These ladies were nice enough to help me make a cup of tea,' Louis said to Jeffery, as he finished putting the shopping away and then began the long and exhausting journey back to his chair in the corner. 'Nice to have a bit of company, you know?'

He gave Jeffery a look over his shoulder and Jeffery looked back guiltily.

'Sorry, Louis,' he said. 'I've been so busy with work and with Eleanor's estate. You know how it is.'

Jeffery couldn't visit as often as Louis had originally complained to them, Margery thought.

'How are the funeral arrangements coming?' Louis asked, finally sitting back down in the armchair with a thump. Andrew approached slowly and sat down next to him. 'Well, I hope?'

'The police haven't released the body yet,' Jeffery told him. 'And she didn't leave a penny for the preparations, so it's been difficult to set a date.'

'Just send me the bill and I'll sort it,' Louis said quietly, his face crumpling.

Margery decided that they should leave immediately. Louis had told them he hadn't placed the bid. Whether he was lying or not, it didn't seem right to sit and listen to their personal and painful conversation. She stood and grasped for her handbag. Andrew flinched as she reached for it, surprising her.

'Well, thank you very much for the tea,' she said to Louis. Clementine stood, as though she had read Margery's mind.

'No problem at all, ladies,' Louis said. 'Will you be all right showing yourselves out?'

They were, finding themselves back out in the car park before they knew it. Margery turned to Clementine and shook her head.

'I'm not sure what just happened,' Margery said. 'Louis certainly has the money to put down that huge bid for the vase, but you heard him, he's denied everything. Why would he lie?'

'Why wouldn't he?' Clementine said with a sigh. 'Everyone lies when they think it's better than being caught out, don't they?'

'So, what's next?' Margery asked.

Clementine shook her head, her eyes tired and her face drawn.

Chapter Eleven

With no other leads to follow, the dinner ladies had no choice but to continue the plan to visit the pottery class. However, they couldn't do that until Sunday.

Gloria was the one who made the booking. Margery had tried to pay for the entire thing herself, but the team had been so excited about a dinner lady day out that they didn't mind chipping in. Margery sat in front of the television while Clementine washed up the dinner things in the kitchen. She wasn't paying attention to the programme that was on, letting it blare in the background while she tried desperately to think of ways that she could help Clementine and Maria. Clementine's angst was the most important problem to solve, in Margery's opinion. It remained to be seen what Maria's true intentions were and Margery still wasn't entirely convinced that she was fully innocent. After all, an innocent person would have an easily confirmed alibi.

After Mrs Mugglethwaite's accusation, Margery had wondered if there was some truth to her words. Clementine had been loudly clattering around the kitchen in her usual manner. Margery didn't realise that she had stopped until Clementine was standing in the living-room doorway, taking the rubber gloves off her hands.

'You think Maria did it, don't you?' Clementine asked her. There was no malice in her voice, but it made Margery whip around to stare in horror anyway.

'No... I...'

'It's all right,' Clementine said, putting the rubber gloves on the counter nearest to her. 'It's looking harder to believe she didn't kill Eleanor, isn't it?'

'Things certainly aren't adding up,' Margery admitted.

Clementine moved to come and sit next to her, flopping down on the sofa. Her hand brushed Margery's, her skin still damp from taking the gloves off. They sat like that for a moment, seemingly peacefully, but Margery could feel that the air was charged with an undercurrent of something much darker.

'I just keep thinking about what Martha said,' Clementine said, staring off at the television. 'But we know we're related, don't we? The test said we were. But what if it was wrong? People think you and I look alike, don't they? But we aren't related.'

'People only decide we look alike because they're trying to work out who we are to each other and they've decided we're siblings, or they think all middle-aged women look exactly the same,' Margery told her. 'The test said you were siblings. Where's the letter gone? It's all there in black and white. What's brought this on?'

'I just feel like I should know what's going on,' Clementine said with a sigh, slumping back even further into the sofa cushions. 'I feel like we're supposed to have some sort of weird sibling bond, and I should just know where she is and how she feels. It's even worse now I don't know where she is.'

'I don't have that sort of bond with my brother or my sisters,' Margery reminded her. 'And neither do you with your brother… and you grew up with him.'

'That's true,' Clementine said, a small smile reappearing. 'And Vincent and I talk all the time.'

'Exactly,' Margery said, patting her on the arm. 'Don't blame yourself for this. It's not your fault.'

'It is, though, isn't it?' Clementine said. 'She was looking for me before Eleanor was found dead. If she'd found me then maybe this wouldn't have happened.'

'Or you'd have been involved,' Margery said, leaning back on the sofa. 'Which would have been much worse. Because there's no way I could get you both out of prison on my own.'

'That's true,' Clementine said, nodding.

'And there's still hope, isn't there?' Margery said. 'The police might have found the auction items here, but that just proves petty theft, not murder. They wouldn't be able to keep her forever for that.'

'Yes, that's true,' Clementine agreed, a black fog seeming to clear from her. She turned her head suddenly, looking towards the front door. 'Come on.'

'What?' Margery asked in alarm, as Clementine got up from the sofa and went to the front door. She found the keys to Maria's van on the row of hooks on the wall.

'Let's just double check there aren't any more clues in the van,' Clementine said. 'The police found the auction items, but we might find something that can actually help us.'

'Like what?' Margery asked her. Clementine thought for a moment before a smile spread across her face.

'Her phone,' Clementine said, her expression steeling at the words before settling again so that she looked more like herself. 'Where's her phone, Margery?'

'They found it,' Margery said, her brow furrowing in surprise. 'It was in her locker at the school...'

Clementine shook her head. Margery was confused. She had seen the police search Maria's locker herself. Had walked right past as Officer Wilkinson was staring down at what they had uncovered, a gleam in his eyes.

'They found her phone,' Margery began again. Clementine interrupted her.

'They found her *new* phone,' Clementine said. 'Not her old one.'

'Well, what do you think is on that phone, then, if it's here?' Margery asked. 'Surely the police would have found it already? They ripped the house apart. My sock drawer will never be the same.'

Clementine shook her head. 'I don't think so. They'd have had much more to say if they did, I'm sure.'

Margery followed her out to the van and watched as Clementine pulled herself up inside by the handrail. The van wasn't much, just a hard-looking built-in bed and a table and chair before the driver's seat in front of it. There was a tiny electric fridge in between the table and the bed, and a sink above it. The door underneath the sink had been left open and the plastic bottle that it ran from was on display. The police hadn't ransacked the van, which Margery was glad of, but they had certainly searched every inch of it judging by the bedspread that had been rolled off the bed and the books strewn on the table. The van didn't look too much worse for wear since the police had been inside it. In Margery's opinion it was cleaner than it had been when Maria had been living in it, but she daren't say that to Clementine.

They began looking through the cupboards and under the narrow bed... even inside the fridge and under the seats. Margery even went to the front of the vehicle and opened up the bonnet, peering inside at the engine hopelessly.

'She wouldn't have hidden anything here,' Margery said finally, wracking her brain for any other ideas. Clementine poked a toe at the rough piece of carpet lining the floor, her arms crossed against her chest. Margery was about to suggest that they give up. Maria obviously had her secrets and maybe they should leave it at that. Maybe she'd lost the phone or broken it. There must have been a reason she had got a new one in the first place.

Suddenly, an idea arrived in a blinding rush of light. Margery gasped and almost lost her footing on the steps of the van, catching herself with the handrail at the last moment.

She leaped back down onto the driveway, then rushed back into the house, not waiting a moment before stumbling through the kitchen and out the back door. She had realised where Maria might have hidden the phone – it had been playing on her mind for weeks, but she hadn't really been able to fully articulate the idea. Maria hadn't taken the money tin to steal the money. She had stolen the tin, yes. But not for the cash inside it.

Margery went straight to the newly dug stretch of garden, over to the spot with the single wooden stake stabbed into the ground. She grabbed the trowel Maria had never put away in the shed and began to dig, hoping beyond hope that it wasn't too buried too deeply. After a minute of frantic digging, the trowel hit something hard and metal with a clank. Margery grasped for it, pulling the teabag tin out of the ground, a flurry of soil and seeds coming with it.

She wiped the dirt off the tin as best she could, then popped the top open. She pulled out the bags of notes and coins and bits of paper on which were written Clementine's IOUs, and then found the old Nokia mobile phone underneath at the bottom. It was the sort of phone that Margery had owned until very recently, when she had finally been persuaded by Ceri-Ann to buy her old smartphone. This sort of phone couldn't send an email but would probably be perfectly fine if dropped from a third-floor window into a swimming pool and then dried off with a napkin from a fast-food restaurant.

'Did you know she'd buried this here?' Margery asked Clementine, who had appeared behind her and was kneeling down in the grass next to her.

'No, of course I didn't!' Clementine said. 'I'd have already dug it up, wouldn't I?'

If it had been any other phone, Margery would have thought that it would have run out of battery in the time it had been in the money tin in the cold ground, but the old screen lit up as soon as she touched one of the buttons. It had a PIN code and Margery looked to Clementine expectantly.

'Ahh, why are we always foiled by a password?' Clementine groaned. 'Why does everyone lock everything now? When I was younger, we left everything unlocked, front doors, windows, cars… I mean… we did get burgled once and they did take the car because we left the keys out…'

'Do you have any idea what the code might be?' Margery asked. 'It's four numbers.'

Clementine thought about it and the determined look returned to her eye. 'What about her son's birthday?'

Margery almost flinched at the mention of Maria's dead son, but she nodded.

'Well, what's that?' she said when she felt she had enough words to.

'I don't know,' Clementine admitted. 'Hang on... she had a calendar up in the van.'

Clementine disappeared back into the house and Margery stood up, taking the money tin over to the garden patio table and sitting down on the nearest chair. Clementine left Margery with her memories of Thomas, watching him fall in slow motion as she dropped down into the freezing water back-first and all the air exploded from her lungs. He had deserved what was coming to him, she told herself. She had told herself for years now that she had to believe it, even though she knew deep down that she didn't. Really, she believed that anyone could be redeemed, especially someone so young. Before she could escape further into her grief, Clementine returned, holding the battered *Cats Wearing Hats* calendar. The photograph for August was of a kitten wearing a sunhat and reclining on a deckchair.

'Try the fifth of August,' she said. 'That's Thomas's birthday. If it's not that it might be something else in here. I brought the calendar in with me just in case.'

Margery tapped *0508* into the phone when prompted and it opened onto the main screen. Despite her conflicting emotions about Thomas, she felt the smile return to her face at the beam from Clementine's.

'Okay,' she said as she tapped through the phone settings. 'What are we looking for? You know, usually I'd ask someone younger to help me with this, Ceri-Ann maybe. But I feel like I can work one of these.' She gestured to the screen. 'Most of her text messages are from you and Louise asking why she isn't at work… oh…'

'Something else?' Clementine asked. She craned her neck to try and see the screen better.

'A text from someone, she hasn't saved their phone number,' Margery explained. 'It just says, "is it done?"'

'Well,' Clementine said, her mouth pulling into a grimace, 'that's not ideal. Maybe look in her phone calls?' Clementine sat down on the chair next to Margery and looked at the phone over her shoulder again.

Margery did as she was told, but found nothing of interest in the outgoing settings, and moved on to the missed calls. 'She's had a few missed calls. One's a local number judging by the area code and the other is a mobile, the same number as the text message.'

'Ooh!' Clementine squealed excitedly. 'What's the local number? I'll goggle it.'

'Do you mean "google"?' Margery said, showing her the number.

Clementine scoffed – a loud *phft* that reverberated around the quiet garden. 'It should be called Goggle, Margery. Because it's got so many eyes on everything.'

She typed the first number into her phone, leaving Margery free to search through Maria's notes. There was nothing there and she had no voicemail messages. Margery went to the text messages and scrolled down to the bottom of them. Most were from Clementine, but she finally found another one that wasn't. Margery gasped when she read the contents.

'That number is the school,' Clementine said, her brow furrowing, oblivious to Margery's surprise. 'Wait, what was the other one?'

'It was a mobile number. Clem…' Margery said. 'Maria—'

'Well, you can't really goggle them,' Clementine told her. 'It probably won't pop up as anything, but I'll try it anyway… are you all right?'

Clementine had finally noticed the look on Margery's face. 'What? What have you found?'

'Maria was the secret bidder,' Margery said, showing her the message Maria had sent to Eleanor, and Eleanor's enthused response. 'She was the one pretending to be Louis Fisher.'

'What?' Clementine gasped, grasping for the phone.

Margery handed it over, watching as Clementine's face fell into despair once more.

Chapter Twelve

'I'll be amazed if this works,' Margery said, touching her new false nose gingerly. It squished horribly under her fingers.

She hadn't asked Grace and the rest of her gang of Summerview's theatrical make-up department what her new face was made of, deciding as they were gluing it onto her original face that she didn't want to know. Clementine had been much too excited about it, spending much of the time in the make-up chair grinning at her own reflection in the mirror.

'You'll have to do me a different colour wig next time!' Clementine had shrieked in joy, flipping her hair around. 'I bet I'd make a good redhead.'

Clementine's wig was as dark as her hair used to be and certainly made her look a few years younger. Margery was wearing a red wig, which she hadn't been sure about at all, having been blonde before she began to go grey. Somehow it seemed to suit her and she did look like a completely different person. It apparently hadn't been enough for Rose to concoct this mad experiment, but she had also demanded that she be the one to choose their outfits.

Margery wasn't sure how Rose managed to get through the day with the huge dangling earrings and large shawls

– wearing them herself, she felt as though her ears might fall off.

Clementine was enjoying herself, though. And she did look smart in Rose's designer trouser suit, even if it was slightly too small for her.

'We have to come up with different names for ourselves,' Clementine said, as they joined the group outside the ceramics studio. 'You be Barbara and I'll be Sandra.'

'All right,' Margery said, 'but what are our surnames, and how do we know each other?'

'I own a hotel,' Clementine shrieked in excitement. 'And you're my accountant, but I fired you for cooking the books and you went to prison for a time, but you're out now and we're still married because our love can survive a little bit of tax evasion and general fraud. Though actually, I don't know if we should be married, really. I've never found you less attractive and I think it's because you're wearing Rose's cape… oh my, this is going to be so much fun.'

'It's not supposed to be too much fun, Clem. We need to find some information to help Maria, remember?' Margery said with a laugh, regretting it as soon as Clementine's new face fell at the reminder. It had been a long few days and Clementine had been entirely miserable since they had realised that Maria was the secret bidder. Margery wished she hadn't said anything.

'Of course,' Clementine scoffed.

They still didn't know what to do with the revelation that Maria was the one who had placed the mystery bid under Louis Fisher's name. All signs pointed to Maria being involved with Eleanor's murder after all. Margery only had a very thin sliver of hope that they might find something out today that would exonerate her. 'Okay, so what's the plan again?'

'I'm not really sure,' Margery said, crossing the road. The rest of the dinner lady team were waiting for them outside the building and she waved at them. Gloria gave a hesitant wave back. 'I think we just go in and then one of us will try and cause a distraction with the teachers and then you and I will snoop about a bit.'

'This truly is a dreadful wishy-washy plan, isn't it?' Clementine groaned. 'I wish I could tell Maria – she'd think it was hilarious.'

'Oh my God.' Ceri-Ann laughed as Margery and Clementine arrived in front of them. 'What do you both look like? Did you fall into Rose's wardrobe?'

'Is it too much?' Margery asked, reaching for the earring that was precariously dangling from her earlobe and resting against her shoulder.

'Mate, it's perfect!' Ceri-Ann grinned. 'You look exactly like the type of people who do pottery!'

'As do we,' Gloria said, glaring at Ceri-Ann in uncharacteristic annoyance. 'I'm very excited about it. I want to make a ceramic holder for my bible. Two hands open, you know, like Jesus's.' She gestured with her own hands, pretending to open a book.

'I want to make a teapot.' Karen beamed. 'And Sharon's going to make a set of cups to go with it and then we're going to drink Prosecco out of them when we finish next week's parkrun to celebrate.'

'Mate, this is a two-week course on making an egg cup,' Ceri-Ann said, still smirking at Margery and Clementine's disguises. 'Maybe you could buy your own clay or whatever when the course ends and we've all become experts.'

'An egg cup!' Karen shrieked. 'What am I supposed to do with that? I don't eat eggs…'

'Yes, we're both vegan,' Sharon said, her eyes welling with tears.

'I saw you eating a chicken and sweetcorn sandwich yesterday after work,' Gloria said, her eyes narrowing accusatorily.

'Yeah, well, I don't like birds, so I can eat chicken,' Sharon told her. She paused thinking about the egg cup. 'I suppose I could store earrings in it.'

'Or ping-pong balls,' Seren suggested.

There was a flurry of nodding among everyone else as Gloria rolled her eyes.

Margery decided to intervene before the conversation got too far away from them. 'Shall we go in?' she suggested.

The dinner ladies made their way inside in a gaggle.

'Hello,' a woman called from the back of the room. The class was all set up ready, with a few pottery wheels and bags of clay sitting next to them in a pile. 'Are you my class?'

'We are!' Ceri-Ann said, stepping forward to greet the woman. 'We booked over the phone.'

'Ahh yes.' The woman beamed. 'The dance troupe! I'd love to see a routine after if we've got time…'

'Yeah, that's us,' Ceri-Ann said, turning to Margery to give her a huge wink that must have looked incredibly conspicuous. 'We'll have a bit of tap-dancing ready to go straight after, don't worry, and then Seren will do you a bit of ballet to top it off.'

Margery hoped the teacher wasn't expecting anything suspicious. It would be obvious that they weren't who they said they were if she did. Especially after the class when they all started tapping and flopping about all over the place. For one thing, Seren had a packet of cigarettes sticking out of the pocket of her shirt and Margery felt that she and Clementine were much too old to appear in a dance troupe. Especially with Clementine's mad, made-up story about running a hotel.

'My name is Helen and I'll be your teacher for the next two sessions.' Helen gestured for them to all take a seat. 'Has anyone partaken of the glamorous world of egg cup making before today?'

'I made a cup out of Playdoh once,' Seren admitted as they all sat down. 'I tried to drink out of it, but it melted and my tea went all over me.'

Helen raised her eyebrows, but caught her reaction in time to smile at Seren politely.

'That's great,' she said, skimming over to the next part of the conversation quickly. 'Well, it's quite a straightforward process and by this time next week you'll all be making your own egg cups. Then I'll take them to be fired and you can pick them up the week after.'

Karen raised her hand.

'Yes?' Helen said.

'If we wanted to make a teapot, can we do that instead?' Karen asked.

'No,' Helen said, 'egg cups only, I'm afraid.'

'What about a vase?' Clementine said, clapping her hand over her mouth as she realised what she had said out loud.

Helen just shook her head. 'I do an advanced pottery class that's eight weeks long and has the possibility of making all those sorts of things, but this is the introductory class. The advanced class is much more expensive, and to be honest with you, it's quite… well… advanced. This is just the basics of throwing and shaping. Once you've all mastered that, then I would be pleased to book you onto our more senior sessions.'

'What if I made a very long and tall egg cup that could also be used as a vase?' Ceri-Ann asked. Margery had the suspicious feeling that she wasn't taking the class very seriously at all.

'Let's just see how this goes, shall we?' Helen said with a smile.

There was no guilt in her eyes – nothing suspicious at all, in Margery's opinion. Maybe they had made a mistake coming here. She looked around as Helen began to explain what they would be doing in their first session. The ceramics studio was quite small, and they were all squashed inside it.

There didn't seem to be any obvious clues that Margery could see in the room itself. She didn't really know where to start. There was a door that led to what looked like a storeroom or an office – perhaps there would be something of interest back there? Margery wasn't sure how she could get there, though. She would have to think of a way to cause a distraction.

The room was dusty, Margery suspected that all sorts of art classes went on under its roof and some were not as well tidied away as others. She began to feel a sneeze coming on, trying to hold it in under her new nose. It would ruin everything if half her face exploded off onto the table in front of her.

Helen guided Seren, the first person in line, to the pottery table and sat her down gently. Seren put her hands on the ball of clay in front of her, her eyes roaming around the room nervously at the rest of the team. Margery sensed an opportunity was about to arrive, though she wasn't sure exactly what it would look like.

'Just relax,' Helen said soothingly. 'Wet your fingers first, and then put them back on the clay.'

Seren did as Helen instructed, wetting her fingers in the bowl of water next to her and then returning to the clay on the wheel.

'Right, now gently put your foot on the pedal,' Helen said, pointing to the pedal by Seren's foot and smiling encouragingly.

Seren nodded, and put her foot down on the pedal. Gingerly at first, and then much too hard. The wheel began to spin wildly and the clay that had been resting gently on the surface of it was flung off into the air and splatted against the wall. They all screamed.

Karen and Gloria rushed over to help, but in her panic, Seren pressed down on the pedal harder. A second wodge of clay flew off and hit Gloria square in the face, coating her glasses. She stumbled backward, momentarily blinded, as the rest of the dinner ladies tried to duck and hide from the assault. Helen rushed to unplug the machine, but in her haste, she unplugged the wrong plug. The wheel kept spinning as the dinner ladies cowered behind the nearest table, clay flying in all directions. Seren's foot remained glued to the pedal, the machine whirring violently as Seren shrieked.

Margery took advantage of the commotion to rush into the back room and closed the door behind her, only feeling a splattering of clay hit her as she entered. She breathed heavily, looking around, knowing that whatever she did now would have to be quick. If Helen caught her in here, she would just say that she was trying to avoid getting splattered. Margery was sure that would work. She looked around the room. There was not much to it. Just two shelving units facing each other, pottery waiting to be fired and glazed on one side and finished pottery on the other. And a desk with not much on it.

She ran her hands over the nearest sadly wilted mug, lifting it to look underneath. There were initials printed there. *Everything has initials on*, she thought, as she lifted the next and looked underneath that one as well. There was another piece half hidden behind the rest of the finished pottery and Margery sought it out with her fingertips. It was a simple bowl, nowhere near as grand as the Dewstow Heritage Vase, but still lovely and well made. Much better than the rest of the sad, stunted cups and saucers and dented egg cups that had been fired. There were no initials on the piece, however, nothing to mark it out from the rest of the objects.

She looked around and saw Helen's diary on the desk at the back of the room. It was stained with clay fingerprints and had seen much better days. But Margery found herself drawn to it, and started flicking through the pages. There were mentions on each class date of who had taken a piece home, or was waiting for one to be fired to pick up. There were mentions whenever someone picked something up. It was a detailed record and Margery found herself flipping through the stained pages, finding her eyes widening when she realised that the name Robert Evans was all over the pages, in Helen's tight scrawl.

The door clicked open and she whirled around. Margery clutched her chest, sure she'd been found out, breathing a huge sigh of relief to only find Clementine, covered in clay and looking quite sorry for herself.

'I wondered where you'd got to,' she said, looking around the room. 'It's a total mess out there—'

'Clem, look.' Margery pointed to the pages of the book. 'Robert Evans is written in here a lot. Do you think that could be the Robert *James* Evans – R. J. E. – that we're looking for?'

'Oh yes, maybe!' Clementine gasped. 'So, this wasn't all a huge waste of time then! He might well have the real vase – you never know! Maybe he needed it to make a better copy, maybe he killed Eleanor. I bet he did!'

'Let's not get ahead of ourselves,' Margery said, trying not to let Clementine's excitement catch on. 'Let's go to visit him and see what he has to say for himself.'

'How will we find him?' Clementine asked. 'We didn't have any luck with the phone book, did we?'

'We'll find a way,' Margery promised. Clementine nodded at her confidence and Margery hoped she would be able to keep the promise. 'We're getting closer, I can feel it.'

They slid back into the main room, the chaos still ongoing. Margery said a quiet prayer of thanks for Seren's bumbling clumsiness.

'I'll refund your deposit,' Helen was saying as they entered the room. 'I'm so sorry, ladies, but I think the room will take a while to recover from this and I just… To be honest, I think it would be best if you left so I can clear it up before it sets.'

Karen and Sharon were taking it in turns to dab the clay-covered walls with a paper towel, while Gloria comforted Seren, who was sitting on a chair with her head in her hands. Ceri-Ann was on the phone. Margery could see her through the window to outside. Ceri-Ann had somehow managed to avoid the worst of the clay onslaught. Perhaps she had escaped through the front door as Margery was running into the back. They went outside to meet her. Ceri-Ann almost jumped out of her skin as they exited the building, putting her hand to her chest as she gasped.

'Christ, I forgot it was you under that!' Ceri-Ann huffed, looking between them both with wide eyes. 'Did you find anything?'

'Yes,' Margery hissed. She told her what they had seen in the book and Ceri-Ann nodded excitedly.

'I'll get Symon to look him up,' Ceri-Ann said, pulling her phone back out of her pocket. 'See if there's anything on him…'

'Isn't that very illegal?' Margery asked, worrying her lip. 'You said you didn't think Symon should be involved.'

'Well, yeah…' Ceri-Ann hesitated. 'Yeah, I think you're right, maybe I shouldn't ask him. That Officer Wilkinson bloke isn't very fond of him after all that with Mr Fitzgerald.'

'We'll find out some other way,' Margery reassured her, even though she could feel Clementine seething at her words. 'Clem, it's not fair to get Symon in trouble, he could be thrown off the case and then we'll have nothing—'

'Sometimes I think you don't want to help Maria at all,' Clementine snapped.

'Of course I do,' Margery said, swinging around to look at Clementine in bafflement. 'But we can't get other people in trouble for us, especially seeing as we know Symon is trying to help.'

'Well, we haven't got very far, have we?' Clementine said sulkily.

'No, but we've found out that the second secret bidder does pottery and almost certainly made the fake vase,' Margery said. 'Can't that be enough for now?'

Clementine's face fell. Margery knew her outburst had been to cover that she was close to tears.

'Mr Fitzgerald used to keep everything documented, didn't he? There wasn't anyone in town he didn't have weird notes on,' Ceri-Ann said quietly, looking between them in worry. 'Would he not have something about this guy written down in one of his conspiracy theory notebooks?'

He might do, Margery thought. Mr Fitzgerald had once had a full CCTV system that covered most of Dewstow town centre and had kept written tabs on everyone. You couldn't go on holiday without him writing your departure time down somewhere. It seemed like the next best step.

Chapter Thirteen

They were pulling the apartment above the shop apart for what felt like hours before they gave up. Margery put the kettle on, and then she and Clem relaxed on the deckchairs that they had brought from their own garden shed. At the time, it had seemed to be tempting fate to buy any proper furniture for the flat above the shop. It was almost an insult to Mr Fitzgerald's memory to change that room after they had changed so much of the downstairs already. Now, Margery wished that they had just done it. It had been a long few months with the deckchairs, and they often ended up in the flat when there was a class finishing downstairs.

The room was gloomy in its emptiness. A cool breeze blew through it from the window that badly needed resealing. Sometimes it felt a little too spooky up in the flat, but Margery reassured herself that if Mr Fitzgerald was going to haunt anywhere it would be somewhere with a lot of drama. Perhaps Rose's office at the school, or Mrs Mugglethwaite's mobile phone.

Clementine had dragged down the box of files from the bookshelf so they could look through them. There was a great deal of information about the residents of Dewstow and their comings and goings, but nothing concrete for Margery and Clementine to grasp. It was frustrating to say the least. The pages strewn across the room were just as annoying. They would have to clear it all up before they left. It felt incredibly taboo to ever leave a mess up in the flat for the same reasons they hadn't bought new chairs.

'I've been thinking,' Clementine said suddenly, breaking the silence in the room. 'Wasn't Eleanor one of the residents that complained about our shop?'

'She was,' Margery said, the memory returning to her mind. 'She signed the petition saying we should close up.'

'She was quite miserable then, wasn't she?' Clementine said. 'Maybe she wasn't as well liked as Cecelia at the museum is making out she was.'

'I'd imagine that's true,' Margery said, stirring the mug and removing the tea bag. 'Louis didn't seem particularly happy with her, did he?'

'No,' Clementine agreed with a nod. 'He seemed a bit betrayed that she'd essentially stolen the vase. I imagine it would be quite the blow for your grandchild to not want to keep up with your long-held traditions anyway, that would be bad enough. But for her to downright tread all over them? I expect that smarts more than a bit.'

'You have to remember that she's not long dead,' Margery said, adding sugar to both their mugs. She reached up to the cupboard and took out the pack of bourbon biscuits that lived there, realising as she took it down that it was only half full. Martha Mugglethwaite must have been helping herself in between classes. 'He's probably incredibly upset about that, even a bit bitter. It's probably brought it all up again. We don't know what he was like before, do we?'

'Well, if she was really as awful as we remember, then surely there would be a queue of people who would want Eleanor dead,' Clementine suggested, taking the cup Margery handed her gratefully. 'So how do we find them?'

Margery hummed as she sat down in her own chair and took a sip of the much too hot liquid. It burnt her tongue instantly, ruining it. 'Mrs Mugglethwaite.'

Clementine gave her a curious look. 'Martha?'

'She knows everyone and everything,' Margery reminded her. 'Even if something's not quite true, she'll have heard it at some point. She remembers everything, doesn't she? Don't you remember the day that you left Arthur's birthday present at home and we accidentally went empty-handed to his birthday party? I heard her telling someone on the bus about it last week!'

'That's true. Do you think she'd know who this Robert is?' Clementine wondered aloud. 'Hmmm.'

'We could ask her in an hour or so,' Margery said, looking up at the clock above the sink on the wall of the kitchenette. 'It's nearly time for the WI meeting she runs with Dawn.'

'That would mean speaking to Dawn, though.' Clementine grimaced. Margery chuckled. 'Listen, Margery... I'm sorry about earlier. I know you care about Maria and helping her...'

'Don't apologise.' Margery waved a hand at her. 'Water under the bridge. We'll find out what happened, don't worry.'

'I wish I could stop worrying,' Clementine sighed. 'I wish Mr Fitzgerald really had something here, all these weird spying files and nothing of use.'

'Well, we haven't finished looking,' Margery reminded her. 'It's not over quite yet. We don't know who this person is. They could have been to Summerview school for all we know, a former student. Perhaps Rose could dig out some information that could be of help.'

'What if they're a current student?' Clementine pondered. 'Like the children who did the fake noses for us?'

There was a noise from downstairs, the doorbell ringing. The sound clattered up the stairs into the flat.

'Someone forgot their key?' Clementine suggested, meeting Margery's eyes.

'Who?' Margery asked. 'There isn't a class on yet. I hope Dawn hasn't come early again. I ran out of things to say to her last time. And every time there was a lull in the conversation, she brought up the fact we crashed my car into her pond again.'

Clementine snorted at that. Dawn had never forgiven, nor forgotten Margery accidentally crashing her car into her pond years earlier. Maria's campervan had been the latest in a new line-up of complaining from Dawn, who had put a note through the door every day since it had first arrived. The notes had become more and more unhinged as time went on, but instead of being as worried as Margery had been, Clementine and Maria had thought it was hilarious.

'She'll run out of ink eventually,' Clementine had said, waving a hand over the last all-capitals diatribe. 'Or the shops will run out of paper, one of them.'

Margery knew if Maria hadn't suddenly disappeared then Dawn would never have stopped, even if all the paper in the world suddenly disintegrated into mulch. She would probably just have found out their email address or written it on the pavement in chalk or paint. Margery was hopeful that Maria would reappear soon and Dawn would be able to restart her rude correspondence.

Margery decided there was no point in waiting to find out if Dawn was early or ignoring it. Dawn would be able to get inside once Martha arrived and then they would need to explain why they hadn't answered the door to her. She heaved herself up from the deckchair and went downstairs, careful to use the handrail and take each step one at a time until she reached the shop floor. She could see a figure through the glass in the door of the shop door and went to it, opening it and peering out. It wasn't Dawn Simmonds at all.

'Hello,' Margery said. 'How can we help you?'

'Oh,' Jeffery said, looking just as surprised as Margery felt. He peered past her into the shop at the shelves of craft supplies and the tables and chairs stacked against the wall. 'This isn't an antique shop any more?'

'No, we took it over when Mr Fitzgerald died,' Margery explained. 'Can I help you with something? We might know where you can find what you're looking for.'

'Well…' Jeffery began. He looked around at the shop behind her with trepidation in his eyes and then back to Margery, his brow knitting in confusion.

She realised with surprise that he didn't recognise her. They hadn't yet taken off the stage make-up, both of them worried that it would take much more than a gentle face wash to remove. And Rose's clothing had so many layers it would have taken a while to unravel themselves. And so she hadn't bothered to change her look.

'It's just you here?' he asked, looking behind her again as though someone else might pop out and greet him. 'Not… not anyone else?'

'Just me,' Margery said, hearing Clementine clattering down the stairs behind her. 'And my associate… Brenda…'

She turned and watched as Clementine paused for a moment, before continuing into the room with a grin on her face. Margery didn't know why she had lied – there had been no need to. Really, she should have just explained to Jeffery that they were helping the students practise costume make-up for a play, but the way he kept looking around in confusion was confusing her. The thing was, the disguises had helped them sneak into the pottery class, and she was sure that it wouldn't be good for that to be found out. It could make things very difficult if the general public found out that Margery and Clementine were using disguises to visit buildings in the town. They were no longer the darlings of Dewstow, not now that the debacle with Maria had happened. It was going to take a while before they would be able to go to town meetings without people looking over their shoulders to gawp at them. Anyway, Margery told herself, Jeffery had just lost a family member. She was sure a surprise wasn't needed at all. He would be gone in a moment and the next time they saw him she would be herself again.

'Oh,' he said finally. 'I had heard a rumour that the Dinner Lady Detectives owned this place now?'

Margery didn't know what to say to that, or why he had asked. Surely, if he'd known that they owned it, he would know that it was no longer an antique shop? Why was he really here?

'They do,' a voice behind them said. Margery turned to see that Clementine had decided to join in. The accent she was putting on was a strange mix, almost as though Clementine was trying to pull every British accent from a washing machine, and they were all tied together by the apron strings. 'We're the custodians.'

'Oh, I see,' Jeffery said, his eyes brightening as he realised he was in the right place after all. For whatever it was he really wanted, Margery thought grimly.

'My sister-in-law has recently passed away,' he said, waving his hands in explanation. 'Her grandfather is the executor, but it's too big a job for him, so he's passed it on to me. Eleanor was a collector of such a great many things. I thought the antique shop might be able to price some of them. I'm sure her son would be interested in the value of some of it.'

Margery wondered for a moment where Eleanor's son was and if she had ever met him. She certainly hadn't seen him around Dewstow. That she knew of, anyway. The sorting of the will hadn't fallen onto his shoulders. Louis did seem to still be the family patriarch on the Fisher side, but who was the Black family's? Eleanor might well have left it all for her son. If that was the case, then it was kind of Jeffery to help. Louis seemed to still have all his wits about him, but he must have been in his nineties and that was being generous. Planning his own granddaughter's funeral was a lot to ask of a very elderly man. It wasn't the right order of anything. Perhaps Louis didn't feel that he could.

'Why don't you come in for a cup of tea and I'll see if I can find you the number for the antique owner we know,' Clementine suggested from behind them. Margery stepped back so Jeffery could enter the shop. 'We sold them a huge amount when we took over— I mean, Margery and Clementine did, of course…'

Margery hadn't wanted to invite Jeffery in at all, had counted on him leaving as soon as possible. For one thing, once Dawn and Martha Mugglethwaite arrived, they would want to know who Jeffery was talking to. It would be very obvious that they didn't know the strangers siting with him and then the ruse would fall apart. She shot Clementine a warning look as Jeffery entered the shop floor and sat down at the table in the middle of the room. Clementine had forgotten all about their tea mugs waiting upstairs for them and was already busily making them and Jeffery a fresh cup. Jeffery seemed interested in the room, looking around in surprise as Margery sat down at the table.

'They've done a good job here,' he said, taking a seat next to her. 'I'd never have known what it used to be. I always felt like I was a second away from walking into a cobweb the last time I visited.'

'I don't think they've managed to get rid of all the spiders, but they live here as much as anyone does,' Clementine joked. 'There was so much dust it was practically a biohazard.'

Jeffery chuckled politely and Clementine brought the drinks over.

'Do you have Mr Bell's number, Cl— Brenda?' Margery asked as she sat down with them, nearly saying Clementine's name by mistake and kicking herself for it. 'I thought he could probably help Jeffery with Eleanor's things.'

'Of course, Ethel,' Clementine said, with a half snort that made Margery flick her head to look at Jeffery's reaction. Luckily, he was busying himself with adding sugar to his mug. Clementine reached down into her bag and pulled out her purse, opening it up to look for Mr Bell's business card.

'How do you know Robert?' Jeffery asked, pointing to the scrap of paper with the name on it that they had taken from the pottery class, and which Clementine had left lying carelessly on the table. 'He's an odd fellow, isn't he?'

Margery and Clementine exchanged a surprised look. Jeffery didn't notice as he picked up the mug and took a sip.

'Yes,' Clementine said, wordlessly agreeing with the look Margery shot her across the table. 'We know him. Very odd man.'

'Great fun, though,' Jeffery said quickly, as if apologising for how strange Robert was. 'I haven't seen him for ages,' he mused, taking the business card Clementine handed him. 'Thanks for this. It'll be a weight off our minds when the house is cleared. Honestly, I thought Cecil had a lot of things, but Eleanor seems to have gone mad buying antiques since he died. She could probably have opened a second museum with it all.'

Margery wondered for a moment if the Black family was cursed. They certainly seemed to have had more than their fair share of misery befall them. She wondered how to switch the topic back to Robert now that Jeffery had begun telling them about Eleanor's house again. Clementine decided for her.

'Robert left something here a while ago, and we've been meaning to return it,' Clementine said casually. Margery felt her eyebrows raising involuntarily. Rose would have wanted to sign Clementine up for the next school play if she could see her acting. 'Do you know where he lives?'

'Of course,' Jeffery said. He was distracted by putting the card into his wallet. 'Do you know the old church house in Ittonvale? It's down the lane behind the school. Ittonvale school.'

Margery didn't know the exact house, but she knew where he meant. They slipped back into an awkward small talk as Margery's head whirled with ideas and apprehension.

'I'm so sorry to ask,' Jeffery said. His voice seemed unnatural, stumbling over his words like a student reading Shakespeare out loud for the first time. 'But you must know the dinner ladies quite well?'

'Yes,' Margery squeaked. 'Quite well.'

'It's just that…' Jeffery waved a hand, trying to explain. 'Look, I may have come here on false pretences…'

'Really?' Margery asked, trying to sound surprised.

'Yes,' Jeffery said. 'I was hoping to see what they were up to. Well, what I mean by that is… this is hard to explain.'

'Did you want to hire them?' Clementine said brightly. 'They're not cheap, you know. But they'll make you an excellent Victoria sponge while they solve your issue.'

'Not exactly,' Jeffery said, his face pulling into a wince. 'I just wondered if they had any leads on the death of my sister-in-law.'

'Is she the same Eleanor that died at the school?' Clementine said, the bizarre accent back at full volume. 'We've heard all about it!'

'Yes, she was,' Jeffery said, nodding and stirring his drink again.

'Is it true that she was killed by your own family vase?' Margery asked, deciding that if she couldn't get Clementine to stop then she might as well join in.

'It was a fake,' Jefferey said, leaning in to whisper to them closely. 'The murder weapon was made to look just like the real vase.'

'How did they know that, though?' Margery asked, her own voice dropping to a calm hush.

Jeffery looked around before turning back her. 'Robert made it decades ago. It had his initials inscribed inside.'

Margery and Clementine pretended to gasp, though Margery could feel the panic rising in her throat. He shouldn't have known that information. It wasn't public knowledge, and they only knew because Symon had told them it was fake. She wondered if the police would have told the family that information, she couldn't imagine that Officer Wilkinson would be very forthcoming with it before the case was solved.

'Shame all that with Eleanor and Robert,' Jeffery muttered finally after a long pause. 'I heard that the police have already been up there to spook him. He wouldn't have killed her, of course.'

'What do you mean by that?' Margery asked, picking up her mug and taking a large sip of the still-boiling tea. 'Have you spoken to him?'

'No, I keep meaning to put him in touch with my solicitor – he's not afraid of bending the rules a little, you know? But I've just been so busy with the funeral and everything else,' Jeffery said with an exasperated gush of air. 'But just because your initials are on something doesn't mean you killed someone, does it? Robert wouldn't have killed her, he barely leaves the house. A recluse.'

'Gosh,' Margery said. She realised that if Jeffery was paying attention, then he would know that Robert wouldn't have visited the shop from his own words. She took another sip from the mug, feeling it burn her inside all the way down.

Jeffery looked up from his mug. 'So, you must know… are Margery and Clementine interested in her death? I expect they have a few suspects in mind. Do you know who?'

That was curious, Margery thought. Very curious. Why did Jeffery want to know what they were thinking? Unless he had something to do with Eleanor's murder in the first place and needed to know whether anyone had made the connection.

'They've given all that up,' Clementine said quickly. 'After Mr Fitzgerald died – he was their friend, you see – they stopped taking cases. And the shop keeps them so busy.' She laughed a little too loudly, a horrible guffaw that rattled the walls, and gestured around at the busy room. 'Well, there's no time for solving murders!'

'Oh, yes, yes,' Jeffery said. He didn't look placated at all. In fact, he seemed as though he might be gearing up to seeing if he could search the building to see what Margery and Clementine were up to. 'Wow, I can't believe they don't have any opinions about it. What with Clementine's sister being the main suspect. I thought they'd be desperate to pin it on someone else.'

'You don't think that she did it?' Margery asked, trying to bait him into revealing more. 'The police seem very certain.'

'Oh no, I'm not saying she didn't,' Jeffery said. 'I just… forget I said anything. But have they had any contact with her at all that you know of?'

'We really wouldn't know,' Margery began.

'Of course, of course!' Jeffery waved his hands to clear the air, which had grown thick with tension. 'Forget I said anything! Maybe let's not mention this to the dinner ladies, hmm?'

The plot thickens, Margery thought. Clementine had fallen silent, considering Jeffery with an eagle eye.

Margery lifted her mug again and then found herself grasping at her face. Her false nose was coming off. She could feel the glue escaping, the nose tearing off in a horrible way as it melted from the warmth of the tea. The steam must have loosened it. She grasped for her nose, gasping as she felt the rubber slide under her fingers.

'So sorry,' she babbled, getting to her feet. The chair slid out from behind her in her haste and fell, landing with a crunch on the wooden floor. 'Nosebleed!'

She rushed to the back of the room and up the stairs again, hoping Clementine would take the hint and see Jeffery out before he realised what was going on. She pulled what remained off the nose off and placed it on the kitchenette counter, taking a deep breath to steady herself. She reached over for her original mug of tea, reasoning that if she was trapped up here for a while she might as well finish it. It was gone.

She looked around the room blindly for it. Maybe Clementine had thrown it away, but the mug wasn't in the sink. The packet of biscuits was almost empty, the wrapper left on the counter with a solitary biscuit inside. Margery took it and bit into it with a crunch, shaking her head at the audacity of Clementine, the biscuit monster.

Chapter Fourteen

Margery drove the car down the lane that led to Robert's house, careful to go slowly as darkness fell. The leaves from the hedgerows brushed against the wing mirrors until they reached the small cottage. She pulled up outside, and she and Clem both peered out of the windscreen.

It had been a very narrow escape, all told. Clementine had managed to shoo Jeffery out of the shop, which had been easier said than done as Jeffery kept insisting that he was first-aid trained and trying to come up the stairs to 'help' Margery with her nosebleed. They had discussed what had just happened on the way to the house and both come to the same conclusion: Jeffery was hiding something, or in the very least, he knew more than he was letting on. Clementine had barely been able to hide her fury. Margery packed all the information away for later.

It was interesting that he had immediately jumped to the defence of Robert. Surely you would blame him for your relative's death given that he had made the murder weapon. Even if you knew deep down it wasn't him, you'd still assign some degree of blame. They had met enough murderers and liars now for it to send her suspicions regarding Robert right to the top of the pile.

The other thing that had struck her about the encounter was that Jeffery should have no reason to suspect Maria didn't do the crime. The evidence all pointed to her guilt at the moment. Unless, perhaps, he was worried that Margery and Clementine were trying to prove her innocence before she was caught – which, of course, they were. Margery hoped beyond hope that Maria had managed to make another daring escape, as she had done all those years ago when she had fled police custody. Though, it had nearly killed her then and she had known she was innocent. Maria was much older now. There was no telling what it would do to her psyche all these decades later.

'Isn't this the old groundskeeper's house for the school?' Clementine asked, as they continued to sit in the car. Margery turned the engine off and dimmed the lights but couldn't bring herself to open the car door.

'Maybe,' Margery said, looking at the whitewashed bricks of the small building. 'Ittonvale used to be a boarding school, didn't it? A long time ago?'

'I bet the headteacher two hundred years ago would be twirling in his grave if they knew that Ittonvale school has its own coffee shop,' Clementine said with a snort. 'I expect it was all more about discipline and lacrosse back then.'

'Do you think he's even in?' Margery asked, suddenly feeling nervous. She gripped the steering wheel a little bit harder, wishing that they hadn't come. Clementine nodded.

'Jeffery said he's a recluse, and the light is on in the window,' she said, gesturing to the front of the house where a warm glow awaited them. 'So let's go and find out what he knows. There's no point worrying about it here, is there? We've come this far.'

They got out of the car and went to the front door. Margery reached out and cracked the old knocker down against the wooden door. They waited for a beat.

Just as Margery had decided that he must be out, the door opened a crack. Margery could just about see the man's nose and one of his eyes as he peered out at them on his doorstep.

'Hello,' Clementine said cheerily. 'Are you Robert? Of R. J. E. fame?'

He opened the door and tilted his head to look at them, his mouth opening but then closing again, his lips pulling together in a tight line.

'You'd better come in,' he said finally, stepping back from the doorway. Margery turned to Clementine to share her trepidation, but Clementine was already following him inside.

'You got me,' he said as they entered the house, stepping over the threshold into his living room. 'Took you long enough to find me and all.'

Well, it was sort of a living room, Margery thought. Perhaps more artist's workshop than comfortable sitting room. Pots and plaques lined every surface, along with half-finished mugs and plates and all sorts of other things Margery was sure were supposed to be a familiar shape, even if they weren't quite fully formed yet. There was a potter's wheel in front of the battered, clay-covered armchair, and a bag of clay sat next to it. Ready for the next use.

'Well, you weren't easy to find,' Margery said. 'We got here entirely by chance in the end.'

Robert smiled, leaning awkwardly on his stick as they looked around. He was older, Margery thought, maybe similar in age to herself and Clementine, and he had the rough-hewn sort of look you usually found in very old dogs whose muzzles are going white. The room they stood in was busy enough to have a life of its own. Margery thought that perhaps Robert spent all his time in it, and alone. The dirty coffee cups piled up on the side table by the worn sofa certainly indicated that. There would be no room for a second person to sit comfortably without hitting an elbow on some piece or other.

'Well, that's by design, isn't it?' he said gruffly. 'I keep myself to myself, really. Don't like to give too much away. It's just, I don't do police.' Robert lowered his voice even further. It was barely audible to Margery's already poor hearing. 'Especially not now with that Wilkinson in charge, and all that with Timothy Fitzgerald. Leaving you two to sort out his death and that he was murdered. They'd have let him rot in the ground with everyone believing he'd had a fall – disgusting behaviour.'

Margery nodded. She still missed Mr Fitzgerald. The town seemed much emptier now he wasn't around. Margery missed seeing him pottering up and down the high street with Jason the dog or trying to sell them another necklace with a locket containing a picture of Princess Diana. Margery suddenly realised what Robert had said, a chill running down her spine.

'Wait… you know who we are?' Margery asked, feeling her voice waver as she spoke, then realised that without her fake nose she was pretty much back to normal.

'Everyone knows who you are,' Robert said, with a small smile. He pointed to her face. 'Even in disguise, Helen knew who you were and what you were doing at her class today. She recognised the rest of your friends, too. Rang me as soon as you'd all left.'

So much for being incognito, Margery scoffed to herself. They may as well have not bothered with their disguises.

Robert continued, 'I'm not surprised you came looking for me. Found something with my name on, did you?'

'We did,' Clementine told him.

'How did you find my address?' Robert asked, his eyes lighting up in interest. Margery found herself becoming annoyed at how lightly he was taking the situation. It all seemed to be a bit of a joke to him.

'Jeffery Black,' Margery told him, watching his face fall in a way she wasn't expecting. That was interesting to say the least. Before she could wonder more, Robert shook his head.

'Thought I'd got away from him for a bit,' Robert said, sitting down on the sofa with a heavy thump. 'I heard about all that at the school – the murder and that,' he whispered. He gasped when he realised what he'd said. 'Well, who hasn't?'

'We know you made the vase that killed Eleanor,' Clementine said. 'Jeffery told us.'

Her voice wasn't accusatory, but Robert's face still fell for a minute and he sat up a bit straighter.

'That prick,' Robert groaned. 'I bet he's the one who called the police.'

Margery shook her head. 'The police already knew it was fake. I don't know how they would have known that, though…'

'The materials aren't old enough, probably,' Robert said. 'Anyone taking a closer look would have realised if they knew their stuff. God, I should have stopped putting my initials on stuff. Never ends well.'

'Why did you make it?' Clementine asked, leaning forward with wide eyes.

'A woman asked me to make it for her,' Robert said, his tone casual. 'Brought me some photos of it. Obviously as soon as she showed me them, I knew what it was, but I humoured her. Wait a sec.'

He reached down by the armchair and pulled out a set of photographs, handing them to Clementine. Margery looked at them over her shoulder. It was the Dewstow Heritage Vase, but the room behind it was the local room in Dewstow Museum, you could see Mr Itton's comb to the side of the display case. Where was it now? Margery wondered. Someone must have taken it, if it had been in the room with Eleanor. There had been signs of a terrible struggle. Margery had been wondering for days now where the vase could be and who, other than Maria, could have swapped it. The thing was, why would Maria go to all that effort to steal the other high-value auction items but not take the vase as well?

'Obviously I saw her in the paper the other day and I thought, *Oh God, that's the one I made the vase for*,' he said, pointing to the *Dewstow Freepress* on the coffee table, nearly completely hidden under a pile of cups and saucers that needed firing.

Maria's face looked out from the paper at them all. Margery felt a shudder go down her spine at the realisation that they had used her mugshot from decades before. Of course they didn't have a new mugshot to use yet, but if anyone in Dewstow hadn't been suspicious of her before, then they surely would be now. Clementine was staring at the photographs in confusion.

'She brought you these and asked you to make her the same?' she asked Robert, who nodded.

'Yep. Well, not exactly. She dropped them off in a box,' he said, his eyes opening wide at the audacity of that. 'Imagine putting anything paper in a box and then just leaving it outside in the rain? Christ!' He laughed, a great wheezing chuckle that seemed to shake the sofa. 'I did, of course – she seemed fun on her text messages, and I like a challenge. Everyone knows the Heritage Vase. Well, maybe only potters care about it. I couldn't see why she wanted a copy, honestly – but hey-ho.'

'So, she came and got the vase, but you hadn't met her before?' Margery asked him. He shook his head.

'No, first time I clapped eyes on her was when she came and got it,' Robert said, his eyes looking into the distance at the memory. 'I hope you don't mind me telling you, but I did ask her if she wanted to go to the pictures with me some time. She was lovely, I thought. I still don't believe all that rubbish about her being a murderer or whatever. She was cleared of it all, she told me she was.'

'Did she say yes?' Margery asked, before she could stop herself.

'Oh God no. She called me a dirty old man,' Robert said, with a grin. 'I told her, "You ain't no spring chicken either, love." She just laughed! Cracking woman. I'll have to ask her again once you get her off the charges.'

'Did she say why she wanted the vase?' Clementine asked. 'She must have had a reason.'

He shook his head again, confusion returning to his eyes. 'No, she didn't say why in her messages. All smoke and mirrors with that as well! Two phones, she texted me from.'

'Two phones?' Clementine asked, perking up.

'Yeah,' Robert said with a nod. 'I never knew which number to message.'

'Can we see the numbers?' Margery asked.

He shrugged, pulling his mobile phone from his pocket. Margery rummaged in her bag for a pen, finding a receipt to write on. Robert showed her each number, both under *Maria* with different emojis next to them, and she wrote them down. Something to think about later.

'She didn't say much about the vase when she came to get it,' Robert said. He put his phone away and then paused, his brow furrowing. 'I reckoned she wanted to give it to you.'

'Me?' Clementine said.

'Yep. You are her sister, aren't you?' he said. 'You've got the same face. It's a shame you aren't single.' He winked at Margery, who felt her eyes narrowing at his leering.

'Why would she give it to me?' Clementine snapped, her face the picture of confusion. 'We've got a million vases already, she knows that. We're practically drowning in them as it is.'

That was true, Margery thought. For some reason, Clementine had a sort of selective blindness when it came to purchasing vases, and whenever she saw a nice one she would buy it and then remember only when she returned home that they already had twenty of them in the cupboard above the kitchen counter. Once she had tried to buy enough flowers for Margery's anniversary surprise to fill each vase, but still a few had remained flowerless.

Robert shrugged. 'Why does anyone do anything? Makes way more sense than what the police thought.'

'Well, what did the police think?' Margery said, feeling as confused as Clementine looked.

'They think she had a copy made to swap so she could steal the real one,' Robert said. 'But that doesn't make sense to me. Why would she want the real one anyway?

And killing the Black family matriarch to get it, at that! She has some balls, if that was her plan.'

All of what he said was common knowledge, which didn't help them at all.

'Is there anything else you can think of?' Margery asked, almost pleading with him. 'Surely you've made things like this for people before if you take commissions?'

'Well, someone else has asked me to make a copy of it before.' Robert nodded. 'But I didn't want to do it because she's, well, quite frankly, I didn't like her at all. Wish I hadn't made one for Maria now and all. I've had the police sniffing about trying to prove I had some part in it. They haven't found anything much to help their little investigation, though, obviously, but didn't stop them taking my phone to look at my messages, did it?'

'Who asked you for a copy?' Margery asked.

'Vivian Black,' Robert said with a shrug. 'Doubt you'd be able to ask her now, really. I don't think she's saying much.' He grinned a horrible tooth-filled smile.

'What on earth would Vivian want a replica of the vase for?' Clementine asked. 'I know Eleanor stole the original, but why would she want a fake?'

'Unless she was planning to swap it with the real one,' Margery suggested. Vivian had certainly been sneaky enough to attempt something like that, but nothing suggested she had actually managed to do it.

Robert shrugged again. It annoyed Margery no end. None of this information was helpful to them.

'I reckon Vivian was going to give the copy to Louis Fisher as a consolation prize after Eleanor wouldn't give the real one back,' he said. 'They'd been fighting over that thing for years, that's another reason I didn't want to make it.' He paused for a moment, thinking. 'I wonder where the real one is now.'

'Me too,' Margery said, realising that the vase might have been more significant than any of them had thought. 'We've spoken to Louis Fisher and he never mentioned that.'

'Maybe he didn't know,' Robert said. 'This was decades ago now, I was just starting out. I was at school with Jeffery. That's how I knew the family.'

'You said you didn't *want* to make her a copy,' Clementine said. 'Not that you didn't make her a copy.'

'Semantics,' Robert said, but he looked away, unable to meet her eye. 'Maybe I did make her it, but it wasn't the best work I've ever done. Bit rubbish, really.'

'Why?' Margery asked.

'I was just starting out.' He laughed. 'Didn't have a clue what I was doing. Anyway, she said it wasn't good enough to fool a flea and refused to pay me for it in the end. Just like her daughter-in-law, she was.'

'Did Eleanor not pay you for something?' Margery asked.

'You can say that again! I don't just do pots, you know,' he said. He narrowed his eyes. 'She wanted a plaque for her stupid museum. Lord Horace of Ittonvale lived here, blah blah. I made it, good work it was too, and then I invoiced her, nothing. I threatened her with small claims court, nothing. I didn't see a bean. I'm telling you, there's a nice, warm place in hell for people who don't pay artists for their work. AI can't make you a set of dinner plates, can it?'

Margery nodded agreeably.

Robert continued his rant. 'I found out not long ago that Eleanor was having trouble keeping the lights on at that museum,' he said, tapping his finger to his chin thoughtfully. 'I heard she'd sold her house and was living in the museum's attic, but you didn't hear that from me. Don't go telling Jeffery that!'

'But why?' Clementine asked. 'The Black family are rich, aren't they? Old money?'

'You'd think they were rich, wouldn't you?' Robert said. 'But Vivian didn't leave any of them nothing in her will.'

'Nothing?' Margery gasped, thinking of Vivian's huge house.

'Nothing,' he said. His blue eyes bored into hers.

Clementine's gaze was distant for a moment before snapping back into the room.

'So, where's the other fake vase now?' she asked. 'What happened to it after Vivian took it?'

'I've never given it a moment's thought.' Robert shrugged. Margery could tell they weren't going to get much more out of the man.

'Wait,' Margery said. 'How did Maria get your number? For that matter, when did you meet her in person?'

'Like I already told you,' Robert snapped, slapping his hand down onto the arm of the sofa. 'I didn't meet her until she arrived to pick the thing up, and she turned me down for a date! Ungrateful, if you ask me…'

'So, you didn't meet her before then?' Margery asked. 'How did you get her number?'

'She must've found me. My details are in the local pages, and I post a few bits and bobbins on Facebook and that.' He shook his head, his cheeks reddening. 'We just spoke by text… and then she turned up looking like a goddess. Much the same as her sister…'

He leered at Clementine, who rolled her eyes.

Robert guffawed, slapping Margery on the back. 'I'm only joking!' he said, wiping a tear from his eye. 'Look, if you find out what happened to that other vase, I'd love to know. Be a bit sad if both of them were smashed. Took me ages both times!'

They left and got back into the car, the thoughts reeling in Margery's head. Clementine was following the same train of thought.

'Oh, Margery, I really don't think Maria was the person texting to arrange for the vase to be made,' Clementine said as soon as Margery had begun to drive down the narrow lane.

'I think she was some sort of patsy in all this. I think she messaged him to arrange for pick up on her actual phone, but someone else was arranging it all.'

'I do too,' Margery said. 'For one thing, we didn't see any messages to Robert on Maria's phone, did we? Surely she wouldn't have deleted them if she hadn't been expecting to get caught. She didn't delete any of the mystery bidding messages. Maybe she didn't have time, maybe she buried the phone to hide the evidence.'

Margery was still holding the receipt. She grasped for her phone, unlocking it and searching through for the number she had added to the contacts.

'It's the same number as the one that texted Maria!' she cried, dashing her fist against the steering wheel in a fleeting moment of triumph that flickered away almost as soon as it had arrived.

'Then we need to find whoever that is,' Clementine said.

Margery dialled the number again. It rang and rang until it finally disconnected. Not even a voicemail service to leave a message on.

'No answer,' Margery said. She felt her hopes being dashed at every turn. 'This is all mad. Two fake vases. One used as a murder weapon, and the real vase still out there somewhere. I don't even know where to start.'

They drove in silence, thinking over what they knew.

Margery barely realised that she was driving down the street to their house before they were already at the driveway. She parked on the street out front as the van was still blocking their access. They clambered out of the car and began to enter the house, but Clementine grasped for her arm before they reached the door.

'Margery!' Clementine gasped. 'Did we leave the van door open?'

Margery knew that when they had finished searching it, they had locked the van door again, and kept the keys in the house. The van's sliding side door certainly hadn't been left open, hanging from its hinges.

Clementine marched straight over and wrenched it open the rest of the way. She took a step inside, then stumbled straight back out, turning to Margery with a look that was so shocked it would have been comical in any other light.

'What is it?' Margery asked, stepping forward so she could look inside the van door.

On the driver's seat sat the Heritage Vase. Margery turned to Clementine and knew she was mirroring her expression. Utter shock mixed with unease.

Chapter Fifteen

'What on earth!' Margery cried, then clapped a hand over her mouth. 'Clem,' she hissed, hoping that the neighbours weren't listening. 'What on earth?'

Clementine shook her head. 'Did Maria bring this here?' she whispered back. 'No. She can't have brought it here. She's not stupid! So, where has it come from?'

'Is this the real vase?' Margery wondered aloud. 'Or the fake?'

She stepped into the van properly and reached for it.

'Margery, your fingerprints,' Clementine whispered.

Margery pulled her fingers back as though they'd been burnt before the tips could brush the ceramic. She held her hand out for a second longer, willing it to make sense of the scene in front of her.

'Should we tell the police?' Margery asked.

Clementine didn't reply. Margery turned and found her looking as conflicted as Margery felt.

'I don't trust that Officer Wilkinson,' Clementine said finally. 'Maria is an easy win for him. The vase is just evidence that she took it. If we take it into the station then he'll accuse us of having something to do with it. You heard him the other day.'

'We could tell Symon?' Margery suggested. 'I think it's more likely to be the other fake.'

'He can't help. You heard Ceri-Ann the other day,' Clementine said, rubbing her brow. 'What about Officer Thomas?'

'Nigel?' Margery said. Nigel had retired from Dewstow police force years earlier, but Margery and Clementine knew they could still call on him for help if they needed it. She wondered why they hadn't thought of him before. Of course, he wasn't on the force any more, but his wife, Mary, still worked on the reception desk and Nigel played golf with several of the higher-ups. He may well have some idea what to do.

'That could work,' Clementine agreed. 'Well, let's go.'

Margery rushed into the house and fetched the washing-up gloves under the sink, pulling them on and returning to the van. Clementine had got a box out of the recycling bin and between them they managed to get it into the house, out of the watchful eyes of Dawn and the rest of their nosy neighbours. Margery felt more as though she was trying to handle a bomb than an antique vase. Once they had placed it gently on the coffee table, they stepped back to stare at it. Margery found her mouth dropping open in horror at the sight of it sitting there so innocently, when Eleanor had been killed by its replica. Who had brought it to their house? And was it the real vase or Vivian's fake? It was all too close for comfort.

'Are we sure there wasn't anything with it?' Margery asked, wringing her hands.

Clementine reached out with gloved hands and tipped the vase upside down carefully, looking inside. Something slid out, nearly impaling her in the eye. The pencil landed on the floor with a soft crack and rolled away underneath the sofa. Clementine managed to get away with just a small dot from the graphite on her cheek.

'Crikey,' Clementine said, putting the vase back down and inspecting her own face in the mirror above the mantelpiece. She pulled off her gardening gloves and began to scrabble down the side of the sofa for her phone and pulled it out, dialling Nigel's number as Margery bent down and searched for the pencil. She found it but couldn't quite get a grip on it. It kept slipping away from her until it was firmly lodged underneath the sofa.

'Nigel,' Clementine said into the receiver as the dial tone clicked out, not waiting for him to greet them. 'Nigel, we need your help.'

'You and half of Dewstow police force, I think,' Nigel replied. Margery could hear the smile in his voice. 'What's the problem?'

'We've had a vase delivered,' Margery explained. 'A replica of the Heritage Vase that killed Eleanor Black. Or maybe the real thing… we're not sure. I'm sure you know all about that by now?'

'You had one delivered?' Nigel asked, sounding incredulous. 'What do you mean by that?'

'Someone dropped it over here,' Clementine explained. 'They put it in Maria's van.'

There was a pause as Nigel digested this new information.

'Well, that's not good, is it?' he said, his voice taking on a joking tone. 'Why don't you smash it and then do a little bit of a mosaic in your garden? That would look lovely in the summer, the light glinting off it as you sat out there with a glass of chardonnay while the sun sets…'

'Nigel, please! This is serious,' Clementine said, her voice rising in panic. 'Why would someone set us up?'

'Well, for the same reasons they set Maria up if it turns out she wasn't involved in this mess,' Nigel said.

'Tell you what, can you bring it over here? I've got a fingerprinting kit that I stole… I mean… borrowed from the station before I retired. Mary's here too. She might know something more about the case.'

He rang off, leaving Margery and Clementine to delicately put the vase into the car and somehow get it to his. It was a tall order, one Margery wasn't sure that they'd be able to complete.

—

It didn't take long to reach Nigel's house. Dewstow wasn't a large place.

Nigel lived near Rose, in the new housing estate that hadn't been new since it had been built twenty years before. That didn't stop older locals from calling it the new estate. Margery and Clementine still thought of it as new too, with its huge box-like houses with many bathrooms to clean. They parked on the street outside the house and made their way to the front door, the vase carefully wrapped up in a bundle of tea towels. Margery held it as carefully as she would a newborn baby.

'Isn't that a police car?' Clementine asked, looking in bafflement at the car on the drive. 'A really old one?'

It was, Margery thought. Perhaps Nigel had borrowed that from the police station too.

Nigel opened the door. He must have been expectantly waiting for them inside since they hung up the call. Margery wondered briefly if that was what retirement was like. You simply sat by your living-room window and waited for something interesting to happen. The world and everyone and everything in it passing you by as you watched from the sidelines. It was enough to keep her from ever wanting to retire from the school. The kitchen kept her active and the youthful energy from the constant stream of students kept her on her feet.

'Come on in!' He waved them inside. 'Mary is just finished making tea.'

He swept them into the hallway and excitedly took their coats. They followed him down the hallway and into the kitchen, where Mary was setting up the table. Tea had been an understatement. In anticipation of their arrival, Mary had laid on an entire buffet, though Margery couldn't work out how she had pulled it off. They could have only been on the phone to Nigel twenty minutes ago.

'Hello!' Mary said excitedly. 'Ooh it's good to see you both. We haven't seen you in so long! The last time must be Nigel's leaving do, do you think?'

'Must have been,' Margery said, smiling at Mary, who beamed at her in return as she took off her apron.

'Gosh, but terrible circumstances to see you in now,' Mary said. 'I'm ever so sorry. Both of you! I heard all about it as soon as it happened, can't believe they put that arrest warrant out for your sister, Clementine, what a shock that must have been for you! And only nine months before Christmas and all… I had all the official report, you know, and then Martha Mugglethwaite rang up to report it and all. "Martha," I said, "You can't just go reporting things you know have already been reported." She'd been at the auction, you know. She knew the police were there, she'd been interviewed by them! She said, "Ooh but I thought you'd want to know." Want to know! I'm the first responder. I knew two minutes before anyone else did!'

Margery suddenly remembered Mary's way of making small talk last a very long time. It wasn't enough to tell you she had visited the chemist. You had to know which particular chemist she had been to, what she had been prescribed, why she had been prescribed it, which staff were on in the chemist. Then when you thought that you were getting to the end of the story, it would loop all the way back around to what she had thought of the doctor's surgery waiting-room furniture when she had visited there to be prescribed the medication.

'Sit, sit,' Mary said, gesturing to the spread on the table as she took a wobbly-looking quiche out of the microwave. 'I made this for Lorraine on her last visit, but she didn't eat it. I had to freeze it, but at least we can enjoy it. Kids, hey!'

'She's thirty-two,' Nigel said, in explanation. 'And she lives miles and miles away. In London! Imagine that, our little girl in the Big Smoke!' He said it so proudly, it brought a smile to Margery's face.

'Yes, well.' Mary's face darkened. 'It would do her well to remember her poor old mum and dad when she's off gallivanting with the Met, wouldn't it?'

'She's very busy, she's part of the mounted unit,' Nigel said, with a proud grin. 'I knew one day all those gymkhanas we took her to would pay off. Anyway, Mary, she's one hundred and fifty miles away! You can't blame her for not coming home for dinner more often.'

'Does she not have a car, or does she legally have to use the horse?' Clementine asked. 'I imagine it would take a long time on the motorway, even at a gallop.'

'Ooh, I don't know,' Nigel said, tapping his finger to his chin in thought. 'I bet it would save a lot of time on the M25—'

'You'd think she only used the horse the amount she does come home!' Mary interrupted with a scoff. 'And every time she does, she wants to get takeaways or go out to eat. Doesn't want my beef stew and dumplings any more, just a thirty-pound pizza. Richie Rich, she is.'

Margery was worried that they might never get around to discussing the strange appearance of the vase, but then Mary turned an eagle eye to it.

'Is that it, then?' Mary asked, pointing to the bundle of tea towels still in Margery's arms. 'Gosh, Nigel told me it was in your Maria's van! A set up, I reckon! Ooh, who could want to set you up, though…?'

'I hope we can work that out,' Margery said, unwrapping the vase and placing it gently on the middle of the table.

'Gosh, it doesn't look like much, does it? I bet I've got a nicer one for my daffodils under the sink,' Mary said, coming closer to scrutinise the vase, her nose almost pressing against it.

Clementine helped herself to a generous portion of potato salad and pickled onions and Margery fought the urge to tip the vase off the table and be done with it.

Mary continued. 'I'd imagine my Bristol blue glass would sell for more than that. That Eleanor was a wrong 'un, wasn't she? I always thought so. I said when she died, "Someone will have offed her," didn't I, Nigel? Maria, well, she's had a hard time of it, hasn't she? A diamond in the rough, not a killer. I've always said that, Clem, haven't I, Nigel?'

'You have, my love,' Nigel told her. He approached the vase with his fingerprinting kit, looking much too excited, his grin showing from behind his moustache. 'Let's have a look, then.'

'Have you heard anything about Maria's movements down at the station?' Clementine asked Mary, with pleading eyes.

'Nothing,' Mary said, suddenly serious. 'Wilkinson is absolutely desperate to find her. Between us, he's done more than a few illegal property searches. I wanted to report him, but young Symon told me to hang on. I said, "Symon, you couldn't have run me a bath a year ago. Just because you've got all your certificates now doesn't mean…"'

Margery saw Clementine breathe a deep sigh of relief as Mary continued to ramble. Unfortunately for Maria, it didn't look like Officer Wilkinson was going to let her go without a fight.

'The evidence doesn't look good for her at the moment, though,' Mary continued, cutting Margery a huge slab of quiche and piling it onto the tiny side plate before handing it to her. It was so dense and heavy, Margery had to hold the plate with both hands, suddenly realising why Lorraine didn't visit for dinner much. 'I dread to think what they'll do when they finally catch her, if Wilkinson is freely breaking the law to look for her. I've been trying to talk him down but I honestly don't know how. I'm not a big talker, you know…'

She plunged a ladle into the trifle on the kitchen counter and scooped each of them a huge bowl of it. The custard was so thick that Margery was sure she could have plastered the room with it, and the jelly was as stiff as a board. Margery could tell she was staring at it a bit too much but couldn't drag her eyes away from the hundreds and thousands on top of the cream that was so overwhipped it was almost split.

'Nothing on it,' Nigel said finally, clicking his tongue at the vase. 'Not even your fingerprints, so you did well there. Another replica, hey? What an odd case this is – makes me wish I wasn't retired. Something to really sink my teeth into.'

'You'd have much less time to play golf,' Mary reminded him. 'And you'd have to remember to do your paperwork, which we all know you struggled to keep up with even when nothing was happening. All these murders, you'd never get all your work done.'

'Yes, I think I made the right decision,' Nigel said with a chuckle. 'Much better to let the young lads get on with it. If you ever did set up that detective agency, though, you know I'm free for some consultancy work. This is on the house, obviously.'

He lifted the vase and inspected it again.

'There's no initials on it,' Margery said, scanning it as Nigel turned it. 'Not like the other fake had, I saw them myself. And look at that chip there...'

She pointed at the tiny hairline crack that ran up the vase, where it met a tiny chip at the top. Nigel turned to look at her, still holding the vase. It was hard to tell his expression behind the moustache, but Margery thought he seemed shocked.

'So?' Clementine asked, her tone as clipped as the newspaper cuttings announcing Maria's guilt.

Nigel put the vase down on the table and looked at it incredulously.

'And someone brought it to your house?' he asked.

Margery and Clementine nodded.

'I can't believe it,' he said. 'I think this is the real deal. The real vase.'

'What?' Margery said.

Next to her, Clementine's jaw had dropped. She was staring at the vase as though it might explode into flames. 'So, it is the real one?'

'Looks like it! The real one was reported missing decades ago, it had a crack just like this,' Nigel explained. 'I'd only just joined the force. It was one of my first cases. Obviously, we found it immediately.'

'What? So, who had it?' Clementine asked gloomily.

Nigel laughed again. 'Louis Fisher stole it from Vivian Black and she called up the station and said it was missing and we needed to arrest him. Of course, we didn't arrest him, but he never missed the swap-over date again. No one did, until Eleanor decided to keep it, obviously.'

'Didn't Vivian care then?' Margery asked.

'Oh yes, of course she did,' Mary said, coming back over to inspect the vase again now they knew it was real. 'Made a right stink. But ownership laws are strange, aren't they? Eleanor had a genuine claim to it. It wasn't a police matter, it was a civil one.'

'I thought that was why Vivian had the fake vase made,' Margery said. 'She definitely thought she could swap them at some point.'

'I wouldn't have put it past her,' Nigel said. 'I doubt she would have mentioned it to anyone else in the family. I imagine she had a replica made and then moved on with her life when she knew Eleanor wasn't going to let her within two feet of the real one. Bet that made Christmases quite awkward.'

'So, this is definitely the real deal?' Margery said. 'That would mean that the fake vase Vivian had made is still out there somewhere?'

'I'm almost positive it's real,' Nigel said. 'For some reason, the details of the case really stuck with me over the years – the families fighting over that old, chipped vase. It always seemed just so pointless.'

'This means Maria can't have killed Eleanor or taken the vase,' Margery said firmly. 'She wouldn't have any reason to.'

'Yes, I suspect whoever did had a motive that involved the family and the history of it all,' Nigel agreed.

'That makes sense,' Clementine said. 'But what can we do to prove that to the police?'

'You'll think of something,' Nigel said. 'Right, does anyone know where you are?' he asked. They shook their heads. 'Good. Here's what you do, then. You leave the vase here and then you go home and pretend you know nothing about it. I suspect you might have a few visitors soon enough.'

'What do you mean?' Margery asked.

Clementine was still staring at the vase silently, though Margery could tell her mind was racing from the expression on her face.

'The way I see it, two things could be going on here,' Nigel said, examining the vase again. 'Someone has either gifted this to you in a very bizarre way, which probably isn't good – maybe the killer themselves did it for reasons I don't want to think about. Or option B, someone – also possibly the killer – has planted that at your house to call attention to you.'

'What's option C?' Clementine asked. 'They just loaned it to us for a bit so we could enjoy displaying some nice flowers?'

'I'd tell you to call the police, but I have a feeling the police might try and connect it to Maria or you somehow.' Nigel scratched his moustache. Behind him, Mary nodded.

'I don't mean to be rude,' Mary said. 'But you don't want to hear what Wilkinson calls you down at the station. I don't think it'd do any good to involve him any more than you have to.'

This was not good, Margery thought to herself. They had no choice but to leave the vase with Nigel and hope for the best at home. The odds didn't feel like they were in their favour.

Chapter Sixteen

'We've got to speak to Maria,' Clementine began. 'Leave it to me.'

'What do you mean?' Margery said, drumming her hands on the steering wheel as they slowly rolled down the hill, picking up speed.

'I bet I can find her,' Clementine said quickly, slumping back in the passenger side seat.

'How?' Margery asked, feeling her brow furrow in confusion. 'Not even the police can find her with all their resources. How will you find her?'

'I just will,' Clementine said stubbornly. 'Call it sisters' intuition, Margery.'

'That's not a thing,' Margery told her. An idea struck her. 'Clem, do you know where Maria is? Are you helping her hide out somewhere?'

'No, no, no!' Clementine said, shaking her head so vigorously, Margery worried it might fall off. 'But if anyone is going to find her, I think I can.'

'All right,' Margery said after a pause, turning her eyes back to the road before she scraped the hubcaps on the pavement. 'The thing is, Clem, Maria did pick up the fake vase that killed Eleanor, so even if you spoke to her, we'd still have to prove that she didn't do that maliciously.'

She had been waiting for Clementine to come to the same conclusion she had. That Maria had more than a little to do with what was going on and Eleanor's untimely death. Maria had been sneaking around the school days before the auction looking at the items on sale. Maria had had an argument with Eleanor in front of Rose and a number of other staff. Maria had been at the school auction and had run from the police. And all that was without the most important and damning information discovered so far, Maria had gone to pick up the replica vase that killed Eleanor at the very minimum. All roads led to her guilt. Still, however Margery thought about it, there was something more to all of this and Maria wasn't there to defend herself. Maria hadn't got the postman to drop the real vase at theirs, there was something missing there. And Margery couldn't for the life of her fathom why Maria would want to kill Eleanor. By mistake perhaps, but even that seemed like a stretch. The thing was, she thought, the more stones they unturned, the stranger it all became. Someone had wanted Eleanor dead and Margery wasn't entirely convinced it wasn't Maria.

'Finding her is our best hope of asking her what's happening,' Clementine said surely. 'She'll tell me what happened, I just know she will. She's my sister—'

'But if she killed Eleanor then you can't help her,' Margery snapped, regretting the words as soon as they had flown from her mouth. 'I mean…'

'I know exactly what you mean,' Clementine said, her voice cold. 'If you won't help me, then I'll… I'll… I don't know what I'll do, but I'll do it without you.'

'What?' Margery spluttered. 'Without me? You can't do anything like that without me, I'm your wife! We're supposed to stick together in thick and thin…'

'Yes, exactly,' Clementine snapped. 'And you aren't keeping your end of the bargain, are you?'

'Oh, for goodness' sake, Clem,' Margery said, shaking her head until her vision span. 'It's "sickness and health", not "sickness and defending your wife's estranged sister who might or might not have killed someone, but is almost certainly a thief—"'

'How did she send the vase, Margery?' Clementine asked. 'How on earth would she send it to us if she's in hiding?'

'Royal Mail first class? Oh, I don't know,' Margery admitted. 'But, Clem, even if she didn't kill Eleanor, she's got herself wrapped up in something terrible. Which is the exact opposite of what she said she was planning to do when we told her she could stay.'

'But—'

'She told us she was going to relax in the van over the down season and work a little bit at the school to make some money. And then she was going to go back off in the van when the weather gets warmer,' Margery reminded Clementine. 'Does any of that sound like what she actually did? Even if Eleanor hadn't died, they certainly didn't like each other, and Maria was scoping out the auction items in the office. And even if you don't believe she took them, they ended up in her van and there was security camera footage of her taking them home.'

'Not her van…' Clementine began.

'Well, she took them in someone's van,' Margery reminded her. 'So, she's all wrapped up in something she shouldn't be, isn't she?'

'Fine,' Clementine snapped. She sat back in her seat, folding her arms against her chest so tightly that Margery worried that the material of her cardigan would stretch.

They fell into an uneasy silence. Clementine usually spoke to Margery in a joking tone or in a soft way that no one else ever got to hear. It was not like her to be cold – and definitely not to Margery. She knew she had crossed some invisible line they had both been dancing around since Maria's arrival. It had not been easy living with Maria, but the absence was even worse. Margery constantly found herself wishing they had never met her. If they had never met her then their lives might be finally getting back to normal. She clutched her fingers tightly around the steering wheel until her knuckles paled, feeling anger simmering under the surface. She was just about to turn to Clementine and tell her exactly what she thought, but before she could, she pulled the car into their street and found it full of police cars.

'What on earth?' Clementine cried, forgetting for a moment that she was supposed to be giving Margery the angry silent treatment. 'What's happened now? Has someone forgotten to pay for their TV licence?'

Across the street from their house, Dawn Simmonds was busily putting her washing out on her driveway, the light drizzle of rain misting over her glasses as she pinned socks onto the obviously electric clothes horse. The electric plug lay on the floor next to it, sadly resting on the tarmac. She wasn't the only neighbour who had decided that this was a good time to catch up on the gardening. Mrs Bright was painting her front door with a tin of what Margery was sure was the salmon-pink emulsion her husband had painted his shed. Under any other circumstances, Margery knew she might have been terribly embarrassed by the neighbours' attention. As it was, Dawn had been complaining about the van and the washing line and Maria in general for so long that she felt quite immune to it all.

Margery would have usually parked in her usual spot behind Maria's van on their drive, but to her horror she found that there was a police car waiting for them. Officer Wilkinson stood by their front door with a number of other officers in riot gear. One held a battering ram and they looked ready to smash their front door into a trillion pieces. Clementine had already jumped out of her seat and rushed over to them, and Margery had no choice but to stop the car and leave it on the street. She followed Clementine, feeling trepidation wash over her as she hurried up the drive. The vase… the police were here for the vase, just as Nigel had suggested they would be. The police were the ones who were coming for them, Margery somehow hadn't expected that. She had been much more certain that someone would come in the night and try and kill them. It was a juxtaposition to her feelings on Maria and her innocence, leaving her confused and worried.

'What are you doing?' Clementine was yelling at the police officer with the battering ram. 'Put that down. You'll knock over my lavender plant!'

'What's going on?' Margery asked Officer Wilkinson, who looked incredibly pleased with himself. 'We've only just had our new door fitted. You can't knock it down like that.'

Margery found that he was usually on the wrong end of smug as it was, but this was an even worse upset. His mouth lifted up into the facsimile of a grin, but without any warmth to it at all. Just a strange sneering that pulled at Margery's stomach and made her feel sick.

'We need to search your house,' he said, taking a piece of paper out of his pocket to thrust into her hands. Margery looked down at the warrant with dismay. 'We have it on good authority that you have something here that belongs to Eleanor Black.'

'You already searched our house,' Clementine spluttered, though she already had her keys out to unlock the front door. 'And you didn't find anything useful then, did you?'

Margery realised immediately what was happening. It was just as Nigel had said it would be, option B. Whoever had planted the original Heritage Vase had known exactly what they had and were using it to try and set Margery and Clementine up. Margery closed her eyes for a second, thanking Nigel and Mary in her mind for keeping the vase at their house. If the police had walked into the house and seen the vase sitting on their coffee table, it wouldn't have looked good, and then they would never find out where it had come from. Of course, it would mean that they would have several conversations with Mr Tamble, but as their solicitor instead of with Maria. They had been set up to discredit them and make it look as though they were helping Maria. Which they were, Margery thought solemnly.

Trying to, anyway. When she opened her eyes again, Clementine had unlocked the door and Officer Wilkinson was beginning to direct his team inside the house.

'What are you expecting to find that you didn't before?' Margery said, trying to sound innocent, but unable to hide her anger. 'We don't have anything else here.'

The officers began to search and even though Margery knew they wouldn't find what they were looking for, it didn't make her feel any better about it. Across the road, Dawn Simmonds gaped at them. Margery stormed across the street without waiting for Clementine or considering how suspicious it might look to the officers gathering in and outside the house.

'Dawn!' she yelled, as Dawn gathered her washing back into the basket, flinging clothes into it in an attempt to escape before Margery got to her. 'Dawn!'

Margery got there first. Dawn bristled but stood proudly by the washing basket with her arms folded.

'Yes?' she said, in the infuriating voice she used when she had gossiped much too close to the sun with Martha Mugglethwaite and her wings had melted. 'It's perfectly legal to stand on my own driveway, Margery. You'd know if either of you ever followed the law of the land...'

'Dawn,' Margery said, panting at the exertion of her leap across the road. 'You don't have a camera, do you? A Ring doorbell? Something like that?'

'No,' Dawn said, her brow furrowing as she thought about it. 'Why? Do you think I should get one?'

'I think we ought to get one,' Clementine said, from behind Margery. Margery turned to see her join them. 'They were on sale recently and I did think about it then, but I couldn't work out where you're supposed to plug them in. We can't all be like you, Dawn, with your electric pavement to plug your washing line into.'

'I wish we'd got one too,' Margery sighed. 'Gosh, I wish the whole street had them. It would solve a lot of issues.'

'The clothes horse was on offer at Home Bargains,' Dawn began smugly.

'I mean a camera, Dawn,' Margery interrupted.

'Well, if you would both join the neighbourhood watch then you could have suggested that at one of the meetings,' Dawn said, with a wave of her hand.

'Dawn, seriously, though, did you see anyone at our house at any point?' Margery asked. 'Anyone or anything at all.'

'What do you take me for, some sort of busybody?' Dawn said, clutching a hand to her chest in mock outrage. She stepped sideways slightly and nearly tripped over her washing basket.

'But did you?' Clementine pleaded.

'Maybe I did.' Dawn sniffed. 'A lady stopped at your house for a time. I wouldn't know how long because obviously I don't notice these things.'

'A lady?' Margery gasped. 'What did she look like?'

'I'm not sure,' Dawn said, in a voice that Margery knew was made of the truth. 'I didn't have my glasses on, but she was wearing a peachy-colour cardigan, and I remember it because I thought it was lovely.'

'You didn't see anything else?' Margery asked.

'No.' Dawn shook her head. 'Honestly, I don't watch your house all the time, I just noticed her especially because of the cardy. If you see her, will you ask her where it's from?'

Margery agreed that she would, but in reality she suspected that if they met the woman there would be much more serious conversations to have. They left Dawn to go inside and then Margery turned to Clementine.

'Who do we know who wears pink cardigans?' Margery asked.

'Well, both of us do,' Clementine said, gesturing to Margery's own salmon-coloured cardigan.

Margery thought about it. 'Cecilia from the museum wears a lot of cardigans, doesn't she?'

'She does,' Clementine said, her eyes widening. Margery could see her thoughts racing behind her eyes.

'And she would have access to all sorts of things at the museum, wouldn't she? Eleanor might have known there was a fake vase all along.'

'That seems like a leap,' Margery said, 'but not entirely out of the question.'

'Well,' Clementine said as she stared back at their house, the police officers weaving in and out of it like busy ants building a nest. 'There's only one way to find out.'

—

By the time they were allowed back into the house, it was much too late to do anything but eat a bit of toast and jam and then sink down onto the living-room sofa next to one of the cats. Margery wondered what to do with herself now. Clementine was sitting on the other side of the sofa, watching the television that blared in the corner, and tapping away at her phone aggressively. Margery hadn't asked her who she was texting. She was sure Clementine would ignore her after their earlier argument.

They had reached an uneasy truce, but their disagreement was not quite sorted, and Margery felt the sting of being ignored. She wondered whether they ought to call out of work tomorrow so they could try and clear things up. She decided against it in the end. Clementine was still angry at her, and she couldn't bear the idea of sitting in the quiet house being ignored for an entire workday. It would be awkward enough at work as it was.

Margery couldn't stop running the events of the auction around in her mind. What if they were wrong? What if Eleanor knew about Vivian's fake vase? What if she had then brought Vivian's fake vase to the auction and been killed by the fake vase Maria had picked up? But that still didn't answer why the real vase had ended up with them, or who had put it in the van. When the police had finally left, she and Clementine had slumped down on the sofa in the living room and sat in silence while they looked around in dismay. There wasn't a single part of the house they hadn't searched through and although the officers had been polite and respectful, it was not a nice thing to happen.

Margery reached over to stroke Pumpkin's soft head, wondering if she should just go up to bed, call the day a loss and hope for some improvement tomorrow. There was nothing else to do today. They couldn't rush over to the museum and demand that Cecilia tell them what was going on. It was much too late for that, and they didn't know where she lived. Also, they weren't sure if it had been Cecilia at their house after all, they only had Dawn's very brief recollection of a woman in a cardigan to go by, which would never have stood up in a court of law. She had briefly mentioned it to the officers, but their faces had told her that they thought she was trying to plead her own innocence and she had left it at that.

The police had left the house in a respectable state, but still things were not quite right. Clementine had spent a good half an hour rearranging all the ornaments in the display cabinet and moving furniture back to where it had been. Officer Wilkinson's expression had gone from smug frog to angry bear in a matter of minutes. When they had all finally left, Margery was sure he was several shades more purple than he had been when he arrived. It served him right, she thought.

Pumpkin's much younger sister, Crinkles, bounded into the room at the very notion that Pumpkin might be getting some attention and came straight over to Margery. She launched herself between the bottom of the sofa and slithered along it like a terrifying sort of snake creature. Pumpkin sat up in alarm, looking over the side of the sofa to watch. Crinkles was fighting something under the sofa, Margery thought, the cat's front legs batting underneath it. She looked down to see what it was just as it rolled out from underneath.

Margery picked it up, ignoring the cat's batting paws. It was a pencil. She wondered where it had come from for a second. She hoovered under all the furniture at least once a week. More if the cats were shedding in the weird bit of weather that always occurred between the spring and summer months. She turned it over in her fingers, sure that neither she nor Clementine had ever owned a bright pink pencil. With a gasp she realised that it must be the one that had fallen out of the vase earlier that same day.

'Clem!' Margery cried, waving the pencil in the air. 'Look!'

'What is it?' Clementine asked with a jump, her brow furrowing as Margery drew her attention away from her phone, which she placed face down on the coffee table.

'It fell out of the vase! I knew something had,' Margery explained, jumping to her feet in excitement. 'Look what it says on it.'

Clementine reached over and took the pencil, reading out loud, 'Dewstow Historical Society, what's that? Oh!'

'Yes!' Margery cried. 'It's Mrs Egbert's group. Do you think she might something to do with this?'

'Could do,' Clementine said, nodding fiercely and looking happier than she had for weeks. 'She wears cardigans too, doesn't she! Do you think that's where the vase came from? Why would she have dropped it here?'

For a moment, Margery wondered if they really should be pinning all their hopes on the mysterious visitor being a cardigan wearer, but they really didn't have much else to go off.

'I don't know, but if she did then we need to find out why,' Margery told her seriously.

Margery sat back on the sofa and thought about it. There was something about the logo on the pencil. She hadn't paid much attention to it before, but she knew about the historical society. It was always a big feature part of the school's newsletter. They were constantly printing photographs from the Year Sevens' thrice-annual school trip to St Fagan's Museum of History. She considered for a moment that they were barking up the wrong tree. If a giant ever picked the house up and shook it, about seven hundred pencils would fall out of it. They could probably have opened a small branch of WH Smith with the contents of the coffee-table drawers. That was why it had taken the police so long to rummage through it all before admitting there was nothing of interest there. Margery had tried not to feel annoyed at the sight of so many police officers looking baffled at her collection of antique thimbles and Clementine's set of interesting bells.

'I think I know where we could start,' Margery said.

They would have to go to school early, before Margery had to leave for the day at Ittonvale school Rose had organised. It was too late to cancel and Margery couldn't bring herself to try, but she just couldn't fathom finding anything of interest there.

Chapter Seventeen

The next day, a few hours before they were due into work, Margery and Clementine hurried through the hallways of the history department. It had been hard to sneak past Rose without drawing attention to themselves. She was usually prowling the main entrance from very early on in the day ready to welcome students as they arrived. Margery couldn't afford to be seen, as she was supposed to be getting ready for her day at Ittonvale school.

Luckily, Rose was deep in conversation with James as they passed her office, Jason the dog on her lap. Margery had been so nervous about the professional development day that she had only just managed to psyche herself up to go. That was after trying on several outfits. Once she was in the kitchen, she reasoned that she could just wear her usual kitchen clothing, but she had to face Ittonvale's fierce-faced headmistress, Mrs Hallow, first. She hadn't anything smart in her wardrobe, really. She had even tried on an old white shirt that made her look like a waitress and a purple polo shirt that would have made her blend in with the students themselves. In the end, she had just decided to dress in her cardigan and plain linen dress combination, as she normally would on the commute.

In the meantime, Gloria had assured Margery that the kitchen would be fine in her absence. 'Seren will be able to drop just as many plates without you here, don't worry.'

Still, Margery did worry. A lot was riding on the day. Rose had written her a list of questions and suspicious activities to be on the lookout for at Ittonvale school, and that was enough to be dealing with without having to actually do a job at the same time. She couldn't just sail through the day on autopilot as she normally did when things got stressful. She would have to pay attention to what Ittonvale's kitchen manager told her, pretending to take it all in. It was not going to be an easy feat.

They rounded the corridor and found the head of the history department, Mrs Egbert. Margery had worried that she wouldn't be in yet, but she was sitting in her tiny office with the door open already and engrossed in whatever she was looking at on her computer with her brow furrowed. Margery rushed to the door and knocked gently, trying not to startle the woman out of her concentration.

'Oh hello,' Mrs Egbert said. She clapped a hand over her heart, looking up at Margery and Clementine. 'God, you frightened me a bit!'

'Sorry about that,' Margery said. Clementine waved sheepishly.

'Oh, don't worry,' Mrs Egbert said, sliding her half-moon glasses back up her nose. Her short purple pixie cut stood on end around her ears. Margery had always liked it. 'What can I do for you two? Are you parents... or... no... you work here, don't you?'

'We do,' Margery said with a nod. 'We work in the canteen...'

Mrs Egbert clicked her fingers together with a crack and pointed to them each in turn. 'Mrs Butcher-Baker and Mrs Butcher-Baker! I should have recognised you both! Ever so sorry. What can I do for you? Is it about the tea trolley we've requested for Isambard Kingdom Brunel's birthday? You've got weeks to sort that out—'

'No, that's all fine,' Margery said quickly. 'We came to ask you about something else. I have this… gosh, this is going to sound silly…'

She stumbled on her words, trying to think of a way to explain why she was holding a pencil without seeming mad.

'Do you know where this pencil came from?' Margery asked her finally, passing the pencil to Mrs Egbert, who took it with confused ease.

'I don't know. A student's pencil case? Under a desk? Certainly a shop that sells stationery,' Mrs Egbert said, sounding confused.

Margery found herself feeling stupid under Mrs Egbert's gaze. They had never spoken more than a few words to each other before. Of course Mrs Egbert would think they were idiots for arriving with a pencil and thrusting it under her nose as if it would mean anything to anyone.

'We mean the logo,' Clementine said finally.

'Oh,' Mrs Egbert said, peering down her glasses at it. 'Oh, right! Oh, I had these printed. Would you like another?'

She opened her desk drawer and pulled out a bag of them, trying to offer Margery a handful.

'I think we've got off on the wrong foot here,' Clementine said, after a pause in which Margery didn't know if she should take the pencils or not. 'We found this pencil in our house, and we want to know how it got there.'

Margery examined Mrs Egbert's face to see if guilt flickered across it, but there was nothing written on it but confusion.

'Did you come to one of our events?' Mrs Egbert suggested with a kindly smile. 'I give them out like sweets, you see. When I ordered them, I accidentally had ten thousand of them made instead of one hundred. Honestly, it's been impossible to get rid of them!'

'Can you remind me, where do you hold your meetings?' Margery asked. She knew for a fact that they hadn't gone to any meeting but wondered if they were held in a location that they did occasionally visit. That might narrow down where the pencil had come from. Perhaps they had borrowed it to sign something, or it had rolled into one of their bags.

'We meet every last Tuesday of the month at Dewstow Museum,' Mrs Egbert said, holding her shoulders up as her chest swelled with pride. 'Mrs Black opens late for us, well... you know, she did.'

'Will you still be doing the meetings now that Mrs Black has passed?' Clementine asked.

Margery processed the revelation that if the historical society met at the museum, then that could very well mean that that was where the pencil had come from. Could the vase have been hidden there? If so, did that mean that it was Cecelia who had put it in Maria's van?

All good questions, but with no answers as yet.

'Her assistant has assured me she'll honour our agreement,' Mrs Egbert said, suddenly seeming snooty. 'We're meeting tomorrow night, in fact.'

'Really?' Margery said, thinking fast. 'Do you take new members on?'

'Of course!' Mrs Egbert beamed, her demeanour changing instantly. 'We'd love new members, are you interested in joining? Gosh, let me get you a leaflet. It's got all the details.'

She began to rummage through her desk eagerly, pulling out a leaflet and passing it to Margery. Margery took it and stared for a moment at the main photograph, which was a picture of Ms Egbert and a group of students in front of the display of Mr Itton's ivory comb.

'Oh, not us. We have a few history buffs in the kitchen,' Margery said, interrupting as Clementine opened her mouth to speak. 'I know that they'd like to join.'

'Well, that's fab!' Mrs Egbert said, still smiling from ear to ear. 'Will we see you tomorrow? It's at six o'clock, at the museum.'

Margery and Clementine made their goodbyes and then began the short walk to the kitchen.

'Are we not going to the meeting?' Clementine asked. Her voice was nonchalant, but Margery could hear a tinge of worry underneath the question.

'Not exactly,' Margery said, feeling quite pleased with herself. 'But our history buffs Gloria and Ceri-Ann definitely are.'

'Oh!' Clementine said. She turned to look at Margery as they passed through the double doors to the school canteen. 'You know Ceri-Ann only knows the history of what the Spice Girls got up to after they split up, don't you?'

'Yes,' Margery said. 'But that's no matter. She'll just have to pretend she knows more than Geri Halliwell lyrics for an hour. And while she's doing that, we can sneak in around the back of the museum and see what we can find out. Between all of us, I can't see how it can go wrong!'

Clementine nodded agreeably, but Margery couldn't raise her enthusiasm any further than that. She stopped just before they reached the canteen door and turned to Clementine.

'Are you okay?' Margery asked her. She reached for her wrist, searching her face for any upset, rubbing her thumb over Clementine's pulse point.

'Of course,' Clementine said. She nodded and let Margery give her hand a squeeze, though Margery felt as though she really wanted to pull away. 'Sorry, I know I'm being a bit off, it's just…'

'What is it?' Margery asked.

'Nothing,' Clementine said, giving Margery's hand another squeeze. 'Really, I'm fine.'

—

Margery had somehow managed to get to Ittonvale school in plenty of time, and by the time she arrived, all thoughts of Clementine's upset were gone. Mrs Hallow had barely noticed Margery, let alone what she was wearing, and she had soon been passed off to Ittonvale school's kitchen manager without a second glance. Paul had come to meet her with Mrs Hallow at the entrance, beaming at her immediately and pressing a paper cup of coffee from the onsite coffee shop into Margery's fingers.

'Solved any murders lately?' Paul joked as they donned hairnets and stepped into Ittonvale's gleaming school kitchen.

He was an odd man. Younger than her by at least a few decades and full of a chaotic energy that didn't match his well-groomed face. He was stocky – the nape of his chef jacket stretched tightly around his large shoulders and neck – but his beard was trimmed short, and his fingernails were clean and manicured with clear polish. Margery found herself drawn to him, his joking and laughter reminding her of her own kitchen. Kitchens were all the same, really, she tried to tell herself as she stared wide-eyed at the extensive array of expensive catering equipment, and the people in them were the same. The only people who stayed in the food service industry after the age of twenty-five were lifers, as far as she was concerned, and they all had the same air of frivolity about them. Paul's team didn't stray from her ideology. They were a slightly mismatched gang, just like her own team.

'No murders,' Margery said, adding on a dramatic sigh for Paul's benefit. 'Which is good news, really. I wish people would stop killing each other long enough for me to finish my stocktake.'

'Or for drama teachers to stop writing plays?' Paul said. He raised his eyebrows mischievously as Margery felt her own furrow.

'Plays?'

'Yeah, like the one Rhonda's been rehearsing,' Paul said, his face dropping when he realised that Margery didn't know what he was talking about. 'Forget I said anything.'

'That'll be hard to do,' Margery said, the conversation reminding her suddenly of their promise to help the art students with their missing equipment. In all the commotion of the past week she had almost forgotten entirely. 'Would you mind if I went and had a word with Mrs Blossom after lunch?'

'Oh yeah, of course,' Paul said with a wink. 'No worries.'

He raised his finger like he'd just remembered something. 'Oh, Mrs Smith told me you wanted to see our ordering system. We use the same as you, you know,' he said, rushing over to the tablet resting on a prep table. 'But we've been using it ages. I've got loads of shortcuts to show you. Literally, you can get your rota for the entire year done in about ten minutes.'

'You know…' Margery said, thinking of what Rose had said about the secretive nature of Ittonvale kitchen's catering. 'I've heard marvellous things about your cakes and biscuits… particularly your brownies. Do you have a special recipe?'

'Nah, not really,' Paul said with a shrug. 'I just use BBC Good Food for stuff like that. Nothing special.'

Margery smiled back, finding herself enjoying the morning and the newness of it all. It had been a long time since she'd worked in another person's kitchen and she found she didn't mind it.

The lunch queue formed in a much more orderly way than it would have back at Summerview, the students snaking through in a line, holding their trays. The food wasn't that much different to her own at Summerview, but the atmosphere in which it was served was.

Summerview students grappled and jostled in the line. Ittonvale students stood calmly, chatting among themselves but at a reasonable volume. Margery wondered if that was trained into them from the very first year. Some of the Summerview students were much too far gone to behave like that now, even if they had wanted to behave themselves for a single day. Margery concentrated on serving with the others, until a student caught her eye.

'Hello, Andrew,' she said. 'How are you?'

Andrew Black didn't answer. Instead he turned and rushed away. The tails of his blazer whipping through the air of the canteen as he barged past his fellow students. Margery stood for a moment, dumbstruck. Then the queue rolled forward again and she found herself serving once more, wondering what on earth she had done to provoke that reaction.

—

Paul was true to his word and let her leave straight after lunch.

'If you go now then you'll catch them in the act,' he had said with a wink.

Margery had found her eyes widening at that. Still, she had made it to the school hall, where she could hear the tinkling of a piano and the full choir singing. She couldn't quite make out the lyrics and as she pushed open the double doors and stepped into the hall, Mrs Blossom stopped them with a fierce wave of her arms.

'Mrs Butcher-Baker!' she cried from her place at the piano. 'How are you?'

'Fine,' Margery said. 'How are you?'

She watched, bemused, as Mrs Blossom excused the waiting students for a break and then clambered out of the orchestra pit. Margery was briefly reminded of the time that they had helped Rose to infiltrate this very room. She had thought it seemed like a much nicer hall than Summerview's at the time and it was even nicer in comparison now. Summerview's school hall had never quite recovered from the freak fire that had nearly destroyed it. Margery watched the students file out, most of them wearing the odd hat or jacket. *The costumes*, Margery thought. Mrs Blossom seemed to read her mind.

'Rose didn't say that I couldn't borrow them,' she said in the same haughty tone that Margery had heard Rose use more than a few times.

'You should probably give them back before she realises that you have them,' Margery said, trying to choke down her chuckle. 'She's been looking everywhere for them… sorry…' Her attention had been caught by something moving near the legs of the piano. 'Is Ada Bones wearing a cat outfit?'

Mrs Blossom reached back down into the orchestra pit and pulled Ada Bones up with great difficulty. 'Yes, and?'

'But…' Margery felt confused. 'Why?'

'We're doing *Cats*,' Mrs Blossom said, the words coming out in a rush but also as if Margery was the stupidest person in the world. 'For the end-of-summer-term play. I know we're a term early, but it's a very complex show—'

'But the students aren't dressed as cats…' Margery began.

'No,' Mrs Blossom said. 'No, that's just the choir…'

'But we went to watch *Cats* in the theatre once,' Margery said. 'And I didn't recognise the song you were just performing.'

'It's a director's cut,' Mrs Blossom said. 'Came with the sheet music.'

'Okay,' Margery said, realising that she was probably not going to get much more out of Mrs Blossom. She made a mental note to ask Rose about it all tomorrow. There seemed to be something else going on, however. Mrs Blossom was probably still rattled from finding Eleanor Black's body, so Margery decided not to push it and said, 'I'll let Rose know you're going to return the costumes.'

'Please do,' Mrs Blossom said. 'Now, if that's all, I'll get back to *Cats*… we're going to be performing "Memory" in a minute, if you'd like to stay and listen.'

'I'd better get back to the kitchen,' Margery explained quickly before she was forced to stay. The last time that had happened, she and Clementine had ended up drafted into the school's Christmas concert. Margery hurried back, but the worry lingered. One mystery was solved, but it had opened several other doors.

'Anything left to do?' Margery asked Paul when she finally returned.

'Just the bins,' he said, sighing as he finished his checks on the tablet. 'Don't you worry, I'll do it in a minute.'

'You'll do no such thing,' Margery said. She reached for the bin bag and the recycling bag and hefted them up. 'Let me do it.'

She ignored Paul's concerns and, stepping out of the back door to the kitchen, turned right and headed for the bin area she had driven past on her way into the car park that morning. To her surprise, Andrew was sitting by the bins, tears rolling down his face.

'Are you all right?' Margery asked him. At the sight of her, Andrew looked for a second as though he might run, but then he wiped his face with his hands.

'Yeah, I'm fine,' he said, still sniffling.

'Well, you don't look fine,' Margery said, trying to sound as kind as she could. 'Are you feeling okay? Should I call your dad for you?'

'No,' Andrew sobbed, a fresh set of tears falling. 'Anyone but him.'

Margery set the bin bag into the bin and then sat down by him, feeling that Paul wouldn't mind if she took a few moments to help a student.

'Has something happened with your dad?' Margery asked gently.

'I'm not supposed to talk to you,' Andrew said.

'Oh,' Margery said, her mouth dropping open in surprise. She really didn't know what to say to that. 'Why not?'

'Because you're not supposed to know anything,' Andrew said. He slapped his hand over his mouth, his eyes filling with regret. 'I've got to go.'

He leapt up, not waiting for Margery to respond. Before she could even react, he was halfway across the path. *How very odd*, she thought. There was a lot more to all of this than met the eye, she knew. Perhaps Jeffery had more to tell than he was letting on.

Chapter Eighteen

When Margery arrived home in the late afternoon, Clementine wasn't there. Which was odd in itself. Margery had been about to call around to see if anyone knew where she was, but then Clementine had arrived home with a bag of supermarket shopping and made them both dinner. She had asked Margery about her strange day and listened with interest to her story about Andrew, but after that the silence had fallen again. It was not so easily washed away and Margery didn't know how to fill it.

Instead, she decided to focus all her brain power on their plan for the historical society visit. Margery had originally wondered what they would need to do to convince the dinner lady team to help them with their plan of visiting the museum. Especially Ceri-Ann and Gloria, who would need to carry the entire thing off inside. She really couldn't trust Karen and Sharon to keep their stories straight and Seren would fold like a dropped flan at the first question she didn't know the answer to. Ceri-Ann and Gloria were their best hope. Ceri-Ann because she could talk about whatever for hours, even if she didn't know anything about the subject. Gloria because Margery imagined she might enjoy watching Ceri-Ann talking.

Margery needn't have worried. That evening, she had barely posted the message on their kitchen team group chat before Seren had sent back a thumbs-up. As if Margery had just announced that they were being forced to go to war with Ittonvale school's dinner lady team and they were going to have to hold a siege from the safety of their own canteen. Ceri-Ann had then spent several minutes helping draw out a proper plan, using a highly confusing mixtures of celebrity GIF reactions and emojis. From what Margery could gather, they were all happy to do it.

As planned, Ceri-Ann and Gloria would visit the museum and join the historical society meeting while Seren waited outside to cause another distraction if needed.

Margery and Clementine would then sneak in through the back and find out what they could. If there was something hidden at the museum, then they would find it. And if the person who had brought them the vase was there, then they would find them too.

'And what will we be doing?' Sharon asked the next day, abandoning the oven she was supposed to be putting roast potatoes in to glare at Margery and Clementine.

'Yeah, you can't leave us out!' Karen said indignantly, as Sharon burst into tears.

'You're on reconnaissance,' Margery assured them both. 'We need you to keep a look out at the back of the building and call if you see anyone coming.'

'We'll wear our running gear and pretend we're out jogging!' Karen beamed.

Sharon immediately cheered up. 'Ooh yes!' she said. 'If anyone comes, I'll pretend to fall and break my leg!'

'That's the spirit,' Margery said, hoping very much that that wouldn't happen. 'Every little idea will help us with the heist.'

'A good old-fashioned heist!' Gloria said, rubbing her hands together in glee. 'We haven't had one of those since, well... I suppose the other day... but does that count? I feel like that didn't count. It took an hour to shower all the clay out of my hair.'

'I've got a good feeling about this one,' Margery said. 'Well... a better feeling than the last one anyway. I don't think we'll need to wear disguises for this.'

Lunch began with a roar of queuing students and once everything had started seamlessly, Margery excused herself to the dry store to begin the daily wrestle with the food ordering.

'Margery... is Clem mad at me?' Ceri-Ann asked, sneaking into the office behind Margery and making her jump. 'I tried to tell her I was sorry. It's just... Symon can't be involved in everything, and we already said he couldn't help. Oh my God, I feel like a right traitor...'

'It's not your fault at all,' Margery reminded her, putting down her clipboard on the top of the chest freezer in her dry store office so she could pat Ceri-Ann's arm in what she hoped was a soothing way. 'We've been searching and searching for proof of Maria's innocence, and haven't found much yet. Clem is just worried that there won't be any at all.'

'Yeah, I know,' Ceri-Ann said with a nod. 'But that doesn't make me feel any better. Symon knew they were coming to your place, but he didn't know soon enough to have told you. Officer Wilkinson made sure he didn't find out until the last moment. He doesn't trust Symon anymore, if he ever did anyway. It's bad, Margery. He's been taking him off jobs and that.'

That wasn't a good thing, Margery thought. Their reckless detective work could really be putting a spanner in the works of Symon's career, and he had a family to think about now.

'We'll leave him well alone, I promise,' Margery reassured her. 'I just wish Clementine could see it the same way.'

'She hasn't said anything to me,' Ceri-Ann said. 'But she's scooping things very dramatically.'

'Let me deal with Clem,' Margery said.

It was easier said than done, Margery thought with a sigh. Clementine hadn't said a word to Margery since they had arrived at work that morning and the evening before had been fraught too.

'Yeah, all right,' Ceri-Ann said. 'But look, if there's anything I can do to help Maria, let me know. Symon can't, but I don't have to worry about my job, do I? I work here. You've never fired me, not even after that day when I accidentally spilled egg mayonnaise onto Mrs George's shoes.'

'I almost made you employee of the month for that,' Margery said with a smile.

Margery left Ceri-Ann to finish sweeping and mopping behind the dry store shelves and went back into the main kitchen area, where she could see Clementine was indeed slopping huge portions of cottage pie and peas at the students, not waiting for them to hold out their plates before sending food towards them. They were ducking and diving behind the kitchen counter to escape the barrage. Margery went up behind Clementine and took the spoon from her gently. Clementine turned to glare at her but quickly looked away.

'Clem,' Margery said softly. 'Why don't you have the rest of the afternoon off?'

'Why? So you can talk with all the others how I've lost my marbles and my sister's a murderer, even though she's got a perfectly good alibi?' Clementine scoffed. 'No thank you. I think I'll stay here.'

'How do you know she has a good alibi?' Margery asked, her brain flickering with suspicion.

Clementine ignored her. The next portion of mashed potato splattered onto the student's plate ricocheted into the air and hit Rose, who, to Margery's surprise, didn't stumble back. Instead, she stared at them with eyes as wide as saucers while mashed potato dropped from her smart jacket and splattered onto the canteen floor.

'Oh dear,' Clementine said. It was a massive understatement.

Seren rushed around the counter to dab at Rose's jacket with a wet piece of blue roll. Rose lifted a bejewelled hand to bat her away gently. Even the line of students had fallen silent, fear of what retribution might befall them if they laughed.

'I think you'd better come with me, Mrs Butcher-Baker,' Rose said, her voice stern.

'She must mean you Margery,' Clementine whispered.

'Now, Clementine,' Rose said, turning on her heels and swooping from the room.

'Good luck, Clem,' Gloria said. 'God speed.'

'Do you think you'll make Clem employee of the month now, Margery?' Ceri-Ann asked, from behind them all.

'You're just as bad as everyone else,' Clementine told Rose. 'You told us you might have footage from your office and then you don't even show it to us! What are you hiding?'

'Now, Mrs Butcher-Baker,' Rose said, years of patience winning out over Clementine's outburst. For better or worse, Rose was so used to dealing with angry students, she didn't even flinch.

Clementine sighed, throwing the spoon down into the cottage pie, where it made even more mess, and then going to follow Rose.

'Clem,' Margery said, reaching for her hand.

Clementine shook it off and continued her journey, not looking back.

'She's really angry at you,' Gloria said. 'To be honest, I don't think I've ever seen Clem this angry about anything. And I remember that day Caroline put the wasp nest in her locker.'

'That was a bad day,' Margery agreed, 'but you're right. Oh, Gloria, what am I going to do? It's not that I don't want to help, it's just that I don't see how we can help. We've already broken enough rules, and we haven't found anything. All the roads lead to Maria so far. I want to be there for Clem, but we can't continue to break into places and do illegal things. We aren't the police, we could be arrested and then Maria won't be any better off.'

'I agree with you,' Gloria said. 'She'll come around, I'm sure of it.'

'Will she?' Margery asked. 'I don't know if she will.'

'You too, Margery!' Rose called from the canteen doorway and Gloria gave Margery a sympathetic look.

—

The doom and gloom of Clementine's mood followed them through the corridors, threatening rain. Clementine trudged after Rose, who was surprisingly nimble on her feet, even with her high-heeled shoes on. Margery tiddled along behind them both, trying to keep up.

Rose reached her office and turned around to glare at Clementine, then pointed with her finger into the room. Clementine followed it, and immediately slumped down into the chair in front of Rose's desk. Margery sat down in the chair next to her and sighed. This could not possibly be good.

Jason was sleeping in his bed in the corner, and he opened one eye to squint at the intruders, closing it again as soon as he realised who it was. Margery couldn't help but smile, despite herself. He looked incredibly comfortable, and Rose had obviously spared no expense for the bed or the pyjamas that he was wearing. Hanging on the wall next to him on a hook was his own raincoat, and Margery felt a small swell of pride that they had passed him on to the right owner.

Rose made her way around her desk, unbuttoning her potato-covered suit jacket with the fingers of one hand and then shrugging it off so she could hang it from the back of her chair. She reached over to the box of tissues on her desk and pulled one out, wiping the potato from her hands with it.

'I was coming over to the canteen to ask Margery how she'd got on yesterday,' Rose said. 'I wasn't expecting to be assaulted by food. What's going on?'

Clementine didn't say anything, her face becoming steadily more purple.

'Well,' Rose said again. 'Margery, any news?'

'Mrs Blossom has your students' missing costumes,' Margery said. 'At the school. Her entire wardrobe department is stuffed with Summerview things. She admitted it to me yesterday, so that's the students paid back for their help with our pottery-class outfits.'

Rose groaned. 'Of course she does. I'll have to share a few choice words with her and let the students know we'll be getting our things back. That was certainly a good reconnaissance trip. Well done, Mrs Butcher-Baker.'

'About my trip—' Margery said, but Clementine interrupted her.

'You have a tape of your office,' Clementine said. She gestured around as if that made Rose guilty of some crime. 'Why haven't you told us what's on there when it could help Maria?'

'You're deflecting,' Rose said.

'You haven't watched it, have you?' Clementine scoffed. 'Of course you wouldn't care. No one does…'

'That's quite enough of the amateur dramatics, Mrs Butcher-Baker,' Rose snapped. 'I should know… I'm in charge of them here, and there's no time for yours, what with the Year Nines doing *Romeo and Juliet*.' She shuddered at the horror of that.

'So, you have watched the tape?' Margery asked, wishing Rose would just get to the point.

'No,' Rose said. Clementine tutted. 'I don't need to watch it, I know what's on it.'

'Well, what's on it, then?' Clementine asked. 'You can't just say that and then not tell us…'

Margery realised instantly what was on the tape, putting the pieces together from her visit to Mrs Blossom. She knew that the song wasn't from *Cats*.

'It's your play, isn't it?' Margery asked. 'The play you're putting on with Mrs Blossom. You're writing it for the Summer Term concert.'

'How do you know...? It's all completely innocent, I can assure you,' Rose began, but stopped at the look on Clementine's face. She groaned. 'Fine! Hang on... I just didn't want to show you until it was ready.'

She reached for the laptop on her desk, her long fingernails clacking against the keys. She turned it around to show them the screen and then pressed play, slumping back in her seat as soon as she had and folding her arms tightly across her chest. The video opened to the sight of the electric piano that usually lived in the corner of Rose's office. She had moved it further into the middle of the room and it looked set up for her to play. They didn't have to wait long to see if that assumption was right. Rose appeared from behind the camera and sat down at the piano, stretching her fingers out in preparation.

The footage was from a few weeks before, Margery thought. The office space behind Rose was entirely piles of things for the auction, cluttered up all around her. All except the Heritage Vase, which sat proudly on the bookcase behind Rose.

'Now, before this begins,' the Rose who was sitting in front of them said, waving a hand at the laptop, 'you must remember that this is very rough because it was just my little show reel for Rhonda...'

Margery was going to ask many more questions then, but the Rose onscreen set her fingers to the keys and then began to play. The notes built into the grand beginning of something, but somehow remained jaunty and fun. The same tune that Margery had heard the day before at Ittonvale school. Rose played much better on the smaller electric piano than when she used the school hall piano, Margery thought, which was permanently tuned an octave up. It was a nightmare when the school orchestra joined for full Christmas performances and school shows. The Rose onscreen cleared her throat, and Margery hoped beyond hope that she wouldn't start to sing.

'We're just a simple team of dinner ladies,' the Rose onscreen warbled, her tone pitchy enough to make Margery wince. 'But things have been different around here lately. There's a killer on the rise, can we solve it, have we got the time?'

'Thyme, as in the herb,' Rose interrupted from behind the desk, with a smug smile. 'And rise, you know... like bread!'

Margery looked over at Clementine, whose mouth had fallen open, finally lost for words for once. Rose continued into the second verse, which was just as dreadful as the last.

'Our manager went into the freezer, now she's as dead as Caeser,' Rose sang, as the Rose sat behind the laptop mouthed, 'Like the salad!' at Margery. The other Rose continued to sing, 'She went in to defrost the bread, she slipped and now she's dead, well that's what the police have said!'

'This is... what...?' Clementine finally managed to splutter out. 'What on earth is this?'

'It's *Education Centre Nourishment Consultants Solve a Murder: The Musical*!' Rose said, beaming from ear to ear and reaching for the laptop. 'Do you want to hear the rest? There's a duet with you two... I mean the characters of Cherry and Margaret...'

'Oh, please, no thank you,' Margery said very quickly. 'What... why have you written this? Why are Ittonvale practising it, too?'

'Look, I really wasn't hiding anything from you,' Rose said. She looked worried all of a sudden. 'I just didn't want you to see the musical before it was ready. It's very loosely based on some occurrences in this very building…'

'You don't say!' Clementine said.

'Rhonda and I wrote it together,' Rose explained. 'It seemed only natural that we'd join forces as schools. Strengthening our special relationship, etcetera… we're going to perform at both schools. A sort of end-of-year concert world tour, but only Ittonvale and Dewstow… you know. The only two places that really matter.'

The tape continued to roll, and Rose continued to sing. This time it was a sad ballad that Margery noted, wide-eyed, seemed to be about the growing price of onions. Onscreen, there was a knock on the door and Rose jumped up to answer it. They could hear her talking for a moment and then the sound of the office door shutting.

'Is it the story of how we solved Caroline's murder?' Margery asked, trying to sound polite. Rose nodded, smiling still even with Margery's blatant dismay. Caroline would probably be twirling in her grave if she knew, like a giant rolling log. Margery and Clementine accidentally solving their kitchen manager's murder had been the beginning of the last few strange years. Margery herself wasn't sure she wanted to remember it in the form of song.

'Yes!' Rose cried. 'Loosely! Look, I'll just need your permission to use your story, you know.'

'So, the costume the students were making for Jason…?' Margery asked.

'He's going to play both of your cats!' Rose enthused.

'How can he play them both?' Margery asked.

'I've been to your house several times, Mrs Butcher-Baker, and I've never seen them in the same room,' Rose said.

She had a point.

Margery looked to Clementine, who would surely have something to say about the ridiculousness of it all that would shut it down before Rose concocted any more odd songs. Instead, Clementine was grinning.

'Well, it's about time we got some recognition!' she said, Rose matched her smile. 'Tell me, who's playing the murderer? Ooh... who's playing us?'

'I've got a very good GCSE student to play them,' Rose said, her voice dropping to a serious note. 'As for you, I mean, Cherry and Margaret... you have no idea how hard the entire thing has been to cast...'

'Is this why students have been hanging around the canteen?' Clementine asked. 'Are they looking for hints on how to play us?'

'Cherry and Margaret, you mean!' Rose scoffed haughtily. 'But, yes.'

'So, you don't have anything that might be able to help Maria?' Clementine said softly.

Rose paused for a moment before shaking her head. 'No, I'm so sorry, Clementine. I really wish I did.'

Onscreen, someone entered the office.

'Oh,' Rose said. 'Wait, that's not me, is it?'

'No,' Margery breathed.

The figure slipped around Rose's desk and grasped for the Heritage Vase, swapping it with a vase they had under their arm. Then, they turned. Margery and Clementine gasped. Rose made a high-pitched, inhuman noise of horror.

'That's Cecilia from the museum,' Margery finally managed to get out. 'She must have swapped the vase.'

'Christ,' Rose said. 'Oh, Clem, I'm so sorry. I should have watched this before! I'll hand it in to the police. Cecilia, you say? What's the surname?'

'You know, I don't know,' Margery said. 'But it'll be easy enough to find out.'

'Well, it's a start,' Clementine said. Her face was a crumpled paper bag. 'But it doesn't exonerate Maria yet. I know what the police will do, they'll get Cecilia in, she'll lie about it all and then we're back to square one. She'll say Maria put her up to it.'

'But don't you see that this means that Cecilia probably brought the vase to our house!' Margery said. 'This is good, we can use this.'

'Can we?' Clementine muttered.

'Clementine is right, I think, and you know it pains me to say that,' Rose said with a sigh. 'Do you have any other dirt on this woman that you could use?'

'No,' Margery said. 'Well, a bit… maybe?'

'I suggest you get your ducks in a row before you approach the police,' Rose said, her mouth pulling into a grim line.

—

Clementine was quiet on their walk back to the kitchen to finish closing it down with the others. Clementine hadn't said anything since they had left Rose's office. Her walk held a dejected air, her head hanging low. Margery had been sure the small breakthrough might have cheered her up, but it seemed to have had the opposite effect. For once, Margery didn't know how to fix it.

'Are you all right, Clem?' Margery asked her as they plodded along.

Clementine seemed distant. She wasn't letting Margery in to view her thoughts like she usually did. It was cold and frightening for Margery, who was used to being Clementine's one-woman audience. An onlooker might not have suspected anything was different, but Margery knew Clementine so well that she could tell instinctively when something was off. She could realise immediately if Clementine used a different soap to wash her face, let alone the small micro-expressions that she used on a daily basis. Clementine usually had no sense of control over her speech, merely saying whatever mad thing popped into her head. The silence was very odd from a person who had once asked her dentist if he'd ever seen *The Little Shop of Horrors* in the middle of a filing.

'I'm fine,' Clementine said, giving Margery a gentle smile. Margery studied it carefully, not believing that it entirely met her eyes. 'Really, I just don't feel very well today. I think I'm coming down with a cold or something.'

'Oh gosh,' Margery said, stopping her walk and reaching out to press the back of her hand to Clementine's forehead when Clementine turned to face her. The skin was cool under her fingers, but Clementine did seem down. 'Do you need anything? What if I make you a nice cup of tea with lemon and honey when we get back to the kitchen?'

'I'll be fine,' Clementine said. 'But I think I might sit the heist out. Is that all right? You'll be fine without me, won't you? What if I just went home now?'

'Do the heist without you?' Margery asked, feeling her jaw drop. 'But we've never done anything like this on our own. I need you to help me crack what Cecilia's been up to.'

'You'll be great,' Clementine reassured her. 'You don't need me if you've got the rest of the girls to help.'

'Well, let's change the day then,' Margery suggested. 'We could do it tomorrow, or on the weekend—'

Clementine held a hand up to interrupt. 'No, please, you have to find out what's going on,' she said. 'I'll go home and have an early night, and you can tell me all about it when you get in.'

'Only if you're sure?' Margery asked, feeling small and confused.

Clementine nodded, but Margery felt like there was something left to be desired in that.

Chapter Nineteen

Margery sat at the big table in the middle of the antique shop and sipped her mug of tea. There were no lessons tonight, and the shop was quiet and still – a rare event. But the room still bore the signs of life from the baby class that had been in that morning. Margery found it comforting to know the old building was being used for that purpose. She suspected Mr Fitzgerald would have loved it, too, being privy to all the town's gossip and new members.

They didn't charge entry for classes, but they did welcome donations to keep the water and electricity bills paid. What money was left over from the downstairs refurbishment had been set aside when they had sold most of the shop's old items, and that was kept aside for bigger bills and maintenance. It had cost quite a bit. Margery hadn't ever spent such a large amount on anything before, but it had transformed the place.

Gone was the dangerous staircase without railings and old trip-hazard floorboards. The dusty old storeroom had become the new baby change and disabled bathroom and the area down a step that had been where Mr Fitzgerald displayed jewellery now contained a little kitchenette. The entire place had been given a lick of paint and a spruce up. The only area that remained as it had been was the till, where Mr Fitzgerald used to sit with his dog, Jason. The antique till remained on the table and the photographs on display above it remained too. A shrine to the shop's former owner.

The dinner lady team had long gone home to get ready to visit the museum that evening. Ceri-Ann and Gloria had spent the last part of the workday trying to work out what they could wear that might make them look more scholastic. Margery had only just managed to talk Ceri-Ann down from dressing up too formally, fearing that she might arrive at the museum wearing a top hat and tails and a monocle.

Clementine had gone home straight after school as she had told Margery she wanted to. Margery hadn't seen the point of going home before they went to the museum, and Clementine had refused a lift in the car. Margery didn't think it would do any good to go rushing off back to the house, when there was nothing there waiting for her. Clementine didn't seem to want her around, after all. The rejection stabbed at her heart, and she didn't know how to deal with it, or what to do about it. There was something else going on, she just knew it.

Thinking, she took out her phone. It was a smartphone, which annoyed her more days than it didn't. She had much preferred her old brick of a mobile that could have fallen down fourteen flights of stairs in her pocket and still been able to call for the emergency services. Clementine had upgraded her own phone a few months ago, convincing Margery to get the same one. 'So we'll match!' she had said excitedly at the time. Margery wondered if Clementine still wanted to match with her after recent events.

For a moment, her head filled with worry about divorce. That was what happened, wasn't it? Couples were together for years and years, happily unmarried, and then as soon as they got married it all fell apart. She hadn't thought that would happen with her and Clementine when they'd married a few years before, but all the roads seemed to be collapsing under their feet at the moment. Margery wished she could go back in time and agree with Clementine on Maria, or in the very least be more supportive. If she could go back in time, she would said to Clementine that Maria couldn't stay with them.

If she could really go back, she'd refuse Rose's summer holiday plans all those years ago and book the cruise Clementine had been trying to convince her to go on for a decade. Then they never would have even met Maria at all, and no one would have died. And they could have plodded on in delicious boredom on an all-inclusive holiday as they stepped into their sixties properly. Golden beaches through golden years.

But there was no point in regretting any of that, Margery knew. You only got to do anything one time. You had to make your choice in the moment and unfortunately, she told herself, you had to live with whatever you did at the time. There was no point looking back when you couldn't yet tell what was coming. Margery had lived long enough now that the decades had blurred together a bit. She didn't want to do it again. She was sure she'd get it wrong anyway even if she could go back. Wouldn't be able to remember the lottery numbers or which stock to buy.

There was a rattle from the front door. Margery's head snapped up at the sound, her phone forgotten for the moment on the table in front of her. The noise came again. When she looked over to where it was coming from, she saw the door handle turn and then a thump as whoever it was tried to enter again. Clementine must have forgotten her key.

'Clem?' Margery called. She stood from the chair and made her way over to the door. 'I'll just be a second.'

She unlocked the door, expecting to find Clementine waiting for her with her arms folded in annoyance at being stuck in the rain. Instead, she opened it onto nothing more than the street. That was odd. Margery stepped outside and looked up and down. No one. Not even Mrs Prewitt's newsagent was open at this time of night. Mind you, Mrs Prewitt did subscribe to her own very bizarre sort of opening hours… but tonight the shop was firmly locked and shut, with the shutters pulled over the windows.

For a moment, Margery regretted covering most of the windows with wall-to-wall shelving units, she would have been able to see whoever was knocking before they had left. She marched up the street, looking from dark shop window to dark shop window until she reached the solicitors at the top. It was open and Margery paused outside it for a good few minutes, wondering where Clementine could be. Eventually, she decided that she didn't fancy having talking to either Mr Tamble or his assistant Brian, so she made her way back down to the shop again.

She went back inside, locking the door behind her. Her phone sat where she had left it and she picked it up and dialled Clementine's phone number. She couldn't have got far, she would just have to come back so Margery could let her in again. The phone rang, but didn't connect, and then just before Margery assumed either Clementine would answer or it would go to voicemail, the line went dead. *Strange*, Margery thought.

She considered the situation for a moment. She didn't like looking at Clementine's location, although it had been Clementine who had set it up after all, with Ceri-Ann's help. And only then because, 'We've upset lots of murderers solving their crimes, haven't we? What if someone kidnaps you? I'll be able to come and find you!'

Margery sighed and then clicked into her map's app, looking at her own dot on the screen. And at Clementine's, which was hovering in the same place. Margery rose from her chair, leaving her tea mug where it was, and went to the door again, looking out through the glass window onto the empty street outside. Clementine had certainly told her she was going to go straight home. It wasn't like her to lie. It had surprised Margery that she would turn up at the shop, but where was she? She certainly wasn't in the downstairs room. Margery whirled around just in case she had missed Clementine sitting behind a bookcase. The room was still eerie in its silence. It no longer felt like the welcoming place it had been on Margery's arrival.

She decided to check if Clementine was upstairs. If she was here with her phone off and hadn't announced it when Margery had arrived, maybe she was feeling more ill than Margery realised. Margery climbed the stairs, holding on to the handrail very tightly, and crossed into the apartment, which was empty and in darkness. Strange, she thought. Then she heard a noise. A laugh. She whipped her head around to where it had come from and shook her head. Surely there wasn't a sliver of light coming from underneath the cupboard door? She went to it and opened it. The door slid open with a soft creak. What Margery had always thought of as a storeroom now contained a ladder and the hatch above it was open. She could clearly hear Maria and Clementine talking.

Clementine had known exactly where her sister was, had concealed it from her and, worst of all, she had lied to her about it. It was obvious now. That must have been where Clementine had been the night before when Margery had arrived home from Ittonvale school. The anger washed over her in furious waves, exposing the layer of sadness littered in her head like debris. Clementine didn't trust her. Couldn't trust her at all, if she hadn't told her about Maria. What did that mean for their marriage?

She stormed downstairs, leaving without looking back, but let the door slam shut hard behind her not bothering to lock the door. Clementine could do that when she left, she decided bitterly.

Chapter Twenty

Margery waited outside the back door of the museum, still feeling like an overboiling kettle filled with rage. She was just about able to conceal her feelings well enough to carry on with the evening's plan. The cold shower of rain she had been caught in had helped calm her down but not extinguish her anger entirely. Seren was waiting awkwardly by the back door, wearing a large dark cape that flowed around her body and ended at her ankles.

'I asked Rose if she had anything dark I could borrow, and she made me wear this,' Seren explained, as Margery raised her eyebrows at the sight of the cape draping over the ground. She was reminded of the curtains that Ceri-Ann had bought for her living room. She hadn't had a tape measure and hadn't wanted to wait to order them, so she'd used Symon's height as a reference. It had turned out that one and a half Symons wasn't a precise measurement, and the curtains were two sizes too long. Baby Nicholas had once managed to roll himself up inside the bottom of them. 'Don't worry, I didn't tell her what we were doing, but, er… that meant she didn't know what I wanted it for, and you know I can't say no to Rose…'

Margery smiled at the memory of Seren's wedding, when the DJ had announced the mother-of-the-bride speech and Rose had stood up at the same time as Seren's mum, both of them glaring at each other until Rose had won the staring contest.

'It's okay,' Margery said. 'I'm hoping to get in and out without anyone seeing us. Thank you for coming, Seren, I really appreciate it. You're a good friend.'

'Anything for you and Clem.' Seren smiled toothily.

Margery forced a smile at the words. Seren's smart watch bleeped and Seren gasped excitedly.

'That's Ceri-Ann,' she said, looking down at the text that had come through on the watch screen. 'She said they're in the meeting and everyone is really boring. But she looked up Joan of Arc on Wikipedia before they came so she's hoping she can talk about her.'

'Time to shine, then,' Margery said. 'Did she say what room they're in? We don't want to bump into them.'

'The top floor,' Seren said, as another message came through. 'At the back. Ceri-Ann thinks that there's a back room on the ground floor we might be interested in. She pretended to go to the toilet and opened the back door for us. Cecelia is upstairs with them helping with the teas and coffees, so this might be our only chance.'

'Come on, then,' Margery said. It was time to see what else Cecilia was hiding. 'No time like the present.'

Margery reached for the fire escape and found it ajar, just as Ceri-Ann had said she had left it. She snuck in and Seren made to follow her, tripping over her cape and staggering in after Margery. Seren landed heavily against a display case full of coins, knocking all the breath from her lungs with a whoosh. Margery and Seren froze as they waited to be found out. Upstairs she heard a high-pitched scream. Ceri-Ann. Margery and Seren shared a confused look. Then the voices carried on as normal.

'Okay,' Margery said, 'Where shall we look first?'

'Maybe in the Second World War hospital exhibit? I've always wanted to see it,' Seren suggested, peeking in at the room through the darkened doorway. 'I don't think anyone would hide anything there, though. I wouldn't.'

'Where would you hide something?' Margery asked her out of curiosity.

'Oh, well, you know I can't keep secrets,' Seren said, her eyes widening at the very idea. 'If I was going to hide something, the first thing I'd do is have to have my memory wiped so I wouldn't remember where it was. Gary knows I have to tell him what his Christmas and birthday presents are as soon as I buy them for him. I told him if we ever have a baby, he'll have to buy the presents and not tell me what they are—'

'Yes, but if you could keep secrets?' Margery interrupted. She could hear footsteps through the ceiling, creaking with the weight of the meeting.

Seren gave Margery a dazzled look that suggested she had never considered hiding anything in her entire life. 'A... um... maybe inside a pair of shoes?'

There were no shoes that Margery could see in the museum and she didn't think anyone would hide anything in an exhibit. Unless... they wanted to hide it out in the open where no one would ever think to look.

'You're a genius, Seren!' Margery said.

'Oh!' Seren said, giving Margery a toothy grin. 'Are you sure?'

Margery tiptoed her way down the foyer and into the smart Georgian-themed room that Cecilia had shown them when she had given Margery and Clementine a tour on their first visit. Eleanor's special desk was antique, of course, but it was in fabulous condition. The wood shone from how deeply polished and conditioned it was.

The chair didn't look comfortable at all, but Margery suspected Eleanor couldn't care less for comfort as long as the furniture was over two hundred years old. That, and it was probably just for show. Margery thought that she was likely to snap the chair in half if she sat down, it being so old and worn. Margery reached over and rummaged through the desk, which didn't contain much, just a few letters. She took the one on top of the pile and scanned it, gasping as she did so.

'What is it?' Seren asked from the doorway, fiddling with the cape and eyeing the hallway cautiously.

'It's a blackmail letter,' Margery said, continuing to read. 'Or definitely something like it. It's certainly threatening enough... and it's about the vase!'

Just like the letters that Louis had shown them, she thought. For a moment, she thought that perhaps these were just another set of letters that Eleanor had received, but the letters in front of them weren't finished. Whoever had written the letters had practised first, and these were the result. The delicate lettering was littered with spelling mistakes, grammatical errors and crossings-out. Margery couldn't have dreamed of sitting at that tiny chair and writing such a thing, but svelte Cecilia probably could have managed it. Margery imagined her writing away at night once Eleanor had left for the evening. Scrawling her many complaints down on the paper. The notes were much too personal to have been written by a stranger.

'Really?' Seren asked. 'The vase you're looking for?'

'I hope so or there's more than one vase and that would be very confusing,' Margery said, searching the desk and pulling out the other letters. 'Quick, help me take photographs of these. We can't take them, in case someone finds out that they're missing.'

Seren rushed over with her phone and began to take photographs of the letters.

'The ink is strange,' Seren noted as she scanned the last page.

'It's fountain pen,' Margery explained, running her finger over the nearest letter. 'Or a quill. Something like that, anyway. I don't know much about it, but I think I know a person who might. Gosh, some of this is quite nasty, isn't it?'

'Yeah, I'd never have even thought of using that word, I'm sure it's illegal to say out loud,' Seren said, her eyes so wide Margery wondered if she would actually be able to shut them again. 'Do you think this'll help?'

'I'm hoping it will open some roads,' Margery explained.

It was too long to explain to Seren, but Margery now had a good idea of who had sent Eleanor the letters now. Cecilia might have seemed like a mild-mannered woman minding her own business at the museum, but Margery suspected that she was hiding something much darker. After all, they had ended up sent to Eleanor, who Cecilia seemed to have had a secretly fractious relationship with. She had her suspect and her evidence. Now she just had to piece it all together.

Seren emailed her the photographs she had taken, and then they left the room. Margery decided she had one more place to search and led Seren to the door behind the museum's front desk. The tiny back office was wall-to-wall shelving units, all covered with books and bric-a-brac, piled high from floor to ceiling. Margery ignored the shelves and went immediately to the table, picking up one of the envelopes left there. Cecilia couldn't have opened today's post yet, or maybe she was avoiding opening it. For good reason, Margery thought. Joining the pile of letters on the table was bill after bill, all of them final notice. Eleanor really had run out of money, then. She must have been selling the vase for herself. Perhaps it was the only way she could think of to keep the museum open.

Armed with that further proof, Margery and Seren left the office, trying to be as silent as they had been as they entered it. Not quietly enough. Seren tripped over the foot of a suit of armour resting at the side of the hallway and went face first onto the floor. She dropped her phone with a crack on the hard floor of the foyer and nearly pulled Margery down with her.

'Gosh, Seren!' Margery cried, grasping for the woman's arm. 'Are you all right?'

'Yes,' Seren wheezed, picking herself up from the floor. 'Just hurt my arms... and a few of my bones. Maybe an organ.'

Margery helped Seren up to her feet, just in time for Cecilia to rush down the stairs towards them, her pastel blue cardigan flapping behind her. They froze, Margery trying to think of a reason they would be there and failing dramatically to find anything to say.

'Oh, what's happened?' Cecilia asked, rushing to Seren. 'Let me get the first aid kit!'

She rushed into her office, returning a moment later with the first aid kit and beginning to inspect Seren closely.

'Sorry about your statue,' Seren said, waving a bruised arm at the suit of armour, which didn't have a single mark. 'I hope I didn't damage it.'

'I bumped into Seren in the street!' Margery babbled. 'She was just going to... er...'

'I was coming from Slimming World!' Seren lied. 'Margery told me about the talk…'

'Yes, and Seren was intrigued so we decided to come and see what it was all about,' Margery prattled. Seren groaned from the floor as Cecilia inspected one of her arms. 'Are we late?'

'Well, yes!' Cecilia said. 'But no matter, I'm sure Mrs Egmont will be able to pass on any information for the next session if you were planning on joining.'

Cecelia smiled at Seren and began dabbing at the cut on her elbow with antiseptic while Seren winced. The group were beginning to come down the stairs, Ceri-Ann and Gloria were wide-eyed as they spotted Margery and Seren at the bottom of them. Mrs Egmont looked just as confused. The rest of the historical society funnelled around them and began making their way out through the main entrance until only the dinner ladies were left.

'We missed the talk!' Margery cried. She tried to gesture in a noncommittal way, but found herself waving madly, unable to stop the hysteria rising in her throat. She began to panic even more when she realised that Clementine was not here to calm her.

'Well, remind me never to book any catering with you,' Mrs Egmont said. 'I told you exactly what time it was and where. Your dinner ladies managed to get here perfectly on time.'

'Well, Margery always says, "Do as I say, not as I do!"' Ceri-Ann said chirpily. Her hands were full of pencils with the historical society logo printed on them.

'Yes, lovely,' Margery said, fumbling with her words. 'Well, I suppose if we've missed it then we might as well be off. Come along, Seren, let's get you to A&E.'

'It's just a scratch...' Cecilia began, her brow furrowing. She looked down at the small plaster she had stuck onto the tiny graze on Seren's elbow.

'No, I think Margery's right,' Seren said, leaping up to her feet. 'You can never be too careful, can you? What if I'd landed on my head? It was very close! I should probably get an X-ray, just in case.'

'You'll probably need an MRI as well,' Ceri-Ann said cheerily, reaching out to take Seren's arm. 'I'll drive us all there.'

'You told us upstairs that you don't know how to drive,' Mrs Egbert said, her mouth twisting in confusion.

'But what better time to learn?' Gloria said, a little too enthusiastically. 'Come on, ladies, I'm sure we can find some L-plates somewhere.' She began to shoo Seren and Ceri-Ann towards the main entrance, Margery following behind them. 'Come on.'

They managed to escape the building, leaving Mrs Egbert and Cecilia exchanging confused looks.

'What happened?' Gloria hissed as soon as they were out of earshot.

'I fell over,' Seren said. Her face fell. 'I'm really not having a good week, am I?'

Gloria patted Seren's arm and tutted.

'Mate,' Ceri-Ann gasped to Margery. 'They kept asking me what my favourite bit of history is, and I panicked and said, "Princess Diana," and now one of them wants me to come and see her Princess of Wales plate collection. I told her I already had all the plates, so I didn't need to see any more of them and now she wants to come and see my collection! What am I going to do?'

'I like the Romans,' Gloria said, interrupting Ceri-Ann's panic smugly. 'I had a great chat about the Roman road system. All roads lead back to Rome, you know!'

'All roads here lead to the M4, mate,' Ceri-Ann said, looking at Gloria in dismay. She turned back to Margery. 'What did you break coming in? I tried to cover the noise, but I don't know if it worked. Nothing we could do about the second noise, though.'

'It did,' Margery said. 'Thank you.'

'Did you at least find what you were looking for?' Ceri-Ann asked.

Margery nodded and Ceri-Ann smiled.

'That's all right, then,' she said.

They said their goodbyes. Margery offered Ceri-Ann a lift home.

'Same time again next month?' Gloria asked Ceri-Ann as they prepared to go their separate ways. Margery shook her head in disbelief.

Chapter Twenty-One

Instead of doing what she wanted to do after all of that and go home, Margery dropped Ceri-Ann at her doorstep and then drove back into the town centre. According to her phone, Clementine had returned to their house at some point during the evening's events. Probably to pretend that she hadn't been in the attic, Margery thought. The secret attic at that. It made her bristle still, but her curiosity stopped her from continuing to seethe. She messaged Clementine before leaving the car park, deciding that she couldn't bear to hear her voice lie to her. Then she made her way to the shop through the silent high street, only catching sight of a few smokers in the smoking area outside the King's Arms at the top of the hill, nursing their pints quietly.

Margery realised that in her haste to escape the shop earlier she hadn't shut the front door properly. It lay half open. The doormat had ridden up, stopping the door from closing. Surely she hadn't done that, Margery wondered, a sense of cold unease riding along her spine. Surely she would have noticed. She had definitely shut the door when she left. She had heard it slam behind her, the Yale lock snapping into place.

Margery stepped into the downstairs room with small timid steps, looking around. It all seemed relatively normal, except she couldn't help the feeling that things weren't quite right. She couldn't remember what everything had looked like before, but she felt sure there was something out of place. Margery decided that she didn't have time to wonder about what it could be, and instead she made her way upstairs.

She decided to make a pot of tea to calm herself, finding another pack of biscuits in the cupboard – custard creams, nowhere near as good – and simultaneously either a bit too stale or a bit too soggy from the length of time they had been in the cupboard. Nonetheless, it felt good to tuck into one as she read through the half-finished threatening letters Seren had photographed while waiting for the kettle to boil.

The letters to Eleanor were not nice at all, and if the drafts were any indication, then Eleanor must have been very frightened by the finished thing. Margery knew she would have been if someone had threatened to murder their pets and darken their doorstep unless she gave up on selling the Heritage Vase. Margery decided that as they were only the drafts then Cecilia must have written them, right under Eleanor's nose. A horrible thing to do.

It somewhat proved her theory that someone had killed Eleanor for the vase. And Margery knew that Maria hadn't written these letters. She knew Maria's scrawl quite well now, from the letters she had sent Clementine over the last few years. There was no way that Maria would have used a fountain pen either – she had enough trouble with a biro. No, this was beautiful calligraphy that made the horrible words seethe and glisten and come to life on the page. It could only have been done by an artist or, in the very least, someone who took great care over these things, but also secretly enjoyed angry swear words. Cecilia seemed just that sort of person.

Maria was just like Clementine in the way that she never thought for more than three minutes before doing something. There was no way Maria had taken time out of her busy days of helping Clementine spontaneously decide to strip all the textured wallpaper in their hallway or put up a set of shelving without using a level. Anything even slightly rounded she put on the shelf in the spare room rolled off, and unsurprisingly the hallway walls badly needed plastering, which the old wallpaper had hidden well. Margery found herself selfishly wishing Maria would be out of trouble soon, if only so she and Clementine could have a go at patching them up. Maria also wouldn't have had the forethought and patience to sit and write her feelings down. She was the type of person to have an argument in the middle of the street and then have completely forgotten it all the next day.

Margery found herself feeling quite calm, unable to draw up any of the anger that she had felt only a few hours ago. After the discovery of the letters, it had warped into something more complicated.

Just when she began to think that she might have to go up and visit Maria herself, the sound of footsteps on the stairs made her turn her head. Clementine walked straight up into the room, pausing when she saw Margery was waiting for her, and raising her hand in a sad wave. Margery wondered for a moment if Clementine would continue her lie, but the sight of Clementine's flushed cheeks told her she wouldn't.

'Hello,' Margery said, gazing at her from where she leaned against the kitchen counter and folding her arms.

'I'm sorry I didn't tell you what I was doing,' Clementine said, all in a jumbled rush. 'I... arranged to see Maria.'

'How did you find her?' Margery asked.

'She was at Mr Fitzgerald's garage,' Clementine explained. 'I gave her the key weeks ago to get some of the auction stuff… and then… Well, obviously she couldn't stay there… it's got no water or electric or anything!'

'No,' Margery agreed. 'So, you moved her here?'

'Only a few days ago. It took a while to plan,' Clementine said, worrying her bottom lip with her teeth. 'Honestly, I didn't know she was at the garage until the other day. I'd thought over every single place she might have been and then I remembered the key. Once I realised, I had to find another place for her. I didn't think anyone would check the attic here even if they searched the building. It's not that visible, is it?'

Clementine paused in the middle of taking her coat off and waited, seemingly for Margery's disapproval, her face scrunching in confusion when there was none.

'Is Maria all right?' Margery asked. 'I wanted to go up and ask her, but I didn't want to startle her before you got here.'

Clementine's face relaxed, the tension leaving it. 'She's okay. Things have been better.'

'What happened?' Margery asked, finding that she desperately wanted to know. 'Have you found anything out that can help her?'

'Yes and no. That's where I was this afternoon – the attic,' Clementine said. 'I'm sorry I left work without telling you where I was really going.'

Margery waved a hand in forgiveness.

'Did Maria tell you where she was the evening of the auction?' Margery asked, drawing closer to Clementine, as eager as she was for answers.

'Yes,' Clementine explained. 'Margery, I know you don't agree with this, but will you please help me? I can't do this without you.'

'You can't do this again at all,' Margery said. She felt a cool calm collect on her shoulders. A surety in her words. 'We might not agree on things sometimes, but we're still on the same team. You can't run off and do things without me, anything could happen.'

'Yes, all right,' Clementine said, coming over to the kitchen counter and taking a biscuit, rolling it around in her fingers. 'I promise. I kept meaning to tell you, but I didn't want you to get into trouble as well if we got caught, which, let's be honest, we definitely will. There's no way we can keep this up, she'll have to leave sometime.'

She took a moment to collect herself, but when she looked up again she seemed much calmer than she had for days. 'Come on. She can tell you herself.'

Clementine went to the storeroom and reached for the broom in the corner. She tapped three times on the ceiling and then twice more in a rhythmic pattern.

For a moment nothing happened and then the loft hatch opened, and the ladder began to slide down. Clementine steadied it. Maria emerged, clambering down it carefully.

'Hello,' she said weakly.

Margery managed a small smile. Maria didn't look as fine as Clementine had said. She looked dirty and unkempt and dreadfully sad, all the light and spark extinguished from her face. They returned to the kitchenette and Clementine and Maria sat on the deckchairs while Margery made hot drinks. When they each had one, she stood in front of them, feeling a little as though she was conducting a police investigation.

'Maria was working for Eleanor,' Clementine began. Maria nodded, taking a sip from her mug.

'What?' Margery asked, feeling blindsided by this information. She thought that Maria and Eleanor hadn't got along. But Maria had been working for Eleanor? 'Doing what?'

'It's a long story,' Maria said.

'Well, we have plenty of time,' Margery reminded her.

'I owed money to a lot of people,' Maria began with a sigh. 'Not just a bit of money, loads of money.'

'I suspected that, actually,' Margery said. 'Is that why you're back in the country? You only got back a few months ago.'

'Yes, but don't jump to conclusions,' Maria warned with a pointed finger. Margery held her hands up in surrender. 'I was doing okay, working and whatever, but, well…' Maria continued, stuttering off into silence for a moment. 'You know I've got a bad knee?'

'Yes.' Margery nodded.

'I went through a period where I couldn't work and I started gambling to try and win the money so I could live and eat and whatever, which obviously went the way it always does when you run out of luck, which I did quite quickly,' Maria said, fiddling with the mug in her hands. Tapping her nails against it. Clementine took another biscuit, crumbs falling on the floor. Specks on the dark wood. 'I thought that if I came back here then the problem would disappear, but obviously…'

'Your problems followed you over the Channel?' Margery said.

'Swam over, more like,' Maria sighed.

'I wish you'd have told us,' Clementine piped up.

'Yes,' Margery agreed. 'We might have been able to help. We've got some savings.'

'No, I couldn't have taken your money,' Maria said. 'Besides, it's paid back now, no harm done.'

'Okay, start from the beginning again,' Margery said, with a shake of her head. 'So, you're in debt, so you come back to the UK and end up here with us in Wales. Then what?'

'Eleanor hires Maria to help her steal the auction items, which she did,' Clementine explained. Maria nodded along. 'Eleanor promised her a lot of money. She'd heard about Maria's history, said that it's a low-risk venture for Maria. No one here knows her, do they? All easy-peasy stuff for her.'

'Oh,' Margery said, feeling her brow raise in surprise. 'So, who hired the van to steal the auction items?'

'Cecilia hired the van for me at Eleanor's request,' Maria explained. 'But even Cecilia didn't know what the plan was exactly. The plan was that I would steal the things from the auction and keep them in my van till the coast had cleared a bit, then Eleanor would claim on the insurance and give me my share of the money.'

'Gosh,' Margery said. 'Well, that didn't quite work out. She didn't quite get to the selling bit, did she?'

'No,' Maria said gloomily. 'So obviously she didn't pay me because she hadn't claimed the money back yet, she told me I had to wait. The cheek of that when all her dusty old stuff was imminently going to be filling my van to the brim for an unknown length of time! So, I had no choice. I had to put the feelers out for other options to clear my debts.'

'You said you cleared it,' Margery said. 'How did you manage that if Eleanor didn't pay you?'

Maria put a hand up to explain. 'A few weeks ago, I was approached by a member of Eleanor's family who asked me to steal back the Heritage Vase because Eleanor stole it from the Fisher family or something. These people are nuts, Margery. *Who cares about a vase?* I thought. But I took the job because of the cash, they paid me upfront! And it was just a vase, wasn't it. Easy-peasy. I thought I'd play them both, double the money.'

'Who approached you?' Margery asked, the biscuits and tea forgotten.

'He said his name was Louis Fisher,' Maria said.

Clementine chuckled darkly, amusement passing over her features for a second as Margery gasped. 'He lied to us.'

Margery nodded, unsurprised, but confused. 'Louis Fisher said he hasn't left his house for years.'

'I know,' Clementine said. 'I think that's part of the lie.'

'Oh?'

'This man seemed way too sprightly to be ninety years old and housebound,' Maria said with a shrug. 'He definitely wasn't a man who could barely walk to his front door.'

'So, then what happened?'

'He told me he'll pay me more than even Eleanor was going to pay me,' Maria said, her eyes shining with excitement at the memory of the money. 'I was so happy, I could pay off the debt and fix up the van and get out of this dump— I mean... oh, you know what I mean. I miss the open road, you know?'

Margery folded her arms again, wondering when Maria would get to the point. Clementine's face had fallen, only visible to Margery's eye, trained by years of marriage.

'He gives me a huge great wodge of cash.' Maria beamed. 'But then he did threaten to kill me if I didn't swap the vases, so that was a bit of a pickle.'

'I'll say,' Margery said.

'He told me to pick up the vase from that weird man's house, Robert or whatever, and I did. Louis, or whoever he really was, organised it,' Maria said, scoffing at the memory of Robert's eagerness to ask her out, Margery assumed. 'All I had to do was swap them before Eleanor realised, which obviously I didn't manage, did I? You saw her yelling at me in the kitchen. Cecilia saw me and told on me, miserable cow. Eleanor was fuming because she wanted to stick to her plan, and she didn't know what I was playing at. She probably realised what was going on then.'

'So, Eleanor knew there was a fake?' Margery asked.

'Yeah,' Maria said, nodding.

Clementine interrupted. 'But Cecilia had obviously already swapped it with the fake vase, we saw that on Rose's camera, didn't we?'

'What! But... wait, go back a bit...' Margery said. 'So, we know there's a fake vase and a real one still in play. Cecilia had the real one that she swapped for a fake and Maria, you didn't manage to swap them, but you put a secret bid on the vase for the auction...'

'Only because Louis told me to,' Maria asked. 'I never really understood why.'

'This isn't an alibi,' Margery said. 'Do you have one?'

'Of course,' Maria said. 'It's a long story, but basically I rang Louis, or whoever, and I told him that I hadn't managed to swap the vase and he hit the roof!'

'He was angry?' Margery asked.

'Angry? He was livid!' Maria said, shaking her head at the memory. 'I told him I wasn't going to do it and the vase was in my locker at the school and he could do it himself if he wanted to swap them so much.'

'What did he say?'

'He told me that I'd better leave town because he'd be coming to get his money back,' Maria grimaced. 'I was at home in my van panicking because Louis was going to kill me or force me to leave town because, I'd already spent all the money, I couldn't even give it back if I wanted to! I went to the school and found my locker empty, so I knew Louis had decided to do his own dirty work. I thought, I'd better steal the stuff for Eleanor so that I at least had that money to give him, get him off my back, you know?' Maria paused, running a hand through her hair in a nervous motion. 'After I got everything in my van, I came to the auction to find Clem to tell her what was going on. I couldn't find her, so I thought I'd go for a cigarette, but I passed the storeroom and saw that Eleanor was dead. Then I ran because the vase was all smashed and that, all over the floor, he'd killed her with it! It was only a matter of time before he came to kill me.'

Margery felt very tired all of a sudden. 'So, you weren't even running from the police? Surely they could have helped you if you'd told them what was happening before?'

'Do you really believe that?' Clementine asked her. 'What with that Officer Wilkinson on the warpath?'

Margery thought about it.

'No,' she said finally.

Clementine nodded, her face grave and her lips pinched tightly together.

'Margery, this is such a mess,' she said. 'I'm sorry I didn't tell you what was going on. I just thought this would clear things up. All it's done is make things worse.'

'I understand you thought you were doing the right thing, Clem,' Margery said, exhaling a sigh. 'You can tell me your plans, though, I'm your wife! It is "sickness and health" and "sickness and save your sister-in-law", I suppose.'

'Hear hear!' Maria cheered, raising her mug in faux celebration.

'This is definitely making me feel sick,' Clementine scoffed, the biscuit in her hands now disintegrated into almost nothing but crumbs.

'Wait...' Margery said, a thought coming to mind. She picked up her phone from the kitchen counter and then rummaged in her bag for the bidding list Eleanor had written. 'Look, Clem, these are drafts of the threatening letters I found at the museum and the bidding list Eleanor wrote.'

'The handwriting...' Clementine said.

'Yes!' Margery said as they compared the two. 'Does this mean that Eleanor wrote the letters herself? That seems odd.'

'Very odd,' Clementine said, scratching her head and leaning in to take a closer look at the photographs. 'What's that there?'

'Hmmm,' Margery said, zooming in. 'Oh... is that a calligraphy pen?'

'Maybe she did, then,' Clementine said. 'But why?'

'A paper trail?' Margery said, realising it made some sense as she said it, but not being able to quite piece it together, her thoughts racing. She looked again at the image, of the pen resting on the desk. 'Wait! Remember the documents that Cecilia showed us at the museum when we first visited?'

'All about Mr Itton's brand-new ivory comb?' Clementine said, with a roll of her eyes. 'How could I ever forget…'

'It's the same style, isn't it?' Margery asked her, feeling urgency rise in her voice. 'Neat calligraphy, fresh ink… you can't tell me those documents looked old.'

Clementine looked at the photograph again and gasped. Maria looked at them over her shoulder, nodding gravely.

'Cecilia told us Eleanor's grandfather had taught her how to do it, didn't she?' Clementine asked, looking up at Margery again with her eyebrows raised. 'So, did Eleanor write them herself, or was it Louis?'

'Maybe Louis?' Margery said. 'It certainly seems so, doesn't it? He wanted the vase back, and the letters didn't work…'

'So, he tried a different tactic,' Clementine said.

Maybe Louis hadn't written those letters, Margery thought. Not that Louis suddenly seemed innocent, but it did seem a strange thing for him to have done. Perhaps Eleanor had written them to herself in order to garner sympathy from the grandfather she had fallen out with. Maybe Eleanor knew that he wanted the vase back and was trying to pacify him.

'Oh God, does this mean that we have to go back to the museum?' Clementine groaned, leaning back in her chair. 'I thought I'd got out of that one.'

'Yes,' Margery said. 'But maybe we should visit Louis first and see what he's got to say for himself. He might not have been the one to hire Maria, but I bet he'll know who did. I'm not sure if it'll help. The police certainly seem to be trying to build a case.'

'You know I don't trust police,' Maria said, sinking into the chair. She suddenly looked very fragile.

'It's all right,' Margery told her firmly, reaching out to place her hand on Maria's shoulder. 'We're going to fix it.'

Chapter Twenty-Two

The next day, Margery and Clementine buzzed themselves into the retirement village with the password. The nurse on duty let them into the building easily, but when she learned who they were here to see, her manner changed. Instead of escorting them to Louis's room, she sat them down in the office on an uncomfortable sofa. Margery and Clementine shared a worried look. Margery wondered if the reason for their visit had been found out, but the nurse didn't call the police. Instead, she offered them both a glass of water and then she sat down on the office chair in front of them with her hands on her knees awkwardly. She looked at them in a sympathetic way that made Margery's brain reel with worry.

'Can I get you both a cup of tea?' she offered. 'A biscuit?'

Margery shook her head, wondering what this was all about. She finally noticed the box of tissues in the middle of the coffee table between them, realisation appearing just as the woman in front of them cleared her throat.

'I'm so sorry to tell you this,' the nurse began. 'But Mr Fisher passed away last night.'

'What!' Clementine gasped, though Margery had already worked that out. 'How?'

'Old age, unfortunately,' she said. 'His heart.'

Margery found her eyes narrowing of their own accord. Louis Fisher had been old, of course, but he had been in good spirits and good health only a few days before. There was foul play here, she was sure of it. There was a buzz from the front desk and the nurse excused herself.

'Password please,' she said primly into the intercom.

'He can't be dead,' Clementine hissed to Margery. 'Not when we're so close to finding out what happened to Eleanor and getting Maria's name cleared.'

'Just follow my lead,' Margery whispered back.

The nurse finished at the intercom and turned back to them, plastering the wide, fake smile on again. It made Margery feel worse about the lie she was about to tell.

'Would you mind if we went and said goodbye?' Margery asked, before she could continue to try and soothe them. 'To Louis, I mean… well, we know he's not there any more, but we knew his daughter and we always said we'd help him if she went and, well… these last few weeks have been a terrible shock.'

'Oh, of course,' the nurse said, her eyes widening. 'Yes, of course, please do. But obviously, it goes without saying, please don't touch anything.'

'Of course,' Margery said agreeably.

The nurse gestured to the office door, and they went back into the hallway as inconspicuously as they could, only waiting for a few seconds before rushing down the corridor towards Louis Fisher's apartment. The warmth from the afternoon sunlight pouring in through the hallway windows made the already stifling air even worse. Margery had to gasp for it as they barrelled along, her mind reeling with worries.

'What's the plan now?' Clementine huffed as they speed-walked past door after door. 'He can't be dead! This is unbelievable.'

'I think there must be more to all of this,' Margery said. 'He was fine when we last saw. Something awful has happened.'

They rounded the corner, Louis's room loomed at the end of the hallway and Margery rushed to it. She paused outside for a brief second, listening intently. When there was no noise from inside, she reached for the door handle. The door swung open with a creak, and Margery stepped into the room, surveying it carefully. Clementine crept in behind her, her hand resting on Margery's back as if to steady herself. Margery paused at the sight of the room. It looked exactly how it had when they had left a few days before. Only the dirty coffee cups in the sink revealed that anyone had been here. Two cups, Margery noticed. Had Louis entertained a visitor before he died? She gazed down into the sink, looking for anything interesting about the mugs. A smear of lipstick, the smell of almonds revealing poison. Instead, there was nothing but the rings of coffee staining the china with tannins.

'What are we looking for?' Clementine asked.

'I'm not sure,' Margery admitted. 'There has to be something. There always is.'

Clementine didn't seem to agree. She had begun to wring her hands as though squeezing the excess water from a tea towel. It had been all well and good to impulsively go back to his room, but now that they were there, Margery really wasn't sure where to start. It wasn't as though Louis would have left anything obvious lying in wait for them. There had been nothing at their recent visit and there didn't seem to be anything now.

Regardless, they crept through the kitchenette into the living room. Margery paused by Louis's armchair, the arms of it worn from decades of use, the wood a different colour where his elbows would have sat. It looked well made, probably from his former life in the grand family house. A wave of sadness rushed over her, almost bowling her over as it hit. She hadn't known Louis long, she knew that, but there was a despair in the enormity of it. She knew that every second that ticked by would lead to her last second. She felt old *now*. How would it feel to be Louis's age, confined to a room and a chair and maybe a few visits a month to the supermarket cafe if someone was free to take you? Knowing that was all there was, now. Things would never feel better, and the good days were long gone — not appreciated at all while they were happening.

Margery wished she could go back twenty years and enjoy her life again. She wouldn't even complain about Caroline's mad ramblings or the busy workload of the kitchen. Margery would just soak it all in if there was another go around, enjoy the good years while they had lasted. She hoped she might go back there when it was her moment to go, even if just to say goodbye. A shame that there was no second offering of time, for anyone.

'Nothing here,' Clementine said, jolting her back into the present.

'Maybe the rest of the flat?' Margery suggested.

Clementine's eyes widened, uncharacteristically uncomfortable with what Margery had proposed. Margery snuck forward tentatively down the short hallway, looking from one doorway to the other. To her right was a small bathroom, clean and sterile and with barely any personal artefacts except a toothbrush and a razor. A bar of soap and a stick of deodorant rested on the side on the bath. The bathroom mirror sat flush to the wall. It wasn't a cabinet anything could be hidden in. Margery realised that Louis's prescription drugs were probably given out to him by the staff. Perhaps the nurse at the desk could be helpful in discerning the timeline of Louis's death? Maybe, but Margery couldn't think of a way that they could have that conversation and seem innocent.

Somehow it felt taboo to step any further into the bathroom, so instead Margery crossed the hall and turned and peered into the bedroom. The bed was made as though no one had slept in it, the sheets pulled up above the pillows tightly. The bedside tables were almost empty, except for a small analogue alarm clock and a half empty glass of water on the one closest to the door. The patio door opened onto a small piece of concrete that was fenced off from the outside world. Margery went closer and noticed that one of the plant pots next to the wooden chair had been smashed, the soil spread all over the patio and under the seat, shards of porcelain littering the ground.

'Clem,' Margery hissed. 'Do you think someone killed Louis and then escaped this way?'

'Maybe,' Clementine said, looking to where Margery was pointing. 'Or broke in this way? There'd be no record of them then, would there?'

Margery's mind reeled with the possibilities. The nurse hadn't seemed to think anything nefarious was going on, but it seemed too big a coincidence to her.

'Look,' Clementine said. She pointed to the shelving unit by Louis's bed. 'The bookshelf. The dust.'

Margery looked where Clementine was pointing and saw where the dust had indeed been removed by something square-shaped. Margery went to that side of the bed and found a box the same diameter hiding behind it. She reached down to lift it up, finding it much heavier than she had imagined. She set it down on the bedside table and lifted the cardboard flaps, gasping at what was revealed inside.

'The vase?' she said, finding her voice choked in confusion. 'Which one is this?'

Clementine made a strangled noise in her throat. 'Check for a signature.'

Margery lifted the vase by the base, where she found the initials of R. J. E. 'This is the other vase Robert made! The one he made Vivian years ago. There were two— Oh, Clem, we did miss something.'

'What?'

'One was smashed while being used as a murder weapon,' Margery explained. 'And this… this must have been stolen from Eleanor the night she died. Two fake vases!'

'How has it ended up here?' Clementine said. She shook her head, reaching out a hand to touch the vase before thinking better of it.

'What are you doing here?' a voice from behind them called.

Margery and Clementine turned to find Jeffery Black looking at them from the bedroom doorway with his brow furrowed. Margery wondered briefly how long it would take them to escape through the patio door, if they would be able to manage the fence. They didn't get the chance to move. Jeffery's eyes snapped opened wide as he saw what Margery was holding.

'Gosh! Is that the Heritage Vase?' he asked, coming over to touch it gently. 'Oh, maybe I shouldn't touch it, it must be evidence, surely?'

Margery was still holding it upside down, the initials clearly on display.

'We just thought we'd come and pay our respects,' Clementine stammered out.

Margery nodded along with the lie, deciding the truth wouldn't do them any good in the moment. Jeff wasn't listening. He reached out and took the vase from Margery's hands, holding it carefully as though it were a newborn baby.

'I suspect the police will be very interested in this,' he said. 'I'm going to hand it over right away. Maybe it can help their case. Though I don't suppose it will do any good now, will it? Not now Louis is dead.'

'You don't think—' Margery began.

'That Louis killed Eleanor?' Jeff said. 'Well, it certainly seems the case, doesn't it? As he has the true Heritage Vase in his home.'

Jeffery thought that it was real, Margery realised. That seemed too convenient. He continued to babble about the police and how lucky it was that they'd found it, until Margery and Clementine made their excuses to leave. Margery was glad. It would not do to push their luck any further than they already had.

'Well, that's good news, isn't it?' Clementine said, beaming with happiness as they left the building and began to walk to the car park. The sun had come out, revealing a cold but lovely day. 'Jeffery will give the vase to the police and then they'll stop looking for Maria.'

'I'm not sure about that,' Margery said, regretting it as Clementine's face fell. 'Something's off here.'

It took Margery until they reached the car to realise that Jeffery must have seen the initials carved into the bottom of the vase, his friend Robert's initials, and he hadn't said a word.

Chapter Twenty-Three

The more Margery thought about it, the stranger she found the whole situation. Jeffery Black, who knew all about the Heritage Vase, hadn't thought it strange that the initials of a friend were imprinted on it. Unless he knew it was fake. Did Jeffery know what Louis had been up to? Did that mean he had put it in Louis's home to frame him? Or worse? And how would they find out if that was the case? She couldn't think about it now. Not when the students were beginning to arrive and collecting trays and filing themselves into an orderly queue.

A phone bleeped, the sound nearly drowned out by the buzz of the canteen. Ceri-Ann jumped. She reached into the pocket of her tabard and pulled out her phone. 'Yeah, yeah, I know, Gloria, no phones, blah. But it's Symon, so this is for Margery! Let me just see what he says.'

Gloria rolled her eyes. 'You know I'm not your boss, don't you?'

'You're the phone police, though, aren't you? Remember when Sharon wouldn't stop texting and you put her phone in the freezer?' Ceri-Ann smiled, already opening her phone and scrolling through. 'He says no one has handed anything in. Mind you, it's early days, isn't it? Maybe Jeffery hasn't had a chance yet?'

'I'm not sure about that,' Margery said, feeling the gloom descend over her.

'Thing is, he was in the drama studio on the night of the auction,' Gloria said. 'I'm sure of it. I'm sure I saw that Jeffery skulking about by the roulette table.'

'Really?' Margery asked. 'But it was adults only, wasn't it? I remember all the emails about it.'

Gloria nodded.

'Yes, and I'm sure his son was there too. I didn't think much of them at the time,' she said with a shrug. 'I just assumed they thought they were too important to follow the rules, there were a few other students there that shouldn't have been, but Jeffery stood out because he seemed so annoyed about something.'

'The vase being sold, probably,' Margery thought out loud. 'I imagine he was there to watch it be sold. Or maybe something worse...'

She had wondered if Jeffery hadn't yet gone to the police because he was the person who had killed Eleanor.

'Was he there the entire time?' Margery asked.

'I think so,' Gloria said. 'But of course, we don't know when Eleanor died, do we?'

'No,' Margery agreed. 'The police seem to be trying to claim that Maria killed her and then ran straight out of the fire escape, but it can't have been proven by the autopsy and we know that isn't true.'

Gloria hummed and Margery looked over to Clementine, who was still talking to a student, oblivious to their conversation. She suddenly had the thought that maybe she had been too willing to assume Maria had killed Eleanor. If the result had come back as guilty immediately, then she would have gone right along with it. Why hadn't the autopsy been finalised yet? Margery wondered. Surely that would prove exactly when Eleanor had died and then

Maria would be off the hook. They just had to find the real culprit now.

Gloria went to top up the sandwich fridge and the team fell back into their routine, Margery scooping portions of mashed potato. That was usually Clementine's job, but since the incident a few days ago she had well and truly been banned from food service for the moment. Margery had needed to put her on the till, which Karen and Sharon were not pleased about. Still, Karen was doing a good job of scooping the peas, which was more than could be said for Clementine, who had taken to trying to upsell the students' tickets to the summer play while they bought their meals. The spring concert had been entirely forgotten before it had even been performed.

'It's a play about us!' she cried gleefully every time the next student tried to say no, waving their receipts at them in glee.

'Clementine seems to be taking this all quite well,' Gloria said, returning from the fridge with an empty crate. 'Is she all right?'

Margery decided that Gloria didn't need to know that Clementine was so cheery because she was hiding a fugitive in the attic of their shop.

'I really don't know any more,' Margery sighed. 'She think's Jeffery's going to tell them that Louis killed Eleanor and Maria will be cleared. I just can't see him doing that.'

'Maybe one of the other Fishers will confess?' Gloria suggested. Margery shook her head.

'There's no Fishers left, as far as I know,' she told her sadly.

'You've got a fissure?' Karen asked from behind them, causing Margery and Gloria to whirl around. 'I'm so sorry to hear that! God, I wouldn't want one of those. Nasty things.'

'My hubby had one,' Sharon called over from the till. 'He had it while I was in labour. He said it was worse than childbirth. I told him he couldn't possibly know that—'

Before Margery could correct either of them, there was the sound of another beeping phone. It chimed around the room, much too loudly for Margery's liking. She looked around to ask whoever it was to put their phone away.

It took her a second to realise that it was, in fact, her own phone, blaring from her own pocket where she'd placed it after ringing through that morning's orders. Embarrassed, she handed the mashed-potato spoon to Gloria and stepped off the line to take the phone call. The screen told her that it was Dawn Simmonds. Margery's heart sank at the idea of having to speak to her. She battled with herself over answering it, wondering if Dawn would go as far as to call the school if she didn't. In the end, she reasoned that she'd just have to deal with Dawn when they returned home anyway. She answered the call.

'Hello?' Margery said into the receiver.

'Hello, Margery!' Dawn cooed back.

'Dawn, you know we're at work, don't you?' Margery said, feeling her temper flare up. She had been having trouble keeping a lid on it recently. Short and snappy seemed to be both her and Clementine's go-to since Maria had been accused.

'Yes, yes!' Dawn said a lilt of a smile in her voice. She didn't seem perturbed at all judging by her breezy tone. 'But you'll have to come home, it's a police matter.'

'What's happened now?' Margery asked, unable to stop the sarcastic tone rolling off her tongue. 'Has Maria's van become even more of an eyesore? Has one of our cats stolen your washing?'

'No!' Dawn said with a scoff that suggested that she had never complained about anything a single moment of her life. 'Not yet, anyway... Do you think Pumpkin would steal the washing? Only I've had several socks go missing...'

'Dawn, please, I'm at work,' Margery begged. 'What do you want?'

'That woman tried to break into your house again,' Dawn finally said, after a moment of sulky pause. 'Don't worry, I apprehended her!'

'Oh!' Margery said. 'You... oh right! Well...'

'You'll have to come home,' Dawn said, her voice accusing in a way that made Margery roll her eyes. 'You can't expect me to be doing your dirty work, catching criminals. I only joined the neighbourhood watch for the social functions, I'll have you know. Not chasing people down the street. Honestly, first the van, now this...'

Margery decided she didn't need to hear the rest of the conversation at all. She hung up and raced back into the canteen, where Clementine was waiting for her expectantly, ignoring the line of children waiting in the queue.

'Someone's tried to break into our house,' Margery said, all in a rushed sentence. 'Dawn stopped them, I think she's caught them? That's what she told me anyway.'

The idea of tiny Dawn Simmonds being able to apprehend a burglar did seem very out of the ordinary, but who was Margery to argue? She had certainly sounded out of breath over the phone.

'We need to go!' Clementine gasped. 'We need to catch them! Has she called the police?'

'She said it was a police matter, so I'd assume so,' Margery said.

'I'll look after the line,' Gloria said, coming over to take the spoon out of Clementine's hands. 'It's nearly over now. We've only got forty portions of pie left, after that it's just jacket potatoes, I'm afraid.'

'All right,' Margery said. 'Come on, Clem.'

They rushed out of the building to Margery's car, not even bothering to change out of their pinafores. They jumped in and zoomed off down the hill as fast as Margery dared.

'I hope the police get there before we do,' Margery said. 'I'm not sure I'm up to a hostage situation involving Dawn.'

'I hope they don't,' Clementine said. Her hands were gripping the passenger side handle so tightly that her knuckles were white. 'I don't trust any of them, bar Symon of course, and even he isn't very forthcoming with his help at the moment, is he?'

Margery couldn't argue with that and they fell into silence as they travelled.

They arrived at their cul-de-sac, barrelling down Seymour Road at such a speed that Margery worried for a moment that they might crash the car into Dawn's pond again. The small wheels of the car thumped over the speed bumps and hurtled towards the house. Margery parked parallel to it. Dawn was waiting for them on their doorstep holding something in her arms and looking incredibly pleased with herself. To Margery's surprise, there was no one else with Dawn at all, if you didn't count the cats. They were both gathered in the front garden as if at front-row seats to the spectacle.

'I caught her!' Dawn said. She was flinging the material around her head like it was a flag. 'And I'm keeping the cardigan! I pulled it right off her back as she tried to run off.'

'So, you didn't catch her at all, then?' Clementine asked, looking around for the mysterious perpetrator anyway.

'How dare you!' Dawn said, letting Clementine help her to her feet. 'I'll have you know that I very much almost caught her.'

'"Almost" doesn't really cut it, does it, Dawn?' Clementine said, with a scoff.

'Who was it?' Margery interrupted before it could become a full-blown argument. She looked around as though the mystery woman might return.

'I don't know her name,' Dawn said cryptically. 'I know her face, though. It's that one from the museum.'

She stopped her mad waving, unfolding the material in her arms to show them. It was a pastel pink cardigan. Margery knew exactly who it belonged to.

Chapter Twenty-Four

They finally made it to the museum half an hour later, after escorting Dawn home with her new cardigan. The museum's front doors were closed. Margery assumed the worst, but once they tried the handles, they discovered that the great doors were not locked, and Margery and Clementine slipped inside easily. A little too easily, Margery thought as her eyes darted all over the foyer as her heart raced. Cecilia might have been waiting for them to arrive. Waiting to ambush them.

They waited for a moment in the grand downstairs foyer. Margery looked around for signs of life and found none. The room felt too still, the dust settling all around them where they stood. She wished that they had brought Cecilia's cardigan with them for evidence, but Dawn had already put it on as they were leaving and had been preening at her own reflection in the wing mirror of Maria's van. Margery supposed that if the police wanted to see it then they could be the ones to argue with her over it.

'Cecilia!' Clementine called out. 'We know you're here. Come out!'

There was a pause for a moment, but then the office door opened with a heavy creak, and Cecelia made her way behind the front desk. Her mouth was pulled taut, her eyes darting around between them and the door and she was wringing her hands so severely Margery worried that she might give herself a friction burn.

'Are you alone?' she hissed, eyes flicking to the front door again.

Margery stepped forward slowly, as though she were approaching a skittish animal she had caught in a trap. Cecilia evaded her, rushing around her to the front door and slamming the bolt closed. Margery thought for a second that they might have a chase on their hands, but Cecilia took a set of keys from her pocket and then double locked the doors.

She slipped them back inside and turned to face them once more, stepping slowly back into the room and huddling against the front desk, her eyes still worrying at the door but her features calmer than they had been a second before.

'Don't try and hide from us now that we know what you did,' Clementine scoffed.

'You don't understand—' Cecilia began.

Clementine cut her off. 'We know that you forged all those threatening letters to Eleanor.'

Cecilia blinked away from the door to look at her for a moment, before she turned her head again, tilting it to listen.

'Why did you threaten her?'

'She wanted to sell everything we'd collected over the years,' Cecilia said, finally looking at them both properly, the door no longer a concern for the moment. 'You saw what she was trying to do with the vase. Sell it at an auction to the highest bidder.'

'What was the problem with that?' Margery asked her, trying to sound soft and gentle. To coax out the answers. 'The museum hasn't been doing well, has it?'

'The problem is that I told her to do it years before,' Cecilia snapped. 'We don't need all of it, I said that to her. She never listened. We could have easily sold the Heritage Vase back to Vivian decades ago. Vivian would have paid for it.'

'I don't understand,' Clementine said. 'You wanted to sell the vase?'

'In the right way,' Cecilia said. 'To the rightful owner. Not at a public auction to any old sod. Anyone could have bought it.'

'It would have looked nice in our living room,' Clementine admitted.

'Exactly! That's exactly what I mean,' Cecilia said. 'Anyway, Mr Fisher wanted it back. He asked if I could help him.'

'What did you do?' Margery asked.

Cecilia went very quiet, as though wondering what she could and couldn't say.

'We know you swapped the vase with a fake the week before,' Margery told her. Cecilia paled. 'Where did you get that from? Did Louis give it to you?'

'No!' Cecilia snapped. 'No. I was given it from Vivian's estate when she died,' she explained. 'Eleanor knew I always loved the real one, so she said I ought to have the fake one. She thought it was funny that Vivian had had one made… I didn't. Poor Vivian, she'll never know what became of it.'

'What about the other fake vase?' Clementine asked.

'Other vase?'

'We've just found the other fake vase,' Margery explained. 'At Louis's flat.'

'I don't know anything about that…'

'We know you commissioned it from Robert,' Margery said. 'Why?'

'No—' Cecilia stammered. 'No, I didn't do that bit!'

'Really?' Clementine asked with a sneer. 'Then who did?'

'I think you know who,' Cecilia snapped. 'And your sister was working with the family to steal it the whole time!'

'No,' Clementine stammered. 'No, that can't be right. Jeffery told us that Louis killed Eleanor.'

'It is right,' Cecilia said, a flicker of triumph flaring over her face before it disappeared. 'She was more than happy to help me steal all those things from the school, she was the one who suggested to Eleanor that she store them at yours. "No one would suspect a dinner lady," she told her...'

'You overheard all their conversations,' Margery said.

Cecilia nodded, clutching her hands together timidly.

'Maria didn't kill Eleanor!' Clementine cried, her voice ringing around the room and hitting the high ceiling.

'I know she didn't!' Cecilia cried back. They met in the middle, at a stalemate, both glaring at each other and breathing heavily. Margery waited in the middle of them with bated breath. 'But she was still involved in something she shouldn't have been, wasn't she?'

'So, let me get this all straight,' Clementine said, putting her hand to the bridge of her nose and pinching for a second. 'Eleanor is planning to sell the vase, but you don't want her to so you try and stop her by... how exactly?'

'I told her I'd give it back to Mr Fisher,' Cecilia said. 'Can't have an auction for it if you don't have it, can you?'

'But that didn't work because...?' Margery began.

'Eleanor kept up the ruse that nothing was wrong,' Cecilia finished. 'She was certain that people would come for the Heritage Vase so she decided to hide it from me, though I'd already swapped them by that point.'

'So instead of just telling her that you don't want her to sell the vase,' Clementine continued, but she pinched the bridge of her nose as though she had a terrible headache, 'you swap the vases a week before the auction to preserve history or something…'

'I spoke to her numerous times about it—'

'What was your plan for when Eleanor realised she had the fake, though?' Margery asked. 'She would have realised eventually, or whoever bought it would have.'

Cecilia obviously hadn't thought about that, her cheeks flushed pink and she shook her head dismissively.

'Eleanor gets murdered with a fake vase which is covered with my sister's fingerprints because she'd swapped them, and then a bit later you take the real vase which was hidden— where?' Clementine said. Her voice had risen scornfully, her hand gesturing out into the air.

'It was here,' Cecilia said quietly. 'Here where it belongs.'

'All right, so you take the real vase and hide it at our house and then call the police because you're sure Maria killed Eleanor,' Clementine said. 'So, the police turn up and raid our home, thanks for that by the way, and now you're saying you don't think Maria killed Eleanor? Which is it?'

'I couldn't have the vase here because it would have been found and I couldn't hide it at my house, because that would be too obvious a place to hide it,' Cecilia explained. 'I had to take it to yours and then call the police so that they would have it, and it would be safe and then no one would come for me for it when they realised that the vase Eleanor had for the auction was a fake!'

Margery and Clementine processed this new information, while Cecilia began to pace, wandering behind the desk, her hands balled into white fists of anguish.

'I know that Maria couldn't have killed Eleanor,' Cecilia said. 'Because Louis Fisher told me who did kill her when I went to see him a few days ago. A few days before...'

She looked as though she might burst into tears. 'The day before he died. He was beside himself. He didn't want her to get hurt. He just wanted to take her down a few pegs. When he realised who had really killed her... I think that must have killed him.'

Clementine was stunned into a temporary silence.

Margery thought over what they had just been told. 'Who killed Louis, Cecilia?' she asked.

'I...' Cecilia began. 'Look, you need to give me the vase back, that's all. This'll all be sorted if you go and get it for me, right now.'

'No,' Margery said.

'Oh, you must,' Cecilia said, almost throwing herself over the desk in her haste to grab the front of Margery's cardigan with desperate claws. 'I know you still have it, the police certainly don't.'

The double doors rattled as someone tried to open them from the outside.

Cecilia's eyes opened wide, her mouth dropping open.

'You should go,' she said, eyes darting to the door again. 'He'll be here any second...'

'Who?' Margery asked, feeling her temper flare.

'Please,' Cecilia said, rushing around the desk and grasping for Margery's wrist with her thin fingers. 'Please, you need to leave. I never should have left that vase with you.'

'No!' Clementine said. 'You're going to tell us what's going on first.'

'You don't understand,' Cecilia said, her eyes wide and pleading. 'I didn't break into your house for the fun of it, I needed the vase back! Look, you need to leave and then get it for me, or very bad things are about to happen.'

'Well, it isn't at our house,' Margery said. 'It's in a safe place.'

'Then I'm done for,' Cecilia said. She had turned white, all the colour drained from her thin face.

The door rattled again and a booming voice called Cecilia's name. She turned to them in a panic.

'Hide in the office,' she said. 'I'll show you what's going on.'

They did as she told them, though Margery didn't know why. Cecilia tried to slam the door shut behind them as soon as they entered the office, but it rebounded, the old wooden door too warped to fit in the frame without a gentle touch. It left the door slightly ajar. Enough for Margery and Clementine to be able to peer out from the darkness of the room into the brightly lit foyer.

'Hello,' Cecilia said. 'How good to see you again… and so soon.'

Cecilia stood primly, with her hands folded tightly together resting on the front desk. Margery could only see her back and just a tiny amount of the man standing on the other side of the desk.

It didn't matter, though. She knew exactly who it was. And the realisation made her gasp.

Clementine clapped a hand over her mouth to stop the sound travelling. All of Margery's thoughts came together at once and she reached into the pocket of her cardigan, taking out her phone.

'What are you doing?' Clementine hissed through the darkness. Margery couldn't have answered if she had even wanted to with a hand over her mouth. Instead, she unlocked the phone screen and dialled the number that she had saved into her contacts. The number that had been in constant contact with Maria until she had been arrested. The number that never answered. A phone rang out, reverberating through the foyer of the museum, echoing up the grand staircase.

Chapter Twenty-Five

Andrew Black pulled the phone from his pocket and silenced it. Inside the office, Margery's phone rang off. It was Clementine's turn to gasp in surprise. Margery almost laughed out loud, stopping herself before she did.

She and Clementine shared a look of panic before Margery turned her attention back to the foyer, where Andrew and Cecilia were talking.

Andrew stood up straight and tall. A distant relative to the Andrew that Margery had caught weeping behind the bins at Ittonvale school. Clementine reached for Margery's phone and began to tap away at the screen desperately.

'Call the police,' Margery whispered to Clementine.

'I'm doing it,' Clementine mouthed, her face lit up by the screen, ghostly in the low lighting of the office. 'I texted Symon and Nigel. Hopefully one of them will get here in time.'

Margery nodded grimly, but her heart was pounding in her chest.

'You told me you'd have it today,' Andrew said. 'So where is it?'

'I don't have it any more,' Cecilia said. Margery could tell she was trying to be brave by the way Cecilia's fists clenched together tightly, but her voice wavered. 'The dinner ladies have it.'

'No, they don't,' Andrew said, his voice heavy with scorn. 'I didn't see it at their shop.'

Margery was confused, but only for a second. That was why there had been no one there when she answered the shop door. She had thought it was Clementine, but it must have been Andrew lurking out in the darkness. He had been in the shop, she realised with horror. He had snuck in looking for the vase when she had marched off up the street looking for Clementine. The pieces all fell together a little too late. Had he been hiding in the shop when she'd left to go to the museum? It didn't bear thinking about.

'Come on, Ce,' Andrew said. 'You've got to help me out. Do you want to end up like my poor auntie?'

'I know you killed her,' Cecilia said, raising her voice. For Margery and Clementine's benefit, Margery thought grimly.

'I didn't mean to kill her,' Andrew said, the calm exterior cracking immediately. 'You know I didn't mean to!'

'You did,' Cecilia said. It came out as a sob. 'Eleanor didn't deserve that.'

'I know,' Andrew said.

His voice was back to being calm and collected, the voice of someone who had thought a lot about what they had done and considered themself innocent. Margery knew his threats wouldn't remain just that. He had intention about him and Cecilia was in deep trouble if she thought she could get rid of him with words alone. Especially now that the vase was a mile away at Nigel Thomas's house. Margery dug the nails of her fingers into her palms and hoped for a miracle.

'What about Louis?' Cecilia asked. 'Did he deserve to die?'

'I didn't kill him. He was already dead,' Andrew said, his tone sulky. 'You know I loved Uncle Louis. I wouldn't have hurt him.'

'That's just coincidence, then, is it?' Cecilia asked.

'Yes,' Andrew said. 'I went to confront him and he was dead. You can't believe I'd kill him!'

'Why are you here, then?' Cecilia cried, her voice rising hysterically in the second show of real emotion since Andrew had come clattering into the room, disturbing the fragile peace.

'Do you think I want to be here?' He said. Margery could barely see him through the narrow gap in the door, but she could feel that he was shrugging, all the innocence in him gone somewhere else. 'I have to be here, Ce. Dad... he's not going to let this go. He's really angry Uncle Louis got me involved in it all.'

'But that woman... Maria... she'll go to prison for your crime,' Cecilia said. Margery felt Clementine stiffen beside her at the mention of Maria's name.

'What can I do about it?' Andrew spat. 'Dad said she's the one who was helping Louis in the first place, this is all her fault!'

'She was desperate for money,' Cecilia said. 'She didn't know what she was involving herself in, did she? She's not from here. She didn't know your dad or your grandad or your family or what any of you were capable of. Lord knows Vivian wasn't innocent, and neither was Eleanor and you—'

'Yeah, yeah, I'm the worst one,' Andrew said. He waved his hand frivolously, stepping to the side as he did so and giving Margery a better view of him. 'I didn't want to do any of this, Ce!' His voice cracked, though the anger stayed burning in his eyes. 'Dad wouldn't let me go to the police, I wanted to – honestly I did.' Margery could hear him beginning to pace up and down. She opened the door a little wider so she could see better. Andrew ran his fingers through his hair as he paced, and Margery found herself losing her nerve. Andrew was not just making confessions but on the edge of losing control.

Andrew continued, 'Dad said I'd go to prison for the rest of my life. I'm only sixteen! I should smash that vase into millions of pieces.'

His hands clenched into fists, and he banged one down hard onto the reception desk. Margery flinched at the same time as Cecilia.

'All that and you don't even want to keep it,' Cecilia said with a sob. 'I wouldn't tell anyone what you did—'

There was a crash from the foyer, making both Margery and Clementine jump.

'Andrew!' Jeffery Black cried. 'Stop it! Leave her alone.'

'Stay away from me,' Andrew yelled. He reached out for the postcard display and pushed it over. 'This is all your fault!'

There was another crash as the metal display rack smashed onto the floor. Cecilia screamed.

The police weren't going to get here before someone got hurt, the realisation descended on Margery with horror. They were going to have to step in. Before something irreparable happened to Cecilia. Margery stood up and reached for the door. Clementine joined her.

'Leave her alone,' Clementine cried. They left the safe haven of the office and stood next to Cecilia, flanking her on both sides.

Jeffery looked wild with panic, his eyes wide and his breath coming in harsh bursts as he wrestled with Andrew. Margery realised with horror that Andrew was winning easily, twisting his father's arms away from him with the strength from his youth. Cecilia stood back with her hand over her heart watching them, her mouth a black hole of shock. Before Margery and Clementine could do anything, Andrew had tripped Jeffery. He landed on his back with a dull thud and reached for the boy again. Andrew shook him off easily and turned back to Cecilia, seeming to suddenly realise that Margery and Clementine were there.

'You don't need to be involved in this,' Jeffery said, his cheeks flushing red with the exertion. 'Leave and I won't tell anyone you were here.'

'You know we can't do that,' Clementine said. 'Especially when you've managed to get my sister on the hook for a murder you committed.'

'She shouldn't have ever got involved!' Jeffery said. 'I told her not to go to the hall that evening, but did she listen? No. That's why she's going to go to prison and Andrew isn't. He's not stupid, he got out of there as soon as he knew he'd hit her. Sure, he killed her, but we all make mistakes…'

'A mistake is cheating on a spelling test,' Margery said. 'Not murdering an aunt.'

Andrew looked as though he might cry. 'I just meant to swap the vases. I didn't expect her to be there. She was supposed to be too busy with the rest of the auction, I panicked!'

'You hit her with a vase,' Margery said incredulously. 'That certainly shows intent.'

Andrew fell silent at the mention of the truth.

'And you.' Margery turned to Jeffery. 'You've been helping him cover up what you all did. How long were you carrying out plans in Louis's name?'

Jeffery stammered, unable to get an answer out. Andrew turned to stare at him with wide eyes. 'What does she mean, "Louis's name"? I thought getting the vase back was Louis's idea?'

'Well... I...' Jeffery began. 'It may have been my plan initially, but I simply put it in place, I had no idea what the outcome would be...'

'I thought we were protecting Louis as well,' Andrew said. 'But he wasn't even involved?'

Jeffery paused as if debating if he should lie. Finally, he shook his head.

'I just wanted to keep you safe, Andrew,' he said finally. 'You made a mistake, but it shouldn't ruin the rest of your life. We just need to sort this misunderstanding out.'

Andrew seemed to realise that Margery and Clementine were still there. Cecilia had ducked down behind the desk, cowering underneath it.

'Are you recording this?' he asked, looking over at where Clementine still had Margery's phone in her hand.

'Give me the phone,' Jeffery said.

Clementine shook her head, a clear refusal.

Andrew didn't waste time with talking. Instead, his face twisted into a horrible terror-filled expression and then he lunged for her. Clementine managed to evade him behind the reception desk, but only for a moment before he was grasping for her phone again.

'Clem!' Margery cried, trying to stop him. It was no use. He was too strong. He grabbed Clementine's wrist. At the same time, the double doors blew open again and Symon marched in, followed closely by Officer Wilkinson.

Chapter Twenty-Six

'Another lucky escape for the Dinner Lady Detectives,' Officer Wilkinson said wryly. 'And another win – you must be very pleased with yourselves.'

Officer Wilkinson certainly didn't seem pleased. He glared at them both, tapping his pencil hard against his notepad. Margery watched the pencil ricochet off the page each time, leaving little graphite indents as it went. She had a bad feeling about this, her stomach dropping again, even worse than it had when Andrew's phone had rung. She didn't like the way Officer Wilkinson was looking at them, as though they had done something wrong.

Clementine continued to ice her sore wrist, which was bruised and not broken. A first aider on the force had already checked them both over and given them a clean bill of health. Jeffery had survived, but had a broken rib and Cecilia was so shocked that she was still sitting in another room shaking like a leaf and wrapped in a foil blanket like a very large burrito. The officers hadn't managed to get a single word from her yet, but it didn't matter. With Andrew's confession and Margery and Clementine's pieced-together evidence, everything would be well. In a way.

Margery didn't think Maria would be the same again, even now she was free. She suspected that if anything it would make Maria even more distrustful and anxious to get going. A feral cat who had never learned to coexist with anyone else and ran terrified from strangers.

'I think we'd be more pleased if you'd caught the right person in the first place,' Clementine said. Margery nodded.

'You have to admit, it still doesn't look good for Maria. Even with all your evidence,' Officer Wilkinson said, his eyes narrowing.

'What on earth do you mean by that?' Margery snapped, unable to conceal her annoyance. 'This is the second time in a row you haven't got it right. When are you going to start listening to us?'

Clementine gasped at Margery's anger. Margery felt her hands begin to shake with it. It felt out of place in the grand room, the exhibits all around the chaise-longue they were perched on. She toed the old rug in between them and Officer Wilkinson with her shoe.

'I'm not planning to start any time soon,' Officer Wilkinson said with a half-smile. A small and ugly thing that spread over his face. 'Now, where shall we begin with you? First and foremost, I think fraud by false reputation, trespassing… hmm… let's see, what else… what else?'

'You can't be serious,' Clementine spat, gesticulating wildly. 'We just solved your case for you!'

'Did you?' Officer Wilkinson asked. 'Or will some new evidence about Maria come out? It would be a shame if some of the evidence went missing or Cecilia refused to testify, wouldn't it? Especially now you've told us exactly where Maria is. I've got a team heading in that direction right now.'

'You are joking?' Clementine said as Margery felt her mouth fall open. 'What is this? Blackmail? What do you want?'

'I don't want anything from you,' Officer Wilkinson said. He leaned back on the seat, relaxing into it, a cat playing with a pair of mice it had caught. 'I want you to get out of the way so we can get on with police business, and seeing as I've solved this case now, I'm sure the promotion I've been waiting for is on the cards.'

'You'd throw us under the bus for a promotion?' Margery asked, her voice coming out smaller and weaker than she meant it to. 'What have we ever done to you?'

'Got in my way.' Officer Wilkinson shrugged.

There was a noise behind them and Officer Wilkinson's head shot up to glare at the intrusion. Margery watched an array of expressions wash over him, from annoyance to shock, his own mouth dropping open in surprise.

'Sarge,' he said, getting to his feet and brushing himself off. 'What brings you... why are you here?'

Margery turned to see Sergeant Davis of Ittonvale standing in the doorway, wearing an annoyed expression and flanked by several other officers. He really did look as though he would rather be elsewhere, Margery thought, and there was a serious air to the room among the other police officers. They were looking to Officer Wilkinson curiously.

Davis gestured to his officers, and they marched over to Wilkinson, who sat frozen, staring as they apprehended him.

'Mark Wilkinson,' Davis said, gesturing at Wilkinson with a finger. 'It pains me to say this, but you're under arrest for extortion.'

'What?' Officer Wilkinson gasped, though Margery didn't think he looked as surprised as she felt. 'This is preposterous.'

'We'll have a good chat about it down at the station,' Sergeant Davis said.

He didn't wait for Officer Wilkinson to respond, leaving the room. Wilkinson continued protesting as the other officers dragged him out, without even a backward look at Margery or Clementine. The chief's team followed, leaving only Symon standing by the doorway with his hand on his police radio.

'Hiya,' he said. 'You all right?'

'Yes,' Clementine said, though she looked as confused as Margery felt. 'Are you?'

'Yeah.' Symon nodded, coming over to sit where Officer Wilkinson had just vacated. 'Except I've had a million calls from Ceri-Ann trying to find out what's going on.' He chuckled. 'Honestly, it's amazing I managed to become a detective given how many case details she knows. She could be a detective herself, I reckon – she's nosy enough. You might have to give her some freelance work.'

'You're a detective now?' Margery gasped.

'As of a few weeks ago,' Symon said, the happiness lighting his face. 'We thought we'd keep it quiet for a bit, well... the sergeant asked me to.'

'Well, congratulations,' Clementine said. 'But why?'

'Isn't that obvious?' Symon said. 'My first case was to investigate what Wilkinson was up to.'

'Is that why he's just arrested him?' Clementine asked, looking back towards the doorway. 'What's he done?'

'What hasn't he done?' Symon scoffed. 'Extortion, bribery, covering up evidence. Keeping suspects for longer than he needed to for personal vindicative reasons.' He looked at Clementine meaningfully. 'I wouldn't worry, he won't be on the force for much longer, hopefully. That's why I couldn't help you with this.'

'You were too busy trying to crack that case?' Margery asked.

'Yeah.' Symon nodded. 'I hoped you'd be okay, and you were! And honestly, if this hadn't happened it would be hard to prove, but now I have concrete evidence that Wilkinson was still searching for Maria because he didn't like you, even when the evidence was pointing elsewhere. We've had footage of Andrew Black carrying a big carrier bag away from the school with his dad since the beginning, but Wilkinson decided not to act on it. It was pure corruption.'

'We suspected as much before,' Margery said, thinking about the suspicious circumstances that had surrounded Mr Fitzgerald's investigation.

'I did, too,' Symon said. 'And we were right then.'

They sat in silence for a moment, listening to the chatter over Symon's radio.

'What will happen now?' Clementine asked. 'To Maria and everyone else?'

'Maria is still going to have to be charged with petty theft for the charity stuff she stole. There'll be a fine, probably community service,' Symon explained. 'She'll have to turn herself in.'

'Well, that's better than a murder charge,' Clementine said.

'It is,' Symon agreed. 'Them lot in there, Mr Black and his son, I dunno. That's not my job, I suppose. I just find the evidence. I'd imagine manslaughter at least. His son's underage, though, isn't he? It doesn't look good, though.'

'You know, I always think we'll feel better when we solve something like this,' Margery said finally. 'I suppose some people would crack open a bottle of champagne and get on with their life, but I just can't stop thinking about how sad it all is.'

'I know what you mean,' Clementine said, reaching for her hand. 'Even though he killed his aunt, he's still just a boy. He's ruined his life. In some ways it would have been better if Maria… if…'

'I know,' Margery said, squeezing her hand.

The unspoken truth swirled in the air between them. If Maria had committed the crime, then Andrew wouldn't be now sitting in custody, but of course that would mean Maria having the malice to do what he had done. Margery knew for certain now that Maria didn't, but found herself wishing that she had believed in Maria's innocence all along, rather than wasting her energy with doubt. She looked over to Clementine, who was thinking to herself, her brow furrowing with the weight of it all and hoped that Clementine would one day be able to forgive her.

Symon gave them a moment to dwell on it all, but then he cleared his throat.

'You know,' he began, his shy smile reminding Margery of the younger man they had first met years ago. 'I'm going to need you both probably going forward. Would you be up for helping me occasionally? I can see if I can get you on the payroll in some way?'

'Us?' Margery blanched at the idea of it all being legitimate. 'You want us to help?'

'Yes, usually people are desperately trying to stop us from helping,' Clementine said, with a small chuckle that Margery hadn't heard for a while. It sent a jolt of warmth to her heart, and she found her fingers unclenching. Everything might just be okay.

'I know,' Symon said, grinning back. 'But I'm still new to this, and you know everyone and everything that goes on in Dewstow and Ittonvale. Who better to help me? Only if you want to, though!'

'I think we'd like that,' Margery said. Clementine nodded.

'Oh, lush!' Symon said, beaming at them. 'Now, do you want to tell Ceri-Ann what's happened or should I?'

'I think you should,' Clementine said, smiling back at him. 'I don't think my hearing aid can withstand the decibel she'll probably scream in excitement with.'

Symon laughed and got up from his seat, leaving them alone in the quiet room. Margery turned to Clementine and took her uninjured hand.

'Clem,' she began. 'I'm so sorry for not believing—'

Clementine shook her head to interrupt. 'Don't be silly! If Maria had been your relative, I'd have thought twice about it too. She did look very guilty for a bit, didn't she? Anyway, I'm sorry for hiding her from you.'

'I think we've been quite lucky here,' Margery said, with a sigh of relief. 'If Wilkinson had found out where Maria was hiding, this might have all had a much worse ending.'

'It was worth the risk,' Clementine said. 'Thank you for helping me, even when you weren't convinced.'

She squeezed Margery's hand with her own and Margery relaxed back into her seat.

'Sickness and health,' Margery said. 'And whatever else life brings.'

Epilogue

The play had been a roaring success, but that didn't stop Margery feeling a bit strange about it. It wasn't every day that you saw a dramatised version of your own life, after all. Especially a version with songs curated by someone who knew you quite well. It had allowed Rose to go rather in depth with the lyrics and Margery had initially felt a bit embarrassed by them, especially the entire song written around Margery and Clementine's grand splash into Dawn Simmonds' pond. However, despite herself, she had found herself secretly enjoying it. Rose and Rhonda had managed to craft a script that really mirrored what had happened when they had solved that first case all those years ago. Margery knew that Rose must be anxious to hear their thoughts; after all, not only was it about them, but it was the first script Rose had written since the untimely passing of her music teacher, Mrs Large.

She had worried that Rose might have made the script too gruesome for a family audience, but instead she had turned it into a sort of slapstick comedy where the character of Clementine bumbled around in a silly way and then the character of Margery acted as the foil. Which was sort of how it was in real life, Margery supposed.

Ceri-Ann had cackled like a witch the moment her character was revealed, wearing a lot more sportswear and gaudy gold jewellery than she ever would and with a faux cigarette permanently perched in the corner of the student actor's mouth. Gloria had smirked when the tiny student playing her had arrived on stage, while Sharon and Karen had been baffled that the actors playing them were wearing matching costumes.

As they exited the school hall, the only person whose opinion of the play Margery hadn't heard was Seren, who had offered to stay back and help with refreshments. Margery suspected that she had heard and seen enough of the play over the past six months from Rose.

'Did they really have to make the student who played me wear that white wig?' Clementine scoffed as they mingled in the canteen during the intermission. 'It wasn't even a proper one – it was made of cotton wool stuck together. And did she really need to have Jason and Ada Bones playing our cats? It's all wrong, they're not the right species. The cat ears look ridiculous on them. They should have got Pumpkin to play Crinkles and Crinkles to play Pumpkin. Now, that would have been a show!'

They had been given the evening off from providing refreshments by Rose, so that they could watch the play before its big opening the week after. It was going to be nice to work with Paul and his team again, Margery thought. They were doing three nights at Ittonvale school and three at Summerview and all the staff and students were intermingling. It was a nice change from the usual school rivalry. Margery thought it had made some good from the terrible thing that had happened to Caroline all those years ago now.

James Barrow and Mrs George had been brought in to serve teas and coffees and popcorn and crisps. It was amusing in itself to see the former headmaster handing out disposable cups of coffee, but he was beaming from ear to ear and chatting away with the audience members. Mrs George didn't look quite as chipper, her hand bandaged from where she had obviously burnt herself on the water boiler and her face the picture of fury Margery only usually saw during GCSE exam periods.

Margery tried to hide her smile behind her own coffee cup, enjoying the buzz of the evening. The parents mingling with the teachers on duty and the acrid smell of burnt popcorn hanging in the air, all under the familiar strip lights that ran across the canteen ceiling. Margery felt truly at peace for once. Although, she suspected she might have to clean the microwave extra thoroughly tomorrow. James hadn't seemed like the sort to make popcorn in a pan, so she had brought extra bags of microwave popcorn just in case.

'Well, I thought it was a great first half,' Maria said. 'It could have been worse, couldn't it? At least they didn't draw on too many wrinkles. That kitchen manager character had loads, she looked like a painting. Was it all really like that? You never told me you crashed into Dawn's pond! I'd pay a fortune to have seen that in real life. I bet she was fuming!'

Maria was doing well, Margery thought, much better every day that passed. Although she was still much too thin. Her skin was drawn over the bones tightly, showing her angular face.

'We really did,' Clementine said. 'I'm surprised she's never mentioned it to you. It's all she goes on about to me. Her koi carp were all perfectly fine, if a bit surprised. I can't see the problem!'

'What did you think of the story?' Margery asked Maria. 'It's quite similar to what happened... well... Rose has taken a few liberties.'

More than a few, Margery thought, thinking of how the character of the drama teacher, Petunia, was constantly referred to in the script as 'the greatest deputy head alive today'.

'It's good, I can't work out how you're going to solve it in the second act.' Maria smiled. 'And I thought the kitchen manager person was funny.'

There had been a long dramatic introduction played for laughs that mostly starred Caroline Hughes, the school's former kitchen manager. Though the student playing Caroline seemed much nicer than the real one had ever been and with a much better singing voice. Caroline's singing could have been used as a torture method from what Margery remembered of her wailing along to the radio while she did the stocktake.

'Mate, when Caroline came on, I thought I was going to die,' Ceri-Ann said, chuckling at the memory. 'It was well good! I like the one playing me as well, even though I think I've got better hair.'

Gloria sidled over, clutching her handbag close to her chest. Even from a distance Margery could hear the bottles clinking inside it.

'I've got some wine in my bag,' Gloria hissed to the group, her eyes darting over to where Rose was holding court at the front of the canteen. 'Come on quick, follow me to the staff room!'

The group left, leaving Margery, Clementine and Maria in a comfortable silence, their voices muffled by the gathered group of students and parents.

'Do you really have to go?' Clementine asked, turning to Maria and startling her. 'We've had a great time. Can't we just carry on?'

'I just don't think I'm made to settle down,' Maria said, her eyes shifting to look down into her coffee cup. 'But I'll definitely be back to visit.'

'You're always welcome,' Margery told her, meaning every word. Maria nodded, but couldn't meet Margery's eyes.

'Do you mean that or are you planning on just disappearing for years again?' Clementine asked, her face flushing.

'Of course not!' Maria scoffed. 'I'll have to come and visit you, won't I? Thing is, Dewstow's a bit my home now, too… but the van life is calling me. I'm not leaving the country, though. I won't be that far away. Well… first stop's Scotland, so I'll be a bit far away. But nowhere you can't get to in a day, or I can't get back from easy for a visit. And the holiday camp will have a landline I can use to call you and internet so I can email when I'm not running the kitchen. We'll talk all the time, I promise.'

Clementine nodded, seemingly pacified for the moment. Margery wondered how long it would last. Not long, she was sure. Margery imagined that if Maria stopped responding then Clementine would want to go searching for her. Margery was sure they had a lot of adventures still left in store.

'Let's get some dates in the diary,' Maria said. 'What are you doing for your birthday? Anyway, I've been staying with you nearly a year, you've got to be sick of me now!'

Clementine folded her arms across her chest tightly.

'We'll come up to you in the holidays,' Margery said. She thought that she would suggest it before it was suggested, to ease Clementine's mind if there was any doubt that Margery was on her side. 'Wherever you are.

And I'm sure we'll retire at some point and there'll be lots more time for visits.'

'Yeah,' Maria said. 'Honestly, Clem, I'm not going anywhere. Well, I am… but… you know…'

Margery thought that she seemed sincere. Clementine must have realised she was as well.

'Fine, but we couldn't possibly stay in a tent…' she began.

'Hotels all the way!' Maria said cheerily.

'And you can't just not call for months and then except us to drop everything…' Clementine said in warning.

'I'll call you every Friday,' Maria said.

'All right,' Clementine said finally. 'All right.'

The dinner lady team returned in a gaggle, Gloria and Ceri-Ann laughing about something with their heads together, and Sharon and Karen not far behind them. Margery smiled as they made their way back into the canteen. The school bell rang, making Margery jump.

'Are you ready for act two?' Rose called over the crowd as the bell finished chiming. She waved her arms manically over her head. 'This one's even better! There's a duet with the policemen!'

There was a hush of excitement that rolled over the crowd. Margery and Clementine followed the group out of the canteen. Margery turned to wave goodbye to James, who waved back before returning to sweeping up the popcorn on the floor. She let the doors swing shut behind her.

Margery took Clementine's hand and they followed the crowd down the dark hallway, enjoying the feel of the cool air after the packed canteen. They made their way into the even darker hall to find their seats again.

Rose had seated the dinner lady team right at the front, the best seats in the house. Margery found herself nervous for the second act, although Rose had promised that nothing too scandalous would happen. But with Rose, you never quite knew.

Margery turned her head to glance at Clementine and Maria, who were still chatting, though the tension was still there between them underneath their smiles. Margery wondered what the future held, for all of them. The music began to swell, and the murmuring crowd fell silent as the curtain rose. Margery settled back in her seat, determined to enjoy the ride, whatever it might bring. Hoping beyond hope that nothing more awful could happen but accepting that the future was out of her control.

Acknowledgements

Can you believe this is the seventh Dinner Lady Detectives book? It's strange to me, because I wrote the first one just for my own amusement. I was surprised when it was published, then even more surprised when there was a second, and a third.

I had originally planned to stop at book seven. But somewhere along the line, Margery and Clementine, and the world they live in, became very real to me. Their adventures started to outpace the number of books I had on contract. It's easy to keep writing when you can almost believe a place exists in some other universe. And when that happened, I knew I had to keep going, at least a few more, to see them to their ending.

Still, I didn't think I'd be planning ten books in the series. Or that anyone would still be reading by book seven! And yet, here you are, which means you either read it or at least flicked through it because you liked the wonderful cover that Ami Smithson designed. Thank you for picking it up!

Of course, I have the usual (and most important) people to thank for this book existing: Robyn, Emily, Dad, Kirstie, Mum, and Jim. Then there's Louise, Alicia, and everyone at Canelo Crime. A huge thank you to Russell, the wonderfully helpful editor of A Curiously

Convenient Demise, and of course, my fantastic agent Francesca!

I know authors are supposed to have big, grand offices to write in, but since we had a baby, my desk has been tucked into the alcove where our bedroom wardrobe used to be, hidden behind a curtain (which, it turns out, is not soundproof). Because of that, I do about 90 per cent of my writing out and about.

So, here's a big thank you to all the places this book was written, in no particular order:

- Coffee #1, Chepstow
- The Boat Inn, Chepstow
- Pontio Lounge, Chepstow
- Weston-super-Mare Library
- Costa Coffee, Chepstow
- Chepstow Library
- And, on one dreadful day, the car park outside the dentist

Special thanks to *REDACTED NAME* nursery, and to Teresa and Jon for being doting enough grandparents to visit once a week so I can write.

And last but never least, a huge thank you to you for reading this! I hope you've enjoyed this edition of Margery and Clementine's adventures, and I'll see you again for book eight!

Do you love crime fiction and are always on the lookout for brilliant authors?

Canelo Crime is home to some of the most exciting novels around. Thousands of readers are already enjoying our compulsive stories. Are you ready to find your new favourite writer?

Find out more and sign up to our newsletter at canelocrime.com